The Serbian Solution

Eileen Enwright Hodgetts

Eileen Enwright Hodgetts

The Serbian Solution

Eileen Enwright Hodgetts

The Serbian Solution is a work of fiction.. All characters, with the exception of well-known historical characters, are products of the author's imagination and are not to be construed as real.

All rights reserved

Published by Emerge Publishing
© 2011 Eileen Enwright Hodgetts
ISBN 9780998215402

PROLOGUE

What drug had she been given this time? What new formulation of chemicals had finally succeeded in unlocking her memory? How amazing that the memory was still there, still accessible after 34 years, the vivid memory of her four year old self standing by that faraway roadside?

1957 United Kingdom

The journey had been long. Three times Uncle Cyril had been forced to pull the car over to the side of the road. Lizbeth's mother helped her out of the car and watched as Lizbeth stood in the shadow of the big, grey car, heaving and retching and generally hating the whole experience. Someone suggested she should sit on a piece of newspaper, it was supposed to stop motion sickness. Someone else suggested ice cream, it was cold and it paralyzed the stomach. Her mother said, "No, she'll be all right, it's only another ten miles."

Lizbeth leaned against an old stone mile post. With a damp hand she traced the lettering on the granite block. She read the words aloud, proud of herself. "Dragons Green - X."

Eileen Enwright Hodgetts

CHAPTER ONE
May 1991 United States

Lizbeth Price sat up suddenly in the hospital bed. The room was dimly lit by the light from the corridor and the digital read-out on the IV pump at her bedside. Sitting up had been a bad idea, everything hurt. She concentrated on localizing the pain. Her arms and legs were okay, her head didn't hurt, all the pain was at the site of the incision in her abdomen.

The dream was still vivid, the bright blue of the English summer sky, the leafy canopy over her head, her mother in a blue flowered dress. Lizbeth could smell the engine fumes from the old grey car and the acrid cigarette smoke drifting up from the two men who had been sitting in the front seat. It was, she decided, all those hours in the smoke filled car that had made her nauseated. Or maybe not, maybe it was the anesthetic. Someone had given her an anesthetic. The two things seem to blend together, the nausea from the hours in the car and the nausea from the anesthesia. Whatever it was, it was worth all of it to have that sudden clear vision of the milestone. "Dragons Green – X."

She turned cautiously, the incision was only hours old, and located the light switch. Behind the curtain her roommate shifted in protest with a weak groan of resentment and then lapsed into silence.

Lizbeth gritted her teeth, ignored the pain of her incision, and opened the top drawer of the bedside table. She located her purse and dragged it across the bed and onto her lap. She kept her mind focused on the image of the milestone, seeing every detail of the ancient carving. What drug had she been given this time? What new formulation of chemicals had finally succeeded in unlocking her memory? How amazing that the memory was still there, still accessible after 34 years; the vivid memory of her four year old self standing by that faraway roadside.

Whatever the drug was, it was a potent one. Lizbeth's strength was fading fast, and she wanted to lie back down in the pristine hospital bed and sleep. At last she located her address book.

Every five or six years she would buy herself a new address book and mentally and physically toss away the names of the many people who no longer counted in her life: ex-friends, ex-business partners, an ex-husband, acquaintances on both sides of the Atlantic, but she always transferred one number, filed under "S" for Stefan. Last time she had even checked the international code and updated it. Thank heaven, she thought. She was in no condition to be wandering off to find a phone directory and discover the correct code for calling from Pittsburgh, Pennsylvania to Swansea in Great Britain.

By the time she had dialed the international code and her own phone credit card number her mind was fogging over again and the dream was returning. The faraway ringing of the phone blended into the sounds of an English summer day. She could smell the dank, fertile undergrowth and her own childish vomit. Flies buzzed around her head. No, not flies; the rhythmic high-pitched pulsing of a British telephone.

She dragged her mind back into the present and concentrated on a woman's voice announcing a phone number. Lizbeth recalled that the British answered their phones by announcing their phone numbers and then waiting. She had done the same thing herself before she left home and became an American. On the other end of the line the British woman announced the phone number for a second time.

What the hell time of day was it in Europe, anyway?

Lizbeth had no idea. She didn't even know what time of day it was in Pittsburgh. It had been sunset when she had drifted off into the heavily drugged sleep. It was fully dark now and the hospital was quiet. Sometime between midnight and dawn, she thought, which would be daytime in Europe.

"Could I speak to Stefan, please?"

"Stefan who?" The voice was an irritating one, young and high pitched and superior.

"I'm sorry," Lizbeth stammered. "I don't remember his last name, but I've had his number for years."

She knew she was slurring her words and to make matters worse she was sliding helplessly down into her pillows, losing her grasp on the phone receiver. She probably sounded drunk, she thought. She was sure that the woman at the other end of the line could not possibly be impressed by Lizbeth's manner, but a national habit of politeness could not be easily shaken.

"I'm sorry, madam. Perhaps if you could describe the gentleman…"

"Oh, yes." Lizbeth struggled to sit upright. "Well, he'd be elderly now, I suppose. I haven't seen him since 1978."

"1978!" The polite voice had a Welsh accent, and belonged to a girl Lizbeth decided, rather than a woman, no doubt about it.

"It's really important," Lizbeth pleaded. "I'm calling from the States, from America."

"Oh!" The voice was impressed.

"Do you know a Stefan?" Lizbeth asked. "He gave me this number years ago, and it's really important. Who am I talking to, by the way?"

The voice refused to answer that particular question, but she did say, "You might mean Stefan Bubani. He's not living in Swansea anymore."

"But could you reach him?" Lizbeth asked.

The phone was slipping from her grasp again, and reality was sliding away. A canopy of trees was forming itself over her head, shutting out the light. It was very irritating, she thought, leafy English trees intruding into the hospital room like this.

"I could give him a message, I suppose," the Welsh girl said. "Do you want him to ring you?"

"Yes, yes," Lizbeth said, "he should ..." She hesitated. "He should ring me," she said eventually, uncomfortable now in her use of English phrases. "Tell him to call Lizbeth Price, will you please? Thank you very much."

Lizbeth stretched out her arm to replace the receiver and then realized that the thin, far-away voice was still speaking. How strange, she thought, the British were not usually so chatty on the phone. She put the receiver to her ear.

"Hello? Hello?" said the polite voice. "Are you still there? Mrs. Price, Mrs. Price!"

"Yes?"

The Welsh girl was humoring her now, Lizbeth thought, speaking loudly and distinctly for the benefit of this strange American drunk.

"Does he know your number, Mrs. Price?"

"What?" said Lizbeth. "Oh, no, you're right, of course, he doesn't know my number." She hesitated. "I don't know my number. Just a minute."

"Perhaps if you were to ring back later," the voice suggested, "when you're ... feeling better."

"No," said Lizbeth, "he should be told now. I should talk to him right away, while I still remember."

"But perhaps in the morning, you might ..."

Lizbeth recognized the polite hint. No doubt the distant girl was thinking that in the morning Lizbeth might be better able to recall her own phone number.

"I'm trying to find it," Lizbeth said.

She felt defeated. The phone on the nightstand was cloaked in darkness and if there was a number written on it, it was doomed to remain a mystery. Movement was so painful, so incredibly painful, and there was something tied to her arm, something which impeded her movements. She stared at the thin plastic tubing, tracing its path upwards to the stand beside the bed and the plastic bag of fluid. "IV," she said to herself. "Come on, get a grip."

"I'm sorry," she said into the phone. "I can't give you the number. I'm in a hospital, you see."

"Oh, that's a shame," said the distant Welsh voice, sounding not at all sympathetic.

"Nothing serious," Lizbeth reassured her, in response to a question which hadn't been asked, "but it's a little awkward at the moment. That's why I'm calling you see; the drugs they gave me helped me to remember."

"Oh, yes."

"It doesn't matter," Lizbeth said. "Stefan will understand. Tell him that I'm in Northern General Hospital, Pittsburgh, Pennsylvania. I'm sure he'll be able to find the number. Tell him I've remembered."

"Remembered?"

"They've been waiting for years, all of them. They've been waiting for me to remember, but I never could. I was only four years old at the time."

"Of course."

"I'm not crazy!" Lizbeth protested. "You tell Stefan what I said and he'll tell you that I'm not crazy. With everything that's happening now, everything that's going on over there, it could make all the difference. Tell him I remember where it was; please."

"Northern General Hospital," repeated the precise British voice with its sing-song Welsh lilt.

"Pittsburgh," Lizbeth added.

"And you're Lizbeth Price, and you've remembered?"

"Yes," said Lizbeth. She let the receiver fall from her grasp and leaned back against the pillows. She closed her eyes. The trees closed in above her head.

"X," her mother was saying, "is a Roman numeral, not that you have to worry about that, lovie. X means ten."

"X means ten," Lizbeth Price said aloud in her hospital room.

"Only ten miles to go now," her mother said. "Do you think you can get back into the car?"

Lizbeth's child-self quailed at the very thought of re-entering the stuffy interior of the car with its smell of gasoline and exhaust fumes, old leather and cigarette smoke, but she obediently grasped her mother's hand.

One of the men held the door open for them. "She is all right now?" he asked. He had a deep, ugly voice and made the words sound harsh.

"We can go a bit farther," her mother said. "She's a good little girl, she always lets me know in time."

The driver turned in his seat and Lizbeth saw a dark, heavy face, with fierce eyebrows. A stubby little cigarette drooped from his thick lips.

"You should not have brought her," he announced. His accent was thick and ugly like the other man's but Lizbeth was not surprised. She seemed to be accustomed to these accents.

"He's her brother," said Lizbeth's mother, drawing Lizbeth closer to her blue flowered bosom. "The child should see him again. I think if you could put out your cigarette, she might feel better."

The driver tossed the cigarette onto the ground at Lizbeth's feet. She watched its glow die as it settled into the damp grass. It had been raining. She remembered the rain. It had rained almost all the way. The sun had only just come out, just as they crossed the border.

Lizbeth climbed out of her dream. "Border?" she asked herself. "What border?" She turned off the night light, pressed her hands to her bandaged abdomen and fell into a fitful sleep. The dream continued.

"Mummy," Lizbeth muttered, "Mummy."

Overcome with a strong feeling that something terrible was about to intrude on her dream, she tried to wake herself up.

Stop dreaming, she told herself. Stop dreaming and you won't have to see it.

"Mummy," she implored, "talk to me. Please, Mummy, wake up. Why won't anyone wake up?"

She forced her eyes open and saw the shadowy hospital room. She was certain that she had escaped from a nightmare. If she had stayed asleep any longer she would have seen something terrible.

She soon realized what had woken her. A bright light was burning behind the curtain that separated her from her roommate and nurses were talking in loud, annoyed whispers.

"Get back into bed, Mrs. Morrison."

Shadows moved behind the curtain and Lizbeth could see the shadowy forms of Mrs. Morrison and the nurses who held her arms.

"We don't want to get up now, dear, it's the middle of the night," said another tired but patient voice.

Mrs. Morrison's cracked and confused voice offered a protest but she was overwhelmed by a command to "lie down dear, and be a good girl," followed by an explanation from the other voice that Mrs. Morrison was in the hospital, and Mrs. Morrison had a broken hip, and Mrs. Morrison would have to stop trying to get out of bed.

One of the nurses said, loudly and clearly, "Oh shit," and the second nurse said, with an edge of annoyance, "You have to tell us, dear, when you want to go to the bathroom. You can't keep doing this in the bed."

Lizbeth settled herself back against the pillows, confident that she wouldn't be drifting off to sleep in the next couple of minutes. The nurses moved back and forth behind the curtain, rustling sheets and ignoring Mrs. Morrison's complaints.

The activity was interrupted by a masculine voice. "Is all this noise really necessary?" it asked, "I have patients on this floor who need their sleep?"

"Good evening, Doctor, we didn't expect you here so late," said one voice.

"We're having a minor emergency," said the other.

"So I see," said the masculine voice. "How's Miss Price? This is her room, isn't it?"

"She was sleeping the last time I checked," came the quiet reply.

"I doubt if she's sleeping now," the doctor retorted. The curtain was twitched aside and a shadow loomed towards her.

"Miss Price?"

Lizbeth made out the face of the doctor she had seen in the emergency room several hours earlier.

"Doctor....?" She couldn't remember his name.

"Perenyi," he said, "Alex Perenyi."

She nodded.

"How are you feeling?"

"I don't know," she replied. "What did you do to me?"

He moved closer to the bed and she was able to make out his features. He was tall and slim, with straight dark hair and deep-set eyes. He appeared to be unshaven and somewhat rumpled, but as it was the middle of the night she couldn't hold that against him.

"You don't remember?" he asked.

She shook her head.

"I removed your gall bladder and some infected intestine."

"Oh yes, now I remember. It was all so sudden."

"You left it too long before you came into the Emergency Room," he said. "If you had come in sooner we might have found an alternative treatment."

Lizbeth shrugged her shoulders. "I was very busy," she said.

His attention had wandered. He checked the pump feeding her IV tube. He checked the bed controls and the TV remote. He seemed puzzled.

"What's the matter?" Lizbeth asked.

"I can hear a noise. I shall have to turn on the light."

He reached across her and turned on the bedside light. She could see him clearly. He looked tired, distracted and distant.

He made a noise, which Lizbeth could only interpret as a snort of masculine disdain, and picked up the phone receiver which had been buried in the bed clothes and was still emitting a dial tone.

"Was it really necessary to make a phone call?" he asked.

Lizbeth stared uncomprehendingly at the phone receiver. The doctor replaced the receiver and straightened her bedclothes. Lizbeth continued to stare at the phone. Who had she been calling? She couldn't remember.

The doctor picked up her heavy purse and began to collect her various belongings which were scattered across the bed. She tried to concentrate on the purse. What had she been doing? What was she looking for?

"I know women don't like men messing with their handbags," the doctor said, "but you can't leave this all over the bed; you have to get your rest."

He picked up her address book and dropped it into the purse.

"Wait," said Lizbeth. She reached out her hand for the address book.

"Miss Price," the doctor said, "you really must rest. There's no business that you need to conduct at four in the morning."

"Four o'clock!" Now she remembered "Oh, that's all right, I was calling Europe. I guess I didn't wake anyone up."

She laughed, remembering the puzzled but polite Welsh girl who had answered the phone. "They must have thought I was drunk."

Perenyi looked at her quizzically. "I was trying to place your accent; not quite American, I thought maybe Australian."

Lizbeth shook her head "I was brought up in Britain, but I've been in the States for a long time. I don't make an issue of my background. It gets in the way of business."

The doctor nodded. "Lizbeth Price...yes, I've seen your name on *FOR SALE* signs all over the North Hills."

Lizbeth's response was automatic. "Million Dollar Club! Are you thinking of selling or buying, Doctor?"

Perenyi scowled. "You people never miss an opportunity, do you?" he said.

"Real estate's a tough business," Lizbeth countered.

He nodded without speaking and picked up her chart from the end of the bed.

"What are you giving me, Doctor?" Lizbeth asked.

"Tolwin; it's a synthetic opiate."

"It's amazing! I've been having such vivid dreams."

He smiled and Lizbeth found herself liking the younger, kinder man revealed by that sudden smile.

""Don't get too used to it," he said, "it's very addictive. We'll get you off it as soon as possible."

No hurry, Lizbeth thought, remembering the prize that she had finally gained. Dragons Green - X.

"Lie back, please, Miss Price. I want to check the incision."

Lizbeth lay back on the bed. The doctor hesitated, his hand on the sheet, and then called out, "Nurse."

A nurse came from behind the curtain. Lizbeth was relieved that it was the nurse who pulled back the sheet and lifted the hem of her hospital gown. She hadn't been embarrassed when Dr. Perenyi had examined her in the emergency room, but he hadn't looked so rumpled then or so human, and she hadn't seen that engaging smile. He pressed lightly on her navel and she gasped.

"Sorry," he said. He twitched the sheet back into position. "You're doing fine. Would you like a different pain medication, if the dreams are troubling you?"

Lizbeth thought about her last dream. She was with her mother in the back of that old grey car, the car was tilted at a strange angle, and her mother's weight was crushing her. She didn't like this memory or the pain that her child self was feeling, but it was important and she had to see it through to the end. She shook her head.

"I'm all right."

Perenyi reached over and turned out the light.

"Goodnight, Miss Price."

The Serbian Solution

The nurse laid a soothing hand on Lizbeth's forehead. "Try to sleep," she said.

The touch blended into Lizbeth's returning dream. Her mother's touch? No, not her mother; another hand, a man's hand. She could see his face, and his thick black hair, his dark eyes, his fierce moustache.

"Try to remember, Lizbeth," he urged.

Lizbeth tried to remember the pretty little village with thatched cottages huddled around a village green and an old pub with a weather-beaten sign of a red dragon. She tried to make the colors bright and keep the memory happy, but the dream slipped beyond her control. The village green faded, the pub sign slipped away, and she was in another hospital. This dream was vivid, the colors brilliant, the emotions fresh and frightening.

Her bed was in a vast, echoing ward lined with other beds. She could see the row of beds across from where she lay, each with its own nightstand, its blue bedspread, its inhabitant sitting or lying. The ward was noisy. The patients were all children. A nurse stood at her bedside, no, two nurses, one was in a blue dress; she had a starched apron and a small white cap and a blue belt around her waist. The other nurse had an impressive confection of white ruffles on her head, a larger apron and a purple dress. She was grey haired and plump.

"Go ahead and tell her, Nurse," said the ruffled cap.

"Couldn't you do it, Sister?" asked Nurse.

"You have to get used to this some time," Sister insisted. "You might just as well start now. I'll stay with you. Just tell her."

"But," Nurse protested, "there are so many people asking about her. There was someone from the Foreign Office and someone from an Embassy..."

""She's an ordinary little girl," Sister said, "and she has to be told. Do it quickly and then give her a nice cup of tea and stay

with her for a while. She'll be all right, children are very resilient."

"Lizbeth." Nurse's sound nervous and tentative. "How are you feeling, dear?"

"Very well, thank you," said the polite child Lizbeth, but the adult Lizbeth, monitoring the conversation, began to feel strangely sad.

"That's a good girl," said Nurse. "That broken arm will be mended in no time at all, you'll see, and when you go to school all your friends will want to sign your cast."

"Stop shilly-shallying about," hissed Sister, from her position behind Nurse.

Nurse patted Lizbeth's head. "Such lovely ginger hair.".

Lizbeth corrected her. "Auburn; Mummy says it's called auburn."

"Mummy's quite right," said Nurse.

"When's Mummy coming to see me?"

"Tell her now," Sister whispered.

Nurse made an attempt to sit on the bed beside Lizbeth but abandoned it when Sister scowled at her. She leaned forward, her frightened young face close to the child's.

"I'm afraid Mummy won't be coming. You must be brave, dear, very brave. It was a terrible accident, you know, and you were very lucky that you only had a broken arm. I'm afraid that all the others...."

Nurse's voice trailed away. Lizbeth stared at her, wide-eyed, uncomprehending.

"The other people in the car," Nurse continued hesitantly, "weren't as lucky as you were, Lizbeth. The two gentlemen and your mother ..."

"Uncle Cyril and Uncle Nicholas," Lizbeth informed her carefully.

"Your two uncles, and your mother, they're, well,

they're..." Nurse's voice trailed away again.

Sister elbowed her way forward, a thick white china teacup in her hand. "What Nurse Stebbins is trying to tell you, dear," she said, "is that your two uncles and your mother were both killed in the accident. Your mother's dead, dear. Now drink this nice cup of tea."

Lizbeth awoke for a moment. She looked around the hospital room, and reassured herself that she was, in fact, in Pittsburgh and she was no longer a child shying away from Sister and her nice cup of tea.

"Well," she thought, as she drifted back to sleep, "at least I know why I've always hated tea."

CHAPTER TWO

Gregory Gibbons stood at his living room window, a cup of coffee in one hand and a hand-rolled cigarette in the other. He thought about his mother and his sister, and the anger he felt caused his hand to shake and the coffee to spill over into the saucer.

Thirty four years, he said to himself, as he looked out over the dreary English morning which so well matched his mood.

He took a long drag on the cigarette and swallowed a mouthful of the bitter coffee. Why, he asked himself, didn't they ever come again?

A car splashed by on the rain soaked road. The driver sounded his horn and waved and Gregory Gibbons waved back. Viktor always waved to the neighbors as they went by on their way to work and now he would have to take Viktor's place. Nice old Mr. Gibbon, would wave to the neighbors as they went to work. Nice old Mr. Gibbons, except he hadn't always been Mr. Gibbons; he'd had another name, and another language. How surprised the villagers would be to learn that nice old Mr. Gibbons, who lived such a quiet life and cultivated such beautiful roses, had once been Grigori Gruda.

Once he'd had a beautiful mother, and a little red-haired sister, and they'd lived in another place. He'd had a father, too, not Jamie Price, that canting Welsh stepfather with his holier-than-thou face and his constant discipline. No, there had been another father, a fierce, tall, and utterly splendid man who had carried Grigori on his shoulders and introduced him to other fierce men who had laughed and told him he would one day be just as splendid as his father.

Gregory Gibbons gazed unseeingly out at the misty English morning. He knew what he was doing. He was thinking about his father and his sister, and even his mother (who he tried never to think about) so that he wouldn't have to think about the other thing. He couldn't think about that; not yet.

Why hadn't they ever come again, he asked himself although he already knew the answer. They hated him, there was no other explanation. His father had gone and his splendor had vanished from Gregory's life. Then the Welshman had come, and the little sister, but Gregory hadn't been good enough for the little sister. He had done something wrong, something terribly wrong, and the Welshman had sent him away with no one but Viktor for company.

Gregory reined in his racing thoughts. Thinking about Viktor was wrong. Thinking about Viktor only made matters worse.

He sipped his coffee. The rain had stopped and the sun was struggling weakly through the clouds. The mist began to clear and Gregory was able to see across the heath to the village. He could see the yellow stone church glowing in the sunlight, and outside the pub he could make out the outline of the dragon sign which had given the village its name - Dragons Green.

Lizbeth awoke when the nurse touched her shoulder.

"How are you this morning?" the nurse asked.

Lizbeth opened her eyes and looked at the nurse. My God, but she was young, she thought. She made a mental adjustment - maybe the nurse wasn't so young, maybe Lizbeth was getting old; two more years and she'd be forty.

"How are you?" the nurse asked again.

"Not bad," Lizbeth said.

"How's the pain?"

"Under control," Lizbeth assured her, "much better than last time."

"Last time?" The nurse picked up Lizbeth's chart.

"I had a C-Section," Lizbeth said, "years ago, under the National Health and it was very painful. I think I told the doctor about it."

"So you have children?" the nurse said brightly.

Lizbeth read the young woman's name tag - Jackie. "No, Jackie," she said, "I gave my baby up for adoption."

"I'm sorry."

"It was a long time ago," Lizbeth said, "and life goes on."

Jackie replaced the chart at the foot of the bed. "Doctor Perenyi's making his rounds," she said. "I have to get you ready."

"As for royalty?" Lizbeth asked, hoping to lighten the atmosphere.

Jackie laughed. "You'd think so. He's very fussy. Do you want to comb your hair?"

"He's not going to look at my hair," Lizbeth replied.

Jackie began smoothing the bedclothes. "I heard he was in to see you last night."

Lizbeth struggled to sit upright, trying to remember the events of the night before. "I don't remember much," she said, "but I think we had a conversation."

"Quite a long one," said Jackie.

"Were you on duty?" Lizbeth asked.

The nurse shook her head. "No, I came on at seven, but word gets around. Doctor Perenyi doesn't very often talk to his patients, so everyone kind of noticed he was talking to you."

"I don't think he was really talking," Lizbeth replied, "I think he was nagging."

Jackie grimaced. "He used to be quite easy-going before his divorce, but ever since his wife left him he's been impossible. He doesn't ever seem to go to bed and he turns up in the middle of the night and starts ordering people about, like we don't know what we're doing."

She adjusted the curtain to screen Lizbeth's view of the unmoving Mrs. Morrison. "He'll be along in a minute," she warned.

Lizbeth looked at the phone on the nightstand and wondered if she should call the office. No, it was too early. Who would be there at seven in the morning? She'd wait until eight, but then she would really have to get busy. If this ridiculous surgery was going to keep her tied up for a couple of days, someone would have to cover for her. She grimaced, thinking of the commissions she would have to split but there was no alternative, at least not for a couple of days.

The phone rang and she stared at it in surprise. So, someone at the office was going to make the first move, someone was calling her to suggest a split. Who could it be? Who would have the initiative to call so early in the morning? She lifted the receiver.

"Lizbeth Price," she said.

For a fraction of a second she heard nothing but static, and then a man's voice said, "Good afternoon, Lizzie, or I suppose it's morning in the States."

The memory flooded back to her, the dream, the phone call, the message she had left. But this wasn't Stefan, this man had no accent, or at least no Eastern European accent, he was purely Welsh.

"Yes," she replied guardedly, "it's morning here. Who is this?"

"I understand you have a message for Stefan Bubani," the voice continued.

Again Lizbeth hesitated. "Yes, I do," she said eventually, "but you're not Stefan, are you?"

A mild commotion occurred behind the curtain and then the drapes were twitched aside and Dr. Perenyi swept into the room, accompanied by Jackie and another nurse.

"Stefan's not here any longer," said the voice on the phone.

The medical trio waited expectantly at the foot of the bed.

"But you have given him my message?" Lizbeth asked.

Jackie closed the curtain with a defiant swish and the other nurse rattled her plump little hands through a tray of surgical accessories. Dr. Perenyi looked at Lizbeth impatiently through dark framed glasses which he had not been wearing the night before. They made his brown eyes look enormous and soulful.

"Lizzie," said the phone caller, "don't you recognize my voice? It's Joe. Joe Ralko."

A cold lump of anger rose in Lizbeth's throat. So many years gone by without a word, he had no right to speak to her, no right to expect anything of her, no right to come between her and Stefan.

"How do you expect me to remember your voice," she managed to say, "it's been years since I've spoken to you?"

Dr. Perenyi was pulling on a pair of pink rubber gloves. "Miss Price," he said, "we're ready for you now."

She smiled at him, but held onto the receiver and waited for Joe to explain himself.

"Twenty years without a word," Joe said, "and then I find out you're in hospital. What's going on Lizzie?"

"It's nothing serious," said Lizbeth, "certainly not worth the price of a transatlantic phone call, and don't call me Lizzie."

"Sorry, Lizbeth, I won't do it again."

"What do you want?" Lizbeth asked.

"The committee was very interested in your telephone call."

"Don't tell me you're still just a committee; I thought you'd be an army by now. What are you waiting for, Joe?"

"You know what we're waiting for," Joe replied. "We're waiting for you."

For a brief moment Lizbeth was transported back in time. She was a teenager in flared jeans and a tight sweater, chewing her freshly painted fingernails and waiting for Joe Ralko. He was late, but he was always late. He would be with his friends in a dark corner of a dark pub discussing secret meetings in distant cities.

He fascinated her, with his lean athletic body and his brooding dark eyes, and she was incredibly flattered that he had picked her to be his girl, but at times like this, when he arrived late and distracted, she would wonder what she really meant to him. Had he chosen her for herself or had he chosen her because she was Grigori Gruda's half-sister? Every time he asked her "Have you remembered anything, Lizzie?" she would be filled with self-doubt, but then he would put a casual arm around her shoulders and her body would tingle. She didn't care why he wanted her; it was enough that he did.

It was as though the past twenty years had never been. His voice was in her ear, asking the question, "What have you remembered?"

"It may be nothing," she replied, "but Stefan always said that anything, anything at all, that I remembered would be important."

"Yes it would. What exactly have you remembered?"

Dr. Perenyi gave Lizbeth another impatient glance and then motioned to the nurses to roll back the bedclothes. For a moment Lizbeth forgot about Joe and thought about underwear. Underwear would have been a comfort in this situation, she thought. As if aware of her concerns, the doctor tugged the bed sheet into a position which offered her some modesty and then he began to remove the gauze bandage over her incision. Lizbeth glanced at the nurses. Jackie frowned at her. Obviously they expected her to complete her phone conversation and pay attention to the surgeon.

"Lizbeth," Joe asked, "are you still there?"

"Yes, I'm here. They gave me something, Joe, some sort of drug I've never had before, I don't remember the name."

"Tolwin," said the doctor.

Lizbeth looked at him in surprise.

"Tolwin is the name of the drug we gave you," he repeated.

"Thank you," Lizbeth said.

"You're welcome"" he muttered, and took a moment to adjust his glasses.

Far away, on the other side of the Atlantic, Joe Ralko asked, "Do you have someone with you?"

"Just the doctor."

Dr. Perenyi looked at her again. His eyes were very expressive. Lizbeth thought that perhaps "just the doctor" had sounded rather insulting.

"Why don't you tell me what you've remembered," Joe said, "and then you can concentrate on talking to the doctor."

"Don't patronize me," Lizbeth snapped, "I'm not a kid anymore, Joe."

"Did I ever treat you like a kid?" Joe asked, and laughed. Lizbeth felt the blood rush to her cheeks, remembering vividly the adult activities that Joe had introduced her to.

Dr. Perenyi interrupted her reverie. "This will be cold," he said, and he slapped something wet onto her stomach. At last Lizbeth looked down at her own body and saw the pink gloved hands busying themselves over an unbelievably large incision laced with horrible black threads.

"It's so big," she said.

"What?" Joe asked. "What are you talking about?"

"It's no bigger than it needs to be," the doctor said. "Don't worry; it won't leave much of a scar."

"Lizbeth," Joe asked, "can you hear me?"

Lizbeth was irritated: by the doctor, by the ugly wound in her belly, by Joe's constant interruptions. "Just let me talk to Stefan," she snapped.

"He isn't here," Joe said. "Tell me what you remembered. Is it an address?"

"Not a complete address," Lizbeth replied, "but close. I remember being just ten miles away."

There was a hard edge to Joe's voice. "That's close enough. Where is he, Lizzie? We have to have him."

Dr. Perenyi had lifted Lizbeth's gown, exposing her breasts. She felt extremely vulnerable although he was, in fact, touching her only with his stethoscope.

"Lizbeth," Joe said, "just tell me the damned address."

"I'd rather tell Stefan."

"He's not here," Joe repeated.

"It would make him so happy," Lizbeth insisted.

"To hell with Stefan!" Joe snapped. "For God's sake, Lizzie, tell me. Don't play stupid games."

"Breathe in," said Dr. Perenyi, but Lizbeth was already holding her breath. Something was wrong, she'd left a message for Stefan hours ago, he would have called her himself, he wouldn't have trusted Joe. Stefan didn't like Joe, and Lizbeth didn't like the hard edge to Joe's voice.

"Breathe in," said Dr. Perenyi again, jabbing her with the stethoscope.

Lizbeth took a deep breath and spoke to Joe. "Joe," she asked, "do you know the password?"

The two nurses looked at her curiously and Dr. Perenyi said edgily, "This would be easier if you weren't talking."

Joe was angry. "I don't know any bleeding password."

"Ask Stefan," Lizbeth said.

She could hear Joe breathing heavily and she waited, quite certain that she had done the right thing.

"There isn't any password," Joe hissed. "What do you think this is, a bleeding James Bond story?"

"If I don't talk to Stefan, I don't talk to anyone," Lizbeth said, and hung up.

The feeling of power was immensely gratifying. She had hung up on Joe Ralko, something she should have done twenty years before. "I've finished talking," she said to the doctor.

"And I'm finished doctoring," he replied. He pulled off the rubber gloves, rolled them into a ball and tossed them into the trash can.

"How am I doing?" Lizbeth asked.

"As well as can be expected."

"What does that mean?"

"It means you should stay off the phone if you can't stop yourself from getting over-excited."

"It was important," Lizbeth said, "and I don't think it's

over yet."

"I think you'll have to put business aside for a day or two, Miss Price," Perenyi said. He took off the glasses and slipped them into his pocket.

"That wasn't business, that was personal." Lizbeth changed the subject abruptly. "If you would like to talk business—"

"I would not."

"It's just that I heard that you might want to sell your house."

"Where did you hear that?"

Lizbeth shrugged her shoulders. "I understand that you and your wife are—"

Perenyi turned on her angrily. "What are you," he asked, "vultures? Do you know how many of you real estate women called me the day my divorce notice was published?"

"I didn't," Lizbeth protested.

"Maybe you didn't think of it then," the doctor retorted, "but you thought of it now. In the middle of all that business about passwords and mysterious European names, you still had time to think about how to make a few dollars out of my situation. So who told you about me?"

Lizbeth glanced at Jackie, who avoided her eye. "I'm good at what I do, Doctor," she said, "and I live well, but I can't afford to lose my edge. Do you know what it's costing me to be laid up in this bed?"

"Would you prefer that we had let you die?" Perenyi asked.

He didn't wait for a reply. Jackie held the curtain open and he departed, followed by the plump nurse carrying his surgical instruments, and by Jackie, who shot Lizbeth an angry glance.

Lizbeth lay back against the pillow. "Well, I blew that," she thought.

She looked at the phone and then at the clock on the wall. Eight in the morning; lunchtime in Europe. She wondered what

The Serbian Solution

Joe Ralko would do next and how long it would take him.

The pain woke her. Waves of pain seemed to be overtaking her entire body. She was reluctant to move or even open her eyes. God, she thought, I hope it's time for a pain shot. She groped around the bedcovers. She had fallen asleep with the call button at her side, so where was it now?

She opened her eyes wearily, reluctant to lose touch with the last vestiges of her comfortable sleep. The room was in semi-darkness. She could make out the unmoving outline of Mrs. Morrison in the next bed and the sliver of light filtering through the half-open doorway. She moved her arm again searching for the call button and another wave of pain shocked her into immobility. The door opened silently and she saw a figure dressed in white. A nurse, she thought. Thank goodness!

The nurse pulled the curtain across, cutting off Lizbeth's view of Mrs. Morrison.

"Miss Price?" the nurse whispered.

A male nurse! Lizbeth was surprised. He was the first male nurse she'd seen since her arrival.

"Lizbeth Price?"

"Yes. Is it time for my shot?"

"I have some questions to ask you."

He loomed over her in the gloom and turned on the nightlight. Lizbeth blinked. This was no male nurse. This huge man with the drooping moustache was a figure from her childhood, Uncle Nicholas, back from the grave. Surely not, those two uncles had been dead for more than thirty years. Twenty years had passed since she'd removed herself forever from the land where they were buried and put herself in a place where they could never reach her. She was dreaming again, it was the only explanation. If she could reach the call button, then she could wake herself up.

She located the button resting beside her on the pillow but the man's hand shot out and seized her wrist, knocking a couple of pillows to the floor. No, Lizbeth thought, I did it, I knocked the pillows on the floor myself, and my wrist is tangled in the IV tube.

The man leaned forward and spoke softly. She could feel his breath, and the stale scent of cigarettes. "There are no nurses," he said. "They have been replaced."

He walked around behind the bed, leaned down and yanked the phone cord from the wall.

Lizbeth fought against the reality of the dream. He seemed more real with every moment that passed.

Call the nurse, she said to herself. Get a pain shot. Wake up!

"Where is Grigori Gruda?" the dream uncle asked.

Lizbeth groaned. Even in her own dreams she was still asking herself that question. "I don't know where he is," she whispered. "I've never known where he is."

"Tell me what you do know," the man said, "and no one will ever ask you again."

Lizbeth tried to shake her head but even that movement hurt. She heard her own voice saying "No, I won't tell you."

She admired her own courage, but of course it was only a dream and no one could really hurt her in a dream.

The man shrugged. "You are very foolish," he muttered. "What is this man to you? Why do you bother to keep this secret?"

"I don't trust Joe," Lizbeth said aloud, after all, this was her dream so she might as well be honest. "I'll only tell Stefan," she added for good measure.

"We'll tell Colonel Bubani," the nurse/uncle assured her.

She stared at her visitor. He seemed very real. "Whoever you are," she said, "you're not from Stefan."

"My name is Lek Balka," the man replied, "and I am not from Stefan Bubani. The colonel is no longer in control."

Balka lowered himself into a chair at Lizbeth's bedside. She heard the chair creak as he sat down, and finally she knew that this was no dream.

Balka smiled a smile which gave Lizbeth no reassurance. "Times have changed, Miss Price," he said, "and the colonel has not changed with them. He is nothing now, an irrelevancy. Your friend, Josef Ralko, on the other hand, has important friends. He will go far."

"Josef," Lizbeth said. "Did Josef send you?

"We understand your reluctance to confide in strangers," Balka continued, "but believe me, Miss Price, we are quite determined to find out what you have remembered."

He spread his large hands in a conciliatory gesture. "Now that you know that we've come from your old, shall we say "friend" Josef, why don't you make matters easy for yourself?"

Lizbeth gritted her teeth and struggled into a sitting position in the bed. She was quite definitely awake and she was quite definitely in trouble, and her courage was leaving her.

She heard the tremble in her voice as she spoke. "I'm not telling you anything."

The curtain moved and another large figure approached the bed. "There's a doctor coming," whispered the newcomer.

"Is Milos on the desk?" Balka asked.

"Yeah, but he don't look very convincing," the other man replied. "We couldn't get no uniform to fit him."

"Get back out there and see what you can do," said Balka. "I'm not finished with Miss Price yet."

"She being difficult?"

"She'll come around."

"Okay."

The other man turned to leave but he stopped in his tracks as the curtain was drawn fully aside. Light flooded into the room from the corridor.

Lizbeth heard Dr. Perenyi before she saw him.

"What are you doing here? What's going on?"

The doctor pushed past Lizbeth's burly tormenter and stepped into the room. He looked around, assessing the scene with quick intelligence.

"Doctor—" Lizbeth said.

Balka silenced her by producing a deadly looking black pistol from the waistband of his pants and aiming it at her belly.

"Oh my God!" Lizbeth heard herself say. "Do you have to do this? I can't help you, I really can't help you."

The doctor attempted a protest. "Hey, what the —"

Before he could say another word an enormous man with a white nurse's smock stretched tight across his chest stepped up behind him. Presumably this was Milos, Lizbeth thought. She had to agree that he didn't make a very convincing nurse.

"Shut up, Doc," Milos said, wrenching Perenyi's right arm up behind his back and clamping his hand over the doctor's mouth. "Stand still, and you won't get hurt."

Dr. Perenyi stared at Lizbeth with wide, questioning eyes. She stared back in apology.

Balka lowered his weapon very slightly. "Be sensible, Miss Price," he said, "before this whole matter gets out of hand. This is ancient history, and certainly not worth dying for. Think about the good doctor here, you wouldn't want anything to happen to him, would you?"

"Stefan would never let me be treated like this," Lizbeth said.

Balka looked down at the gun, and raised his bushy eyebrows. Suddenly Milos yelped and released the doctor. "He bit me!"

Perenyi backed away. "Wait a minute, wait a minute," he said, "let me speak."

"What?" said Balka.

The doctor's voice trembled slightly, but he kept his gaze steadily on Balka and the weapon he was aiming at Lizbeth. "You want Miss Price to tell you something, is that correct?"

Balka nodded.

"And if she doesn't tell you, you plan to shoot her."

Balka stared at the doctor.

"How are you going to find out anything from Miss Price if she's dead?" the doctor asked.

I should have thought of that, Lizbeth thought. *If I wasn't in so much pain, I'd have thought of that for myself.* She had nothing to fear from Balka. He had no intention of shooting her. She could defy him to his face, nothing would happen.

"He's right," said Milos, "we can't shoot her."

"We're not going to shoot her," said Balka, "I just thought it was worth a try."

"So if I can go now..." said the doctor.

Balka shook his head and gestured to Milos, who grabbed the doctor again. This time he made no attempt to cover his mouth.

"I have to see the other patients," the doctor protested. "There are no nurses on duty. What have you done with them?"

"They're safe," said Milos. "All tucked away safe."

"But the patients—"

Milos smiled. "We've taken care of them, too," he said. "Mark over there, he's pretty good with the bedpans and the glasses of water; aren't you, Mark?"

Mark nodded. "Sure," he said, "let me show you." He stepped forward and picked up the pillows that had fallen from Lizbeth's bed. He arranged them behind her head, smiling at her and showing strong white teeth.

Lizbeth looked down at the floor and saw the thick Home Listing Guide which had fallen with the pillows. Maybe, just maybe...

"May I have my book?" she asked.

Mark shrugged and stooped to retrieve the book. He tossed it onto the bed.

"That's enough," said Balka. "Don't make her too comfortable, she's not going to be here much longer."

Lizbeth's heart skipped a beat. "What do you mean?" she asked.

"Get the wheelchair," said Balka, and Mark hurried from the room. "We're not surprised that you don't want to talk to us," Balka continued. "We were led to believe that you are a very stubborn woman."

"Who told you that?" Lizbeth asked.

"Our friends in Britain. I have a cousin who associates herself with Josef Ralko and his followers, or perhaps I should say that they associate themselves with her."

He smiled at Lizbeth. "Flora is a very strong woman, Miss Price, just like you are. She's asked for you, and she said you wouldn't talk. I was just trying to save time. I'm sending you to her and I would strongly suggest that you tell her what she wants to know, she is not a woman with scruples."

Balka's words sank in. "You're sending me to her?" Lizbeth asked.

The big man nodded.

Lizbeth looked around at the tubing which tied her to the bed. She pressed a hand to her aching side. She felt incredibly weak and vulnerable.

"You can't take her," Perenyi said. "She's a sick woman."

"She has only to tell us what she knows," said Balka.

Lizbeth tried to concentrate but her thoughts were drifting away.

The dreams which had been coming and going all day began to take over again. She saw her brother in the garden of the big house. Grigori was sitting under a tree with Viktor, his tutor. She could see Grigori clearly. He was about 14 years old and thin as a rail. Viktor was reading aloud from a book and Grigori was staring up into the branches of the apple tree while the old tutor droned on in his dry deferential tone.

"Grigo," she called.

He turned and saw her. A smile spread across his face and he held out his arms. "Lizzie," he shouted.

Someone touched her shoulder. She saw Mark standing by the bed with a wheelchair. "Get in, lady," he said.

"You can't put her in there," Perenyi protested.

Balka looked at Mark. "Pick her up," he ordered.

Mark advanced on the bed. He stopped, puzzled. "What about all these tubes and things?" he asked.

"Disconnect them," said Balka.

The doctor interrupted again. "Don't do that. You want her alive, don't you, not dead? You can't unhook her."

"But you can," Balka replied. "So, you fix it."

"Me?"

"Yeah, you, Doc. Fix it up. Do whatever you have to do."

Mark had been standing at Lizbeth's bedside surveying the medical equipment. ""She's connected to an IV," he said. "They have batteries, don't they, Doc?"

Lizbeth could see sullen resentment on the doctor's face. "Yes," he said eventually, "they have batteries."

He walked around behind the bed and disconnected the IV pump from the power supply. "That should last about eight hours," he said. He looked at the bag of fluid. "She'll need a refill before morning."

"Yeah, well, maybe she'll be somewhere by morning," Balka said.

Where? Lizbeth wondered. Where would she be by morning?

"Okay," said Balka, "put her in the wheelchair."

Perenyi seemed to have lost the will to resist them. "Be careful" he warned, "she hasn't been out of bed yet. You really shouldn't do this." He looked at Lizbeth angrily, "Tell them!" he urged. "Whatever it is, it can't be worth your life."

She shook her head. Beneath the pain and the apprehension a faint pulse of excitement was stirring. For years her own mind had protected her from her memories and now the barriers were falling. A journey that she had started years ago and half a world away had been interrupted, but tonight she was starting out again.

Mark slid his arms under the bedclothes and tried to lift her. Something tugged deep inside her body, between her legs, and Mark hastily withdrew his arms.

"There's another tube here," he said, looking back at the doctor.

Perenyi looked puzzled. "Another one?" he asked.

Lizbeth found that she was blushing. "The catheter is still

in," she mumbled.

Mark stepped back. "I'm not doing anything with that," he said.

"Fix it, Doc," said Balka.

The doctor shook his head.

"Alright," said Balka. "I'll do it myself."

He pulled back the bedclothes and Lizbeth's hands shot down to pull on the hem of her hospital gown.

Perenyi elbowed the other man aside. "I'll do it. Go on, get out of the way."

Lizbeth pulled the sheet up over her legs, clutching it tightly.

"Wait out there," said Perenyi, suddenly in control. To Lizbeth's surprise the three men obeyed, moving away from the bed and behind the curtain.

"Open your legs," Perenyi ordered..

"What are you going to do?"

"I'm going to take out your catheter." He lowered his voice. "Where's the phone? Can you reach it?"

She shook her head. "They've disconnected it."

The doctor's hands were on her knees. "Open your legs," he urged. "This won't hurt. I have done it before, you know."

She opened her legs and he slid a hand up beneath the sheet.

He leaned forward. "Tell them what they want to know. You're not fit to be moved, Miss Price. Maybe they don't mean to kill you, but they will.""

"I'm not telling them anything," Lizbeth declared.

Perenyi's response was to pull firmly on the catheter tubing. Lizbeth experienced a brief moment of pain and a longer moment of embarrassment as the doctor held the tube in the air to drain the urine. She was convinced he was doing it to humiliate her.

"Are you finished?" Balka asked from behind the curtain.

Lizbeth picked up the heavy Real Estate Guide. "If I hit him around the head with this, and you grab the gun…."

Perenyi shook his head. "Don't be ridiculous."

"Please," said Lizbeth, "you can't just let him take me."

Perenyi opened the curtain and beckoned Balka toward him. "I have to talk to you," he said.

Balka moved closer, still holding the weapon.

"Miss Price had surgery less than 48 hours ago," Perenyi said. "She's being intravenously fed, she's heavily medicated and there's a grave danger of infection, not to mention pneumonia and other post-operative complications."

Lizbeth tightened her grip on the book.

"I have a responsibility to my patient," Perenyi said.

That was it, Lizbeth thought; that was his agreement. She lunged up and out of the bed and hit Balka squarely alongside the head with the book. Balka released his hold on the pistol and it landed on the floor. The doctor stood, not moving.

"Grab it," Lizbeth shouted.

Perenyi still failed to move. Balka shook his head and staggered forward to retrieve the weapon. Lizbeth hurled herself forward, grabbed the weapon and did what she had been trained to do; she fired.

CHAPTER THREE

The gunshot was incredibly loud, and someone was screaming. Lizbeth! She was the one who was screaming; screaming in pain, screaming in horror. She dropped the gun.
Dr. Perenyi crouched at Balka's side, his hands bloody, and his face furious.

"Is he dead?" Lizbeth asked. "Oh God, tell me he's not dead. I didn't mean to kill him."

"What did you mean to do?" Perenyi asked. He looked at her briefly and then turned his attention back to the man on the floor. He unstrung his stethoscope and pressed it to Balka's chest.

"Why didn't you help me," Lizbeth shouted, "you were supposed to help me?"

Milos picked up the gun and aimed it at the doctor. Perenyi looked up impatiently. "Put that thing away. I'm doing the best I can"

Mark spoke briefly into a walkie-talkie radio and then stood looking down at Balka.

"We'll take him with us," he said. "There's a stretcher in the corridor."

"If you move him, he'll die," Perenyi warned.

Mark shook his head. "It doesn't matter. We can't stop, and we can't leave him here. We take him."

"No," said Perenyi, "if we can get him up to Surgery he—"

"No surgery," said Mark. "We'll take him with us. Milos

will fetch a stretcher."

Mark turned away from the man on the floor, slid his hands beneath Lizbeth's hips and picked her up. The pain was unbelievable. He dumped her unceremoniously into the wheelchair. She squeezed her eyes closed and concentrated on remaining completely still. She closed out the world around her and retreated deep into a world of pain.

She opened her eyes again when she felt the wheelchair moving. They were in the deserted corridor. Ahead of her the doctor pushed a stretcher. Milos was beside him, the gun aimed squarely at the doctor's head.

"We don't mind killing you;" Milos said, "we only need the woman, we don't need you."

"If we go to surgery..." Perenyi said.

"I told you, no surgery," Mark said from somewhere behind her. Lizbeth guessed he was pushing the wheelchair. "Call the elevator," he ordered.

"Help!" Lizbeth screamed. "Someone help!"

She heard Mark's voice in her ear. "Screaming won't do you any good, we've got them all locked away."

Lizbeth tried again. "Help!"

The doctor turned and looked at her; "Don't do that," he said, "you'll hurt yourself."

"Then you do something," she challenged.

"I'm doing something. I'm doing my best to keep this man alive."

The elevator arrived and Mark wheeled her into its bright interior following the doctor with the stretcher. They descended rapidly and emerged deep in the bowels of the hospital. With Perenyi pushing the stretcher and Mark issuing orders, they hurried past the unwelcoming doors of the Pathology Department and the Morgue. No lights shone from under the doors and no workers moved in the silent corridors.

At the rear of the Morgue they emerged onto a loading dock. An ambulance was already backed up against the ramp, its doors open.

"Lift him in," said Mark ordered.

"I can't do any more for him," Perenyi said.

"Get him into the ambulance," Mark repeated. "We're not leaving him here."

Perenyi and Mark lifted the unresisting form of Lizbeth's victim into the ambulance. Milos followed with Lizbeth in the wheelchair, pushing it up the ramp and into the space between the bunks.

Perenyi started to climb out.

"Stay," Milos ordered.

"We can't take him," Mark argued.

"We can't leave him," Milos replied. He shoved the doctor back into the interior of the ambulance. "He comes with us."

Mark and Milos climbed out of the ambulance. The doors closed and the ambulance moved forward. Lizbeth gripped the arms of the wheelchair.

Perenyi took out his stethoscope and pressed it to Balka's chest.

"Is he really dead?" Lizbeth whispered.

Perenyi put away his stethoscope and wiped his hands on a corner of the sheet, and then he lifted the sheet and draped it over Balka's face.

"I didn't mean to kill him," Lizbeth cried. "You have to believe me. I didn't mean to kill him."

"Be quiet, Miss Price," Perenyi said, "you'll only make yourself ill. I'm going to help you out of that chair and onto the other stretcher."

Lizbeth gripped the wheelchair. "No, I can't move."

"Yes you can," said the doctor. "Here we go. Hold onto me."

Lizbeth collapsed onto the stretcher and closed her eyes. She prayed that when she opened them again she would be back in her hospital bed, and that this was all a nightmare. But it wasn't, of course it wasn't. The weapon in her hand had been real. The blood, the pain, they were all real, even the doctor and his failure to co-operate, all real.

The ambulance bumped forward and then the ride settled down. They were on a good road, moving fast, for what seemed like hours. Lizbeth drifted in and out of a drugged sleep, waking occasionally to see Perenyi adjusting her IV, or checking her pulse, or just staring at her. Eventually the ambulance left the paved road and lurched across open ground.

Perenyi looked out the rear window. "Now what?" he asked.

"What can you see" Lizbeth asked.

"It looks like an airfield. Are they going to fly you out of here? How can they do that?"

"They can do all kinds of things," Lizbeth replied. "You don't understand who they are."

"No, I don't, but if you just tell them what they want to know—"

Lizbeth shook her head. "Never."

The ambulance doors opened revealing an early morning summer sky over a rural airstrip. The ambulance had been parked next to a small sleek plane.

"Get her out, Doc," Milos said.

Perenyi shook his head.

"Either you do it, or I do it, and I ain't afraid of hurting her," Milos threatened.

"Okay, okay," said Perenyi. "Take one end of the stretcher, and take it easy."

Lizbeth was carried from the ambulance onto the plane, and then lifted so that she was lying across a row of seats. The doctor adjusted her IV again and then backed away.

Somewhere beyond Lizbeth's view, Milos laughed.

"Oh no, you're coming with us, Doc."

She saw large hands pushing Perenyi into the seat in front of her.

The engines roared and she felt the tug of gravity as the plane hurled itself forward.

Again she drifted into a drugged sleep. When she opened her eyes Perenyi floated into view. She felt his hand on her wrist checking her pulse. His expression was grim and did nothing to invite conversation and after a moment he floated away again.

She awoke again, feeling as though she had been asleep a long time. She felt the plane land and she was offloaded into another ambulance which carried them along a winding road. Through the window she glimpsed hills and trees. She felt a little better. She struggled to sit upright.

"Where are we?" she asked.

A hand pushed her down, not roughly but very firmly. "I have no idea," Perenyi said. "Lie down, Miss Price."

"Why are you still here?" Lizbeth asked. "Why didn't they let you go?"

"Apparently they would like me to look after you. Now lie down."

"But..."

"Lie down."

"My side really hurts," Lizbeth complained.

Perenyi reached up and adjusted the portable IV equipment. "I have you on a very low dose of pain killer, and I've been trying to keep you lightly sedated," he said. "As they've only given me a very small supply and I have no idea where we're going or how long it will take, I am trying to make the supply last as long as possible. I'm increasing the flow slightly, but you must try to tolerate the pain, Miss Price."

"I'm not complaining," Lizbeth said.

Moments later she drifted back into sleep. She was only dimly aware of being lifted out of the ambulance. She opened her eyes and caught a glimpse of a sky heavy with rain clouds. The air was cool, almost cold, and smelled of the sea and fish. She had a brief view of a rusting hull and a metal deck, and then she closed her eyes again.

The return of the pain brought her fully awake with no idea how long she had been unconscious. She was in a tiny metal room, a ship's cabin with a single porthole. The air was full of the sounds of a ship at sea, distant metallic thuds, rattling cables, objects rolling back and forth across the deck. Grey waves broke against the porthole. In the corner of the cabin Dr. Perenyi was hunched over a bucket. She turned away, leaving him alone with his seasickness.

We're on our way, she thought, but where are we going? She knew that the journey would not be over until she or someone else found Grigori Gruda, and that her life and her brother's life would never be quite the same again. But her life had already changed, she thought. She had shot a man. She, Lizbeth Price, Real Estate Agent, had aimed a pistol at a man's chest and pulled the trigger. She closed her eyes and immediately she could see Lek Balka falling to the floor with his hands clawing at his chest and the bright blood pumping out between his fingers.

She opened her eyes and looked at the doctor. He staggered to his feet and turned to face her. His complexion had a green tint and he was obviously exhausted. He lurched across the cabin to lean against the upper bunk. He looked down at her.

"How are you holding up?"

"Better than you, I think," she replied.

He placed a clammy hand on her forehead. "No fever," he said. He took her wrist between his fingers and thumb and waited, consulting his watch. "Not bad," he said. "How's the incision holding out?"

"Hurts like hell but I think it's better than it was," she admitted.

"I wish I could give you something," he said, "but there's nothing left. I'm sorry."

"So am I," she agreed. "I wish you could give yourself something, you look like death."

"It's just ordinary seasickness," he said. "I'll be okay as soon as we reach port. I assume you know where we're going?"

Lizbeth's irritation returned. "How would I know where we're going," she asked, "I barely know when I'm asleep and when I'm awake?"

"You're awake," Perenyi said, "and I would appreciate any information you can give me about where we are."

"I have no idea. How long have we been at sea?"

Perenyi looked at his watch. "About eight hours," he replied. "It's about thirty six hours since...since—"

The boat rolled violently and he groaned.

"Lie down," Lizbeth said. "You're not helping anything by standing there watching me. Lie down and close your eyes, it makes a difference. Believe me I know about these things."

"I wonder what else you know," Perenyi muttered.

He obviously intended to say more, but his face turned a deeper shade of green. Abruptly he scrambled up onto the bunk above her. The canvas dipped to accept his weight, and he settled down with the bulk of his body only inches above her head.

Lizbeth closed her eyes for a moment and then forced them open again to avoid the image that had formed behind her eyelids of Balka rolling on the floor, Perenyi's startled expression, her own horror. When Stefan taught her to shoot to kill, he didn't tell her what it would feel like. He didn't tell her that the scene would play itself over and over again in her head.

She tried to find a comfortable position in the narrow bunk. Rolling onto her side gave her a measure of relief, and the sound of Alex Perenyi's steady breathing gave her comfort. She closed her eyes again and drifted into a restless sleep and a sudden violent dream where the doctor somehow became confused with her memory of the young Joe Ralko.

Joe was driving a green Ford Anglia along the narrow cliff road to Mumbles Head. The windows were open, the radio was playing, and Lizbeth was in the passenger seat. They rounded a corner where high stone walls loomed up on either side. A flock of dirty grey Welsh sheep filled the road, milling about and bleating. Joe laughed and Lizbeth screamed as the car ploughed forward into the grey wooly bodies. Blood spattered up onto the windshield, onto the seats, onto her hands, and Joe stopped laughing. He wasn't Joe, he was Alex Perenyi with a horrified expression on his aristocratic features, and she was laughing and telling him they were only sheep, doomed from birth to become lamb chops. Perenyi ignored her and ran amongst the sheep, trying to stop the bleeding, just as he'd hurled himself onto the fallen Balka.

Lizbeth forced her eyes open and willed herself to stay awake. She had to start thinking. She had to decide what to do. She lay still for a long moment looking up at the sagging bunk above her. She was glad the doctor was with her, she would not have wanted to be alone. She listened to his steady breathing and found herself comforted.

Little by little the motion of the ship began to settle. The seas were smoothing out. Grey light was seeping in through the porthole. Lizbeth rolled onto her other side and wiped the porthole with her hand. The window afforded her a limited view of calm waters, a rain-filled sky and the dark shape of land not very far away.

"Doctor," she said. Nothing stirred. "Doctor." She poked the curved canvas and saw him move. "Doctor."

His face appeared upside down over the side of the bunk. He was no longer green.

"What?"

"I think we're there."

"Where?"

"I don't know.".

His legs came into view over the side of the bunk. "I'm sure you know more than I do," he said.

"Not really."

His legs reached the cabin floor and the rest of his body came into view. His white lab coat was wrinkled and stained but his stethoscope was still around his neck.

He gave her an unfriendly look. "This is your little secret, not mine," he said, "I didn't ask to be invited along."

"I know," said Lizbeth miserably.

Perenyi leaned against the bunk and looked down at her. "Don't you think you owe me an explanation?" he asked.

He was right, of course, he did deserve an explanation, but Lizbeth wasn't anxious to give him one. To anyone who didn't understand, the story would sound so bizarre, so unlikely, so ... she groped for a word ... so *operatic*. Perhaps a little of the truth would keep him quiet.

"They're Yugoslavs," she said.

"Yugoslavs!" he repeated. He leaned across her to look out the porthole. "Is that where we are, Yugoslavia? I thought it didn't exist anymore."

Lizbeth shook her head. "For some people history is everything," she said, "but the answer is no, I don't think this is any part of the old Yugoslavia. This isn't the Adriatic."

He looked baffled, and Lizbeth tried again. "Yugoslavia is an Adriatic country. This ocean looks too cold and too grey for June in the Adriatic."

Perenyi moved away from the porthole. "I don't even begin to understand this," he said. "Don't you have any idea where we are?"

Lizbeth shifted in the bunk. "The only idea I have at the moment, is that I have to find a bathroom."

Perenyi looked at her. "Can you walk?"

She shrugged her shoulders. "I don't know."

"Try it," he urged.

"And where am I going if I can walk?"

He glanced at the bucket.

"Oh no."

Perenyi looked at her impatiently.

"No," Lizbeth repeated.

Perenyi lurched across the cabin to pound on the door. It was opened almost immediately by a tall man in oilskins and yellow sou'wester rain hat.

"And what would you be wanting?" he asked in an Irish accent of vaudevillian strength.

"My patient needs a bathroom." Despite his disheveled appearance, Perenyi spoke with authority.

"The head, is it?" the Irishman said. He nodded and ushered them out of the cabin with a sweep of his yellow coated arm.

Lizbeth was glad of the doctor's hand holding her upright but horribly aware that she was still wearing nothing but the hospital gown which tied at the neck and no other place. She tugged at it, trying to keep it in place.

"Wait a minute." The doctor took off his lab coat and guided her arms into the sleeves.

The journey was along a narrow passage which stank of gasoline and fish.

"Don't lock the door," Perenyi said, helping her inside the foul smelling marine toilet. "I'll wait out here, but I don't want to break the door down to rescue you."

Afterwards, as they made their way slowly back to the cabin with the crewman walking behind them, Perenyi held onto her arm and whispered. "He's Irish, isn't he?"

Lizbeth nodded.

"We flew for about eight hours," Perenyi said. "I couldn't see out of the windows, but I could see the sunlight on the shades, we were flying east. We could have landed in Ireland, couldn't we?"

The crewman locked them into the cabin again, and Lizbeth flopped gratefully down onto the bunk.

She thought about where they could be. "Balka said he had a cousin," she said. "Did you hear him say that?"

"I don't remember," said Perenyi. "I wasn't listening to everything he said."

"He said he was sending me to his cousin, Flora," Lizbeth said, "and that she could make me talk."

Perenyi took a deep breath and looked at her with a pained and serious expression. "Miss Price, do you realize what's happening here? Do you realize what kind of an operation we're involved with? Can you imagine the contacts they had to have to get us onto that plane and out of the States?"

He's patronizing me, Lizbeth thought and I don't blame him, I must seem like a stubborn fool to him.

She nodded her head. "I realiz."

"Then I'm sure you also realize," Perenyi continued "that

there is no point in you keeping quiet about whatever this secret is any longer. You really have to tell them what they want to know."

Lizbeth shook her head. "You're right," she said, "the sensible thing to do would be to tell them, but I can't. You'll just have to take my word for it, Doctor, I can't."

"Can't or won't?"

Lizbeth abruptly changed the subject. "I've been trying to work out where we are. We have an Irish crewman and you say we've been at sea for about eight hours?"

"More than that now," Perenyi said. "It feels like forever."

"Eight or nine hours across the Irish Sea," Lizbeth said and suddenly she knew where they were. It was so obvious.

She cleared the steamy porthole again and looked out, seeing the distant land mass in a different light. Now she recognized all the familiar landmarks.

"Look," she said, "there's the Worms Head, and that, that's Rhossili."

"What does that mean?" Perenyi asked.

"It means they've brought me home," Lizbeth said, "and that's the Welsh coast."

She knew instinctively that they were completing the crossing from Ireland and were in the sheltered waters of the Bristol Channel. She could see the Gower Peninsula to starboard, and knew that the Devon Coast was out of sight on the port side. It was a seascape that she knew like the back of her hand.

She lay back on the bed and stared up at the ceiling. Things weren't so hopeless after all, she thought. She was home! Stefan would be somewhere near, and Grigori wouldn't be far away. She'd find a way to reach him, she'd save him. At last, at long last, Grigori would have his inheritance.

Gregory Gibbons kept a pair of binoculars beside the window in his attic. Without the aid of the binoculars he could glimpse the ocean, but with the binoculars, and on a clear day, he could see across the waters of the Bristol Channel to the Welsh coast. The sun was setting, filling the room with warm light, tinting Gregory's white hair and beard a pleasant pink.

His hands trembled and his view of the distant mountains blurred. He set the binoculars carefully on the shelf and turned away from the window. Evening; and he was alone without Viktor. He had never been alone like this before.

Well, he thought, he couldn't remain alone; there were things to be done and he couldn't be expected to do them for himself. He knew that Viktor had prepared him as best he could for this moment but neither of them thought it would come so soon, or come before he could claim his inheritance.

Now he had to manage by himself. There was dinner to be made, of course, and then he should read the evening newspaper. And after dinner, well, after dinner he must do something about Viktor. He couldn't leave him there in the bed with his eyes open and staring. He would have to do something with the body.

Viktor had told him what to do. "Dig a hole in the backyard," he said, "just like the holes we dug for the pets, and don't forget to throw on some lime, we don't want anything digging me up and spreading me around."

So, Gregory thought, tomorrow I'll take the car out and get a bag of lime.

His knees began to shake and he sat down suddenly in a straight-backed chair gripping the seat with both hands. I can do it on my own, he said to himself. I can drive the car by myself. I can do it. I can do it.

The thought of all of his tomorrows stretched emptily before him. He was never meant to be alone like this. He should have a family. He should have companions and servants.
He shouldn't be alone with no one to wait on him, no one to see to his needs, no one to give him the respect he deserved.

He sighed deeply. How, he wondered, was he to obtain a replacement for Viktor? Viktor had told him he that it would not be possible. Viktor had told him he shouldn't even try, but Viktor didn't understand.

Gregory's reverie was interrupted by the cheerful whistling of the newspaper boy and the sound of a newspaper falling through the slot in the front door and landing on the floor. Gregory hurried to the window and was in time to see the boy riding back toward the village. He'd been delivering papers to Gregory and Viktor for the past year and Gregory knew perfectly well what he looked like. He was a chubby boy with light brown hair and crooked teeth. A sprinkling of freckles spread across his nose and he had a wide engaging smile. He looked strong and intelligent. He would be good company. Gregory watched the boy until he was lost from sight around a curve in the road.

"Why are you watching him?" Viktor said.

Gregory gasped and spun around. "Where are you?" he asked.

"In your head," Viktor replied.

"Why?"

"Because you need me."

"Yes, you're right, I need you. Why did you leave me?"

"Don't be childish; you know perfectly well why I left you. Now tell me what you're planning to do."

"I thought I might ... I might ..."

"Take him?" Viktor asked. "You thought you might take him?"

"I might."

"Remember what happened last time."

"I was very young. I would do better this time."

Viktor was silent.

"So what should I do?" Gregory asked.

"You should do whatever you want," said Viktor. "Don't ever forget that you are a prince, you are not required to behave as other men behave."

"Yes," said Gregory Gibbons, "I am a prince."

Lizbeth could stand it no longer; she was unbearably hot. She kicked off the rough blanket and enjoyed a moment of release before Perenyi spread the blanket over her again.

"I'm hot," she complained.

"And a minute ago you were cold," he said. "You have a fever, Miss Price."

His fingers rested briefly on her forehead and then he lifted her hand and checked her pulse. "We have to get you out of here," he said. "What are they waiting for?"

Lizbeth was beyond caring. She was suffocating under the blanket and the pain which had once been confined to her incision now seemed to have invaded her entire body.

Perenyi tucked her limp wrist back under the blanket and crossed the cabin to pound on the door.

"We have to get out of here," he repeated. "What's the matter with these people?"

He pounded again, and this time the door opened, framing the same crewman they had seen before. He had abandoned his oilskins and wore a thick oiled wool sweater and a knitted watch cap.

"What?" he asked.

"We have to get Miss Price ashore," Perenyi replied. "Her condition is deteriorating rapidly."

The crewman stepped into the cabin and looked down at Lizbeth. She could read nothing in the expression on his long lean face.

"She's running a high fever," Perenyi said. "She needs antibiotics."

The crewman nodded.

"What are we waiting for?" Perenyi asked.

"Dark," the crewman replied. He turned to leave.

"Wait a minute," Perenyi shouted, "just wait a damned minute. I need to know what's going on here."

The Irishman stepped back into the cabin. He leaned nonchalantly across Lizbeth and rubbed a clear space in the steamy porthole. "Look out there Doc, what do you see?"

"Nothing," said Perenyi.

Lizbeth turned painfully onto her side and looked out of the window. Earlier she had seen land, but now she saw nothing but grey-green ocean and watery sunlight.

"If we don't see them, they don't see us," said the Irishman. "Think about that, Doc. and don't go raising your voice to me, it won't do you any good. You're not in any position to be raising your voice."

"How long until dark?" Perenyi asked.

"It'll be a few hours yet."

"We can't wait that long."

The Irishman laughed derisively.

"You don't have any choice. I'm not running you up the channel in broad daylight, that's not the kind of business I'm in. Just hold your water, Doctor, and when you see the lights coming on ashore, you'll feel us moving. I'm not putting you ashore until then."

His cold grey eyes looked at Lizbeth for a long moment. "She looks bad," he said.

He reached into his pocket and pulled out a battered hip flask which he tossed onto the bunk.

"Drink that and don't call me again. I'll come for you when it's time."

When he left he locked the door behind him.

Perenyi picked up the flask and looked at it.

"What is it?" Lizbeth asked.

The doctor unscrewed the lid of the flask and sniffed the contents.

"Whiskey."

"Will it do any good?" Lizbeth asked.

Perenyi shrugged his shoulders. "I don't know," he said.

"Will it numb the pain?"

"I should think so," Perenyi replied, "but..."

Lizbeth reached out for the flask. "I'll try it."

Perenyi still looked very doubtful but he passed the flask across to her and watched her take a long drink.

"Easy," he said, "you can't drink it like water."

"I can try."

Lizbeth took another long pull at the flask. The whiskey burned its way down her throat and spread out into a warm comforting pool in her stomach.

"Oh hell," said Perenyi. He took the flask from her and raised it to his own lips.

"Way to go, Doc," Lizbeth said. "Way to go."

Perenyi sat beside her on the bunk, nursing the flask. "What am I doing here?" he asked.

"You're saving my life," said Lizbeth, "for the second time."

Perenyi picked up her wrist to check her pulse, glanced at his watch, frowned, and kept hold of her hand. His hand felt warm and comforting. They sat in almost companionable silence while the sunlight outside turned from white to gold, to purple, and finally to darkness. The engines began to throb and Lizbeth felt the motion of the boat changing. They were moving.

The doctor gripped her hand tighter. She looked out the window and saw that in the distance the glow of a city lit up the night.

"Look," she said, pulling the doctor down beside her so he could share her view. "The city lights, that must be Swansea, it's the only city along this coast and I'm sure we won't go there. That flashing light, that's the Mumbles lighthouse. I doubt we'll put in there either, too many people. Look over there to the left."

"There's nothing over there," Perenyi said. He was very close to her, his face touching hers as they looked out of the porthole. She could smell the whiskey on his breath, and no doubt, she thought, he could smell it on her.

"That's where we'll go," she said. "The coast is a mass of small bays and inlets. It's very wild and inaccessible. They won't put in there in a boat this size. They'll have to transfer us to something smaller."

Perenyi laughed. His laugh was as pleasant and as unexpected as his smile. "Miss Price," he said, "how do you know so many things?"

Lizbeth grinned. "There may have been a few smugglers among my ancestors, or perhaps a couple of pirates. It's good training for real estate."

Perenyi stopped laughing and looked at her intently. "You've gotten us into a hell of a mess," he said. "Is there any way out of it?"

Lizbeth searched her whiskey-fuddled brain for an honest answer to his question, but before she could think of anything the cabin door opened and the moment was lost.

The effects of the whiskey wore off fast in the fresh air on deck. They were a couple of hundred yards from the land. Patchy moonlight showed them a dark coastline unmarked by signs of human habitation except for car headlights on a distant beach.

The alcohol-induced numbness that Lizbeth had been enjoying did little to ease the pain as she was lowered from the deck of the trawler to the floor of a sleek motorboat which had come alongside,

She forced herself to sit up and pay attention as the boat pounded towards the shore and the headlights came into focus. Somewhere behind her she heard Alex Perenyi complaining of their treatment of her. She heard a thump, and a groan. She turned and saw Alex doubled over in the bottom of the boat.

"Doctor!" she said.

"I'm all right," he grunted, "don't worry about me, worry about yourself."

The helmsman throttled back and the boat settled down into the wave troughs. The shoreline became invisible, lost behind rolling waves, until eventually the boat rode the crest of a breaker which curled beneath her and carried them smoothly onto the beach. It was, Lizbeth knew, a masterful piece of seamanship on the part of the blond haired youth who perched in the stern of the boat, steering with studied nonchalance.

The landing area lit up as they hit the beach. Two vehicles turned on their high beams and Lizbeth saw two figures in shining black wet suits wading through the surf to catch the bow of the boat. Biding their time and waiting for co-operating waves, they hauled the boat effortlessly onto the pebble beach.

"Get out, Doc," someone behind her said, and she saw Perenyi being pushed over the side of the boat. He landed unsteadily and a wave washed in behind him, soaking him to the knees. He staggered and held his ground, his eyes fixed on Lizbeth.

"Hold onto this," someone said, and a blanket landed around Lizbeth's shoulders. She clasped it around herself as she was lifted from the boat into the arms of a giant sized man who stood in the surf waiting to receive her. He carried her ashore as easily as though she were a cooler of beer.

She was aware of Perenyi following the giant up the beach towards the headlights. It took her a moment to identify the two vehicles. She had been away for a long time and their distinctive outline had been forgotten. They looked clumsy and unfamiliar and then memory surfaced, they were Land Rovers, good vehicles for negotiating rocky beaches and steep trails in the dead of night.

Lizbeth was set down in the back of one of the Land Rovers, and Perenyi appeared beside her immediately.

"She needs dry blankets," he said. "Someone get a dry blanket."

The blond giant turned on him, "Shut up, Yank!"

Another voice came out of the darkness. "Get out of the bloody way, Peter and do what the doctor tells you." It was the voice she had heard on the phone. Joe Ralko!

"We have to get her to a hospital," Perenyi said. He took hold of Lizbeth's hand. "You're cold," he said.

Lizbeth couldn't see Joe, he was behind her on the beach, but she could hear him. "No hospitals!".

"She needs treatment," Perenyi insisted. "Who's in charge here?"

"I'll be with you in a minute."

Joe's voice came from somewhere nearby. Lizbeth turned her head and saw him at the water's edge. He turned towards the vehicles and was caught in the glare of their headlights. She saw him as she would a stranger. He was tall and dark, with long black hair with grey streaks that stood out starkly in the white light. A heavy moustache drooped above a generous mouth and a determined jaw. He held a wad of banknotes in his hand.

He handed the cash to the black suited figure who held the bow of the boat and slapped him on the shoulder. He stood for a moment with the waves curling around his ankles and watched as the boat was turned into the waves. As he came up the beach, the motor boat roared away, back into the darkness.

"What's the problem?" he shouted, as he approached Lizbeth and Perenyi.

Perenyi tightened his grip on Lizbeth's hand and opened his mouth to speak. For a moment his mouth remained open and no words came out. Lizbeth sympathized. If she were him, where would she begin? What was the problem? What wasn't the problem? He had been kidnapped from his orderly world and dragged by land, air and sea, against his will, halfway across the world. He had been catapulted onto a cold, inhospitable shore. He had lost track of time and place and had exhausted himself by throwing up for eight hours straight, and now he was wet, hungry and dirty.

"I'm sorry about this," she found herself whispering.

Perenyi ignored her and concentrated on Joe. "My patient is going to die," he said.

"No," Lizbeth whispered.

Perenyi looked down at her and she saw from his grave expression that he was speaking the truth.

"Die?" Joe repeated sounding and looking very foolish.

"What else would you expect?" Perenyi asked.

"Die?" Joe said again.

"Miss Price is recovering from surgery," Perenyi said.

He spoke slowly and distinctly. Lizbeth imagined it was the voice he would use on careless interns, slipshod nurses, or, perhaps, intrusive families. "

She is now running a very high fever and she will need antibiotics, fluids, surgical dressings, respiratory therapy, and pain medication. How close is your nearest hospital?"

"Hospital's out of the question," Joe said, hurrying toward them and pulling a flashlight from his pocket.

"Then she'll die," Perenyi repeated.

"She can't," Joe insisted stubbornly. The beam of the flashlight shone full in Lizbeth's face and she blinked owlishly.

"Liz," Joe whispered. "Lizzie." He reached out and touched a strand of her hair. "What's the matter?" he asked.

"I've already told you," Perenyi said.

Lizbeth stared up at Joe's face, so long forgotten and still so familiar. The years had improved his appearance. His youthful face had been smooth and sullen, but the years had given him a rugged, experienced charm. He looked like the bold adventurer he had always wanted to be.

"Is she really ill?" Joe asked.

Liz sighed inwardly. The years had not, apparently, improved his intelligence.

"I heard she was in hospital, but I didn't think—"

"Well you should have," Perenyi interrupted.

"I thought it was just some minor thing," Joe insisted.

"It was minor" Perenyi said, "and she was making an excellent recovery, until you took her out of the hospital."

"What are we waiting for?" demanded a woman's voice, lightly accented.

The speaker stepped forward, adding the beam of her own flashlight to the circle of light. Lizbeth saw a young woman whose mane of silver hair fanned out in the cold wind.

"The doctor says that Lizbeth is really ill," Joe said.

The woman shrugged. "I'm not surprised."

The beam of her flashlight played briefly over Lizbeth's features and then she turned it on Perenyi, lighting up his wrinkled shirt and haggard face. "You're the doctor?" she asked.

Perenyi remained speechless.

The silver haired woman reached down and took hold of the doctor's right hand, bringing it up into the light for closer examination.

"You have good hands," she said, "healing hands; it is a shame you could not heal Lek Balka."

"I tried," said Perenyi.

"So I was told and we are grateful. You may keep the woman alive for the time being. Get into the car, doctor, there is no time to waste."

Perenyi was hustled away out of the circle of light, and Lizbeth and the silver-haired woman were left alone. Lizbeth blinked as the light played across her face. The woman leaned close and spoke softly.

"My name," she said, "is Flora Balka."

"I guessed," Lizbeth managed to whisper.

"If we did not need you alive, you would be dead already," Flora said.

Lizbeth could think of nothing to say.

Flora reached down and fingered a strand of Lizbeth's hair. "Lek Balka was my cousin," she said. "There is a debt to pay; a blood debt." She pulled viciously on the strand of hair, ripping it from Lizbeth's head. "He will be avenged," she said.

CHAPTER FOUR

Lizbeth and Joe were on the moor. Around them as far as the eye could see were yellow flowering gorse bushes, thickets of blackberries, and hummocks of coarse grass. High up in the clear sky a skylark was singing and closer down on the ground, where they lay, crickets were chirping.

Joe Ralko, young, lean and very strong had his hand inside Lizbeth's blouse. This was her first experience and she found it strange and unbearably exciting to feel the strange hand against her skin. She had allowed his hands to wander around her body before, but outside her clothing, not inside. She tried to trap the hand under her arm but slowly and surely the hand gained its freedom. While his hand was busy, Joe continued to kiss her with grim determination, forcing her head back against the sandy ground. Lizbeth made a conscious decision to relax. It was time.

Her body began to tingle as his hand slid inside her brassiere and closed over her left breast. Her breasts had grown almost overnight and the nuns had told her she should be ashamed of herself, as though these wonderful new curves were a sin in themselves. She wanted to show them to Joe. She wanted to show him that she was now as much of a woman as any other girl he might meet. She wanted him to know that he would never need to look anywhere else.

She sat up and he helped her take off her blouse. She reached around behind her back to unhook her white cotton brassiere but Joe's hands were already there, dealing expertly with the fastening. The bra dropped to the ground. A cool wind was blowing across the heath, but Lizbeth felt warm, very warm. Joe pushed her to the ground.

Lizbeth opened her eyes, fighting off the dream. She felt warm and confused and it took a moment to realize that Dr. Perenyi was leaning over her pressing his stethoscope to her chest.

The doctor smiled, professionally. "How are you doing?" he asked.

Lizbeth felt the blood rush to her face as though the doctor could read her mind and see her dream.

"You seem agitated," he said.

"I was dreaming."

"Are the dreams still as vivid?"

"Oh yes, very realistic."

"That's the Tolwin," Perenyi said, "the effects take a long time to wear off."

His hand moved to pull the sheet away. "I'm going to change your dressing."

Lizbeth breathed deeply. The dream was gone completely and she could take stock of her surroundings. She was in a comfortable bed in a small room with flowered wallpaper. Sunlight was streaming in through windows. An old fashioned light fixture hung above the bed and she realized that everything in the room was old, except for the IV equipment which stood by the bed, and the white metal cart with its array of medical equipment.

The doctor looked at her closely. "Welcome back," he said, "I think you've really surfaced this time."

Lizbeth stared at him.

"You've been more or less out of things for three days," he explained, "but you're back now, aren't you?"

He was looking professional again. Gone was the beard stubble. He wore the same tie, but his shirt was clean and so was his lab coat. The stethoscope was still in place around his neck.

Lizbeth struggled into a sitting position. "I feel much

better," she said, and it was the truth.

She tried to remember something of the past three days. There had been voices, and hands; people had been talking to her, and touching her, but they had been far away and unimportant. Only the pain had been important and now the pain was gone.

"It's been five days since your surgery," the doctor was saying. "In normal circumstances, Miss Price, we'd be talking about discharging you from the hospital. However, your convalescence has been far from normal."

"Where are we?"

"I have no idea," Perenyi said. "I was hoping you would tell me." He forestalled her next question. "The view from the window appears to be urban. I can see some very old looking brick houses, rows and rows of them. There are chimneys and TV aerials, and hills in the far distance."

"That's Wales," Lizbeth said. "There are always hills in the distance."

Perenyi's voice held an impatient and unpleasant edge. "Presumably we are where you expect to be?" he said.

"If we're in a city, we're probably somewhere in Swansea," Lizbeth said. "Joe lives, or lived, at the Star of the Sea Boarding House. Can you see the docks or any ships from the window?"

"No."

"The wall of the prison?"

"No"

"Then it's not the Star of the Sea; you should be able to see one or the other. I don't know where we are."

Perenyi motioned for Lizbeth to lie back against the pillows and she obeyed him. She was momentarily reminded of her dream and of Joe. It seemed to her that Joe's was one of the voices she'd heard over the last couple of days; Joe's voice and a woman's voice. She shivered involuntarily as she remembered Flora Balka. With the memory of Flora came another terrible memory. My God," she thought, I've killed someone. I killed that man. I shot him and he died.

She tried to sit up and Perenyi held her down. "Lie still,

Miss Price." He pulled the cart of medical equipment closer to the bed and slipped his hands into yellow rubber gloves. "Now that you are fully awake, do you intend to tell them what they need to know?" he asked.

"No, never!"

Perenyi kept his head bent, concentrating on his work. His hands were gentle, but his voice betrayed impatience. "Would you mind telling me why not?" he asked.

"I've already told you."

"All you've told me is that this is Wales, and these people are Yugoslavs, citizens of a nation that no longer exists. That's not very helpful information, Miss Price, and it makes very little sense."

Lizbeth watched for a moment as the doctor began snipping and withdrawing the neat black stitches which marched in a row across her belly.

"I have a brother," she said.

He nodded his head and concentrated on his work.

"He's a lot older than I am. We don't have the same father, but we have, or had, the same mother. He's important to these people. In fact he may be important to a lot of people."

"I see."

"No you don't;" Lizbeth said, "you don't see at all. I mean, I loved him, I really did. I was only little but I could tell how lonely he was. He lived all on his own with just this miserable tutor and whenever I went to see him he would just smile and smile and—"

"How old were you?" Perenyi asked.

"Four."

"And you haven't seen him since?"

"No one's seen him since."

Perenyi dropped the scissors back into the tray and began to pull off his rubber gloves.

"I can't let him down," Lizbeth said. "I can't give away his secret, not to these people."

"So no one has seen him in more than thirty years?"

The Serbian Solution

Perenyi asked.

Lizbeth nodded her head.

"How do you know he's still alive?"

"Well, I don't know. I just—"

"So he may be dead?"

What an annoying man, Lizbeth thought. She'd just told him how much she loved her brother and instead of sympathizing he was calmly suggesting that Grigo might be dead.

"Of course he's not dead," she snapped.

"You don't know that," Perenyi said. "However, we do know that Flora's cousin is dead."

Oh, it's "Flora" now, is it? Lizbeth thought. Now I know who he's been talking to while I was asleep.

"You didn't hesitate to kill a man who was quite definitely alive for the sake of one who may be dead," Perenyi continued.

"I didn't mean to kill him," Lizbeth protested.

"Why don't you try looking at this from my point of view?" Perenyi asked. "I do have a point of view, Miss Price."

"Of course you do; and couldn't you call me Lizbeth, after all, we've been through a lot together?"

Perenyi interrupted her. "We've been through a lot, Miss Price, but not together. There has been no agreement on my side that I would go through any of this and I would prefer to keep our relationship on a professional footing."

He rolled the rubber gloves into a ball and tossed them into the waste basket exactly as he had done so many miles ago in Pittsburgh.

"You can get out of bed any time you like," he said, "in fact, the sooner the better. Get as much exercise as you can. You should have been walking days ago."

He dusted his hands together in a dismissive gesture. "I believe that ends our professional relationship, Miss Price. Should I ever get back to the United States I will bill you for my services."

"Doctor," Lizbeth pleaded, "haven't you ever believed in a cause?"

"You have not told me about your cause. I cannot believe

in something I have not been told."

"You have to help me," Lizbeth insisted, but the determined expression on his face told her that he had no intention of helping her.

"No, I don't," Perenyi said. "I don't have to take your side in this; I don't have to take anyone's side. What I have to do, Miss Price, is get back to Pittsburgh."

"You don't think they're going to let you go, do you?" Lizbeth asked. "You don't know these people."

"I've spent the last three days with them," Perenyi said, "I think I know them better than you do."

He turned from her and lifted a vial and a syringe from the tray. He filled the syringe with practiced ease.

What's he going to do? Lizbeth asked herself. What's in there? She struggled as Perenyi took hold of her arm but she was weaker than she realized. His grip was strong and secure.

He looked down at her. He looked apprehensive. "Tell them what they want to know." he urged. "Just tell them Lizbeth, and they'll let us go home. Don't make me do this."

Lizbeth looked at the syringe. "What's in there?"

"Sodium pentothal. Flora gave it to me. I don't want to use it if I don't have to."

"They won't let you go home," Lizbeth said.

"Yes they will."

"Don't you understand?" Lizbeth asked. "I can't let him down. He's my brother."

She closed her eyes and thought about him. She could see him clearly, a dark gangling teenager welcoming her at the door of his new little house on the edge of the moor. "

I don't want to tell them," she said. "Don't make me tell them."

Lizbeth looked at the doctor's face as he plunged the needle into her arm. He looked sad.

The Serbian Solution

She wondered why she had been so unwilling to talk. Talking was so easy and so relaxing that she couldn't imagine why she hadn't talked before when talking made everyone so happy. Perenyi smiled, Joe smiled, even the malevolent Flora Balka smiled, and their questions were so easy to answer. They were disappointed, of course, that she couldn't remember all the details. She described the narrow country road they had followed, where trees crowded in on each side and eventually met above their heads, so that Uncle Cyril was driving the car through a long green tunnel. She remembered a cluster of cottages around a patch of green, and a pretty picture. What sort of picture? An animal? Yes, a red animal, a dragon painted on a sign. She'd glimpsed it from the corner of her eye, but there had been no time to see the details because Uncle Cyril was impatient to arrive. A lot of time had been wasted stopping the car while she threw up.

Everything Lizbeth knew tumbled from her lips in answer to their questions. She had seen a church, with a graveyard but she didn't know the name of the church. It didn't matter how often they asked her, she couldn't tell them the name, because she hadn't seen it. Yes, there had been a sign outside, but she hadn't read the sign: it had been obscured by two big holly bushes. Her mind gave her a clear picture of the dark green foliage obscuring most of the gold lettering of the sign.

Grigo's house wasn't in the village. They'd driven through the village, up a steep hill and out into the open moor where he lived in a brick bungalow, nowhere near as grand as the house he had occupied in Mumbles, but you could see the sea from his attic window.

"Is that enough?" Perenyi asked.

"It's a good start," Joe replied.

"I think she's told you everything she remembers," Perenyi insisted. "From what I've read about sodium pentothal it's a very effective drug. Of course, I've never administered it before, but I think it went well."

He looked at Lizbeth. "That wasn't so bad, was it?" he

said.

She smiled, feeling good. She felt as though a great burden had been lifted. The decision had been made for her. She had told her secret, but not of her own free will. She had betrayed Grigo, but it wasn't her fault. She had nothing to feel guilty about. Only Flora Balka's sudden, malevolent glance gave her a moment of unease.

"Rest now," Perenyi said, "and let the effects of the drug wear off. Flora's arranging for you to be transferred to a private convalescent home. When I come back I'll help you to get out of bed. Another couple of days and we'll be able to ship you back to the States. They assure me they can work it out."

He smiled encouragingly. "You did well," he said.

They left her alone then, lying in the bed, grinning at the ceiling and enjoying the sense of release.

As the effects of the drug began to wear off, Lizbeth's grin faded, and was replaced at first by a puzzled frown and finally by an expression of furious shock. She had talked! She had told them everything she knew.

Frantically she tried to recall exactly what she had said. The border? No, they hadn't asked her about the border, so she hadn't told them about crossing the border. And the milestone? No, no, she was quite certain they hadn't asked any questions about the milestone; they didn't know about the milestone. She felt her spirits lifting slightly. She had been like a computer. Ask the right questions and you get the right answers, but don't expect the computer to volunteer information you haven't asked for.

So what did they know? They knew about the dragon. They would probably look for a village with a pub called The Dragon. They knew about the sea. She'd told them about Grigo taking her up to the attic and pointing out the distant glimpse of ocean. They knew about the church, but every village had a church. They didn't know enough, not yet. They would have to ask her more questions.

She wondered if the doctor would administer another dose of truth drug. As she thought of the doctor she felt herself filled with cold fury. He was a doctor, a healer; how could he do this to her? And if he thought they would let him out of here in one piece, he had another thought coming.

Well, she couldn't spend any more time thinking about him; she had to leave. She had to get out of here before they could do anything else to her. She swung her legs out of bed, rested for a moment, and then stood up.

She felt a little weak, but not too bad. Pushing the IV stand in front of her, she shuffled across the room and stood on tiptoe to look out of the window. The view was as Perenyi had described it, rows and rows of identical red tile roofs, a forest of chimneys and TV aerials, a pale blue sky littered with tiny white clouds, and in the distance the hazy outline of the mountains.

Her heart lifted at the sight of the mountains. She was home. She was back in the land of her childhood, and somewhere out there were people who would help her. Stefan was there somewhere, if only she could reach him.

"Are you supposed to be out of bed?" a voice asked.

Lizbeth turned and saw a girl standing in the doorway, holding a tray of food.

"I was looking at the view," Lizbeth said.

The girl made no comment, closing the door quietly and crossing the room to set the tray on the bed. She was maybe seventeen or eighteen years old. Her hair was long and dark, framing a face powdered dead white with pouting red lips. The hand holding the tray was adorned with a tattoo of a spider. There was, Lizbeth thought, something of Joe in the sullen set of her mouth, and the stubbornness of her jaw.

"She thought you should eat," the girl said, "and whatever she thinks, we do. You'd better eat it or I'll never hear the end of it."

Lizbeth hazarded a guess. "Flora Balka?"

"Flora bleeding Balka," the girl replied, and there was a wealth of dislike in her tone. "God's gift to the revolution," she added.

"So you know about the revolution?" Lizbeth asked.

"Come and eat this food," the girl insisted, setting her mouth in a line so reminiscent of Joe's that Lizbeth had to smile as she crossed the room and sat down on the bed.

"Are you a relative of Joe Ralko?" Lizbeth asked.

The girl raised her eyebrows. "That's a bloody fool question," she said, "of course I am. I'm his sister, Bronwyn."

"He didn't have a sister," Lizbeth said, lifting the cover from the plate and discovering soggy fish and chips.

"He does now," Bronwyn said. "I was a bit of a surprise to my mother."

I'll bet you were, Lizbeth thought looking at the scowling girl. Such a daughter would be a surprise to any mother.

"She thought she was finished with that sort of thing," Bronwyn said.

"I remember your mother," Lizbeth said.

"Eat your bleeding fish," Bronwyn said impatiently, "I cooked it myself."

"Oh," said Lizbeth. "I thought it would come from the fish and chip shop."

"Can't afford the fish and chip shop," Bronwyn said, "I have to do all the sodding cooking at the Star of the Sea. I mean, do I look like I was put on this world to be a bleeding cook for a bunch of old wrinklies? Mum and Dad left it to us both, me and Joe, but he doesn't do sweet nothing."

"I remember the Star of the Sea," Lizbeth said.

Bronwyn looked surprised. "You been in Swansea before?" she asked.

"I grew up here," Lizbeth said.

"Well," the girl said, "you could have fooled me. I thought you were a Yank. Hey, wait a minute, now I know who you are, you're that drunk woman who phoned from the States and wanted to talk to Uncle Stefan. I recognize your voice."

"Was that you who answered the phone?" Lizbeth asked, trying to put together the polite voice on the phone and this sullen, ill spoken girl. "I certainly didn't recognize your voice."

"I use me posh voice on the phone," Bronwyn said,

"learned it from the bleeding nuns didn't I?"

Lizbeth nodded her head. She had a feeling that if she could just be quiet and listen she would learn all sorts of things.

"After you phoned, I was going to tell Uncle Stefan about you," Bronwyn continued, "but Joe told me not to bother. He told me you were just some old tart of the Colonel's wanting to stir up trouble. Is Uncle Stefan really poking you, isn't he a bit old for you?"

Lizbeth was tempted to defend herself on the subject of whether or not she was being "poked" by Stefan, but Bronwyn gave her no chance.

"Not that I don't like older blokes myself," she said. "I mean, they're more interesting, aren't they, but not blokes as old as Uncle Stefan? I see them all day anyway, don't I?"

"Do you?" Lizbeth asked.

"At the Star of the Sea," Bronwyn said. "It's bloody full of old men."

"Stefan's men," Lizbeth said. "Are they still alive? They were there when I was a kid, and I thought they were old then."

"You should see them now," Bronwyn said, "bloody old fools. They spend half their lives on the beach doing their exercises, maneuvers, they call them. They look blooming ridiculous, but it keeps them healthy. They'll live for bleeding ever, they will."

Lizbeth picked up one of the soggy chips and chewed it slowly remembering the old men at the Star of the Sea. They had been a fixture of her childhood. She realized now that Uncle Cyril and Uncle Nicholas, who had taken her to see her brother and died on the way home, must have been part of the same band of men.

She remembered all of them as fierce men with bristling moustaches and flashing eyes. They had smelled of cigarettes and liquor and spoke loudly to each other in a language she couldn't understand. Joe's mother and father had treated them with elaborate respect, always calling them by their military titles. Now Joe's sister called them "wrinklies". It was, she thought, a sad end for the last remnant of the Yugoslav Royalist forces, to be condemned to live out their lives in a boarding house on the south coast of Wales, waited on by a girl whose vocabulary consisted mainly of "bloody, bleeding, and sodding".

"If you ask me," Bronwyn said, helping herself to a chip and sitting companionably beside Lizbeth, "they should all go back where they came from. I mean, there's always someone fighting someone over there in Yugoslavia, or Bosnia, or Serbia or whatever they call the miserable place, and they could probably get in a few shots of their own. At least they'd die happy, you know, instead of lying around here waiting for this great leader of theirs to show up, which he won't."

"You know about the leader?" Lizbeth asked.

Bronwyn looked at her in surprise. "Of course I do," she said, "it's all they ever talk about. Grigori Gruda, the great prince. It's bloody stupid, if you ask me, the man's been missing for thirty years, and he's not going to show up now. He's dead, he has to be. He was probably done in years ago, you know, like the Princes in the Tower. Oh, sorry," Bronwyn looked at Lizbeth again, "you wouldn't know about the Princes in the Tower, would you, you being a Yank?"

"I'm not a Yank," Lizbeth said, "and I know about the Princes in the Tower."

"We had a film at school," said Bronwyn, "about them and me and my friend Carey got a detention for laughing. That's nuns for you, isn't it? I mean, we wasn't laughing at the kids, we was laughing at their tights. Anyway, it's the same thing, isn't it, you know, heir to the throne and all that sort of thing, done away with so he can't inherit?"

"He's not dead," Lizbeth said before she could stop herself.

"Isn't he?" Bronwyn looked at Lizbeth for a long, calculating moment.

"Why should he be dead?" Lizbeth asked.

"You tell me," said Bronwyn. "In fact, there' are a lot of things I'd like to tell me. Who are you? What are you doing here? Why are you so sick?"

"You'd better ask your brother all those questions," Lizbeth replied.

"He'll never bloody well tell me," said Bronwyn. "He thinks I'm too young to understand, and he says I don't have the right blood. He says I've been Anglicized and I'm not a real patriot, not like he is."

She reached out and took another chip. "Big deal," she said, "I wouldn't want to be like him anyway, spending me whole blooming life looking for some old has-been leader, for some country he's never even been to, and doesn't exist anymore."

She stood up and gathered together the remains of the meal. "It's that bloody Flora. Joe was getting quite normal before she came; he even helped me every now and then, you know, with the wrinklies, and then along she comes, and he's at it again, him and bloody Peter and Milos, and all those other great pillocks he hangs around with. He's got them out looking for clues, he says, and he's at home poking Flora. You should hear them, its' bloody disgusting.

It doesn't make any sense to me. I mean Uncle Stefan talks like finding this guy is going to be like finding the Holy Grail, and Joe says they have to hunt him down and kill him. They can't both be right, can they?"

She looked down at Lizbeth. "You alright?" she asked. "You look real pale. You should probably lie down."

"I'm okay," Lizbeth gasped.

She'd known, of course, she'd known all along that they planned to kill him, but to hear this child say it so casually was another matter.

At least she knew now who were her friends and who were her enemies. Somehow she had to leave here and reach Stefan. To do that, she would need an ally and her only hope was Alex Perenyi. They'd been friends, hadn't they, for a few minutes, drinking whiskey on board the Irish trawler? He felt responsible for her, and he was worried about her. He didn't want them to give her more drugs. He could be made to see reason.

"I don't feel well," Lizbeth said. "Do you think you could

ask them to send the doctor up here as soon as he gets back?"

Bronwyn shook her head. "He's gone," she said. "I heard Joe telling Peter to take him to the station. He'll be halfway to London by now, lucky sod."

CHAPTER FIVE

Gregory Gibbons drove the Morris Minor carefully into town. He had never been alone in the old car before and had never felt responsible for its condition. He listened nervously to every squeak and rattle as it bumped down the leafy lane that connected Dragons Green to the outside world.

On the two lane highway the ride smoothed out but the car blew black smoke into the clear morning air and refused to rev itself up to anything faster than 60 mph even on the downhill run to the Garden Center. He turned cautiously into the almost empty parking lot and parked as far away as he could get from any other vehicles, not trusting his ability to locate himself within one single set of white lines.

He purchased a couple of sacks of quick-lime; for his roses, he said as he paid cash. As a last minute measure he bought a new spade. The handle on his old one was beginning to split.

The spike-haired youth who took his money and helped him heft the bags of lime onto his shoulder probably wondered why the old boy had parked his car so far away when the parking lot was more or less empty. Gregory regretted that he had drawn attention to himself as the boy watched him stumbling away under his heavy burden. He stopped and turned to glare at the youth. The boy picked his nose thoughtfully for a couple of seconds and then walked away. Gregory hoped he would give the subject no further thought.

With the lime concealed in the trunk of the Morris, Gregory stopped at the village store. He couldn't face the thought of making his own lunch and he really fancied one of Mrs.

Trewin's meat pies.

"Why hello Mr. Gibbons," Mrs. Trewin said, looking at him over the counter as he came in the door. "Are you all on your own?"

'They think I'm retarded,' Gregory said to Viktor who was safely tucked away inside his head.

'Of course they do,' Viktor replied, "I've encouraged them to think of you that way. I have to keep you safe.'

"But they feel sorry for me," Gregory protested.

"Just think how surprised they'll be," said Viktor, "just think what they'll say when you claim your inheritance."

If I ever do, Gregory thought.

"I'd like a steak and kidney pie," he said to Mrs. Trewin.

Mrs. Trewin smiled the over-bright smile she reserved for children and people of doubtful intelligence and wrapped the pie in greaseproof paper.

"Fifty pence," she said slowly and clearly.

He handed her a five pound note.

"Would you want to pay your uncle's paper bill while you're here, Mr. Gibbons," she asked, "it would save you trouble tomorrow evening when the boy comes to collect?"

Gregory shook his head. The boy must come. The boy must stop and ask for his money.

"I don't have enough cash on me," he said.

Mrs. Trewin looked at the change she was preparing to put into his hand. "You have enough," she said.

"I'm going to stop at the pub for a quick one," Gregory said.

"No you're not," Viktor said.

"Yes, I am."

Gregory took the money from Mrs. Trewin's hand and enjoyed the startled expression on her broad red face.

"Booze is so bloody expensive, isn't it?" he said.

He picked up his pie and left the shop before Mrs. Trewin could say another word.

He hesitated outside the door. Still undecided, he opened

the passenger door of the Morris and set the pie down on the seat. Finally he locked the car doors and went across to the Dragon. Mrs. Trewin was probably watching him from the store window and he intended to be as good as his word.

He was relieved to find that the saloon bar of the Dragon was almost empty, being occupied only by the barmaid and by Bernie Collins and his Golden Retriever. Gregory had seen Collins walking his dog on the moor behind Gregory's house. They had spoken a few times; they weren't friends but they were acquaintances. Bernie was drinking cider and the Golden Retriever had a small bowl of beer. Gregory nodded to Collins and leaned over to scratch the dog's head.

"Are you all alone?" Collins asked.

"My uncle isn't feeling well," Gregory said.

"He does well for his age," Collins observed.

"Yes, very well."

Gregory wondered what he should order. Viktor used to buy cider for him on the few occasions they came into the Dragon but Gregory wasn't in the mood for cider. He ordered a double Scotch.

Viktor warned him to be careful. "Drink it up and get out of here, and don't stand around talking, you'll say too much."

Gregory consumed the Scotch and ordered another. By the time he left the Dragon his head was buzzing pleasantly.

The Morris Minor showed a tendency to misbehave and head towards fences and ditches on its way home to the redbrick bungalow. Gregory was glad when he managed to get it safely put away in the garage.

He carried the spade and the quick lime up the steep slope of the back garden. At the top of the sloping garden where a dry stone wall separated his property from the wild weeds of the moors, he had planted a tangle of rambling roses and flowering vines. Here he set down the bags and began to dig. Soon he was chatting to the occupants of the ground beneath the luxuriant foliage.

"Randolph," he said to the small bone chip that gleamed

on the dark surface of the spade, "you were such a good old dog. 1968 or 69; it's been a long time, Randolph. Rest in peace."

He reburied the bone chip and carefully smoothed the ground. He moved along a few feet and started to dig again. He unearthed another fragment of bone.

"Is that you Tiger?" he asked. "I thought I put you under the rose bush. I'm sure I didn't put you in here."

He wiped his forehead with the back of his hand. He was beginning to sweat. "Must be the drink," he said aloud.

He moved along another few feet and resumed his digging. This time he unearthed a chunk of a much larger bone.

"Leave it alone," Viktor said.

"What is it?"

"Leave it alone."

Gregory turned over another spadeful of earth, more bones.

"No room here," Viktor said and he laughed inside Gregory's head. "No room at the inn."

"Stop laughing," Gregory said, "it isn't funny. I'm tired of digging."

His eyes searched the garden.

"I'll have to move the compost heap. I'll put you here and then I'll put the compost heap on top of you. You'll like that, compost heaps are very warm. I've seen steam coming out of grass clippings""

"No," said Viktor, "do the job properly."

"It's not my fault," Gregory said. "I'm not the one who filled the garden up with bones."

"Then who did?" Viktor asked.

"I don't want to think about that," Gregory said.

He leaned the spade against the stone wall. I'll wait, he thought, until I have someone to help me. I'll wait until tomorrow. Tomorrow the newspaper boy will come whistling up the path and knocking on the door to collect the month's money.

"What about me?" Viktor demanded.

"I don't want to talk to you," Gregory said, "you've been

up to something."

Viktor waited a moment and then he said softly, "Are you sure it was me?"

She had not heard the girl lock the door. Lizbeth sat on the bed, silent and still as a statue and waited, not daring to move. She heard the sound of Bronwyn descending a staircase and the slamming of an exterior door, and then the old house lapsed into silence.

Lizbeth rose cautiously to her feet and found that her strength was returning. She assessed her situation. First the IV would have to go. That didn't seem too difficult a task. She pulled off the Band-Aids and withdrew the needle but it continued to drop a steady flow of liquid onto the floor and for some reason the steadily growing puddle offended her. She laid the needle on the bed where the fluid could soak into the mattress.

Freed of the tethering IV, she was able to tiptoe across the room and try the door handle. Not only was the door unlocked, there was not even a keyhole, there was no way to lock the door. Lizbeth paused to consider what this meant. They had not expected her to get out of bed. How sick had she been, she wondered? Had she really come close to death? Did this mean that the doctor could have left at any time and had stayed only because he felt responsible for her?

She cleared her mind of such thoughts. She would think about him later, when she had the time.

She pulled the door gently toward her and peeked out onto the landing. There was no one in sight. She opened the door wider and cautiously stepped out of her prison. She found herself on a narrow landing with three other doors similar to her own. A flight of steps descended to another, larger, landing and four more doors.
Beyond the lower landing the stairs went on down into a narrow

hallway. The landing on which she now stood was wallpapered in a colorful pattern of nymphs and shepherds. The nymphs and shepherds gave way to pink cabbage roses at the second landing, and down in the hallway the cabbage roses were put to shame by a riot of sunflowers. The whole colorful ensemble was illuminated by sunlight streaming in through a skylight set high above her head.

Lizbeth could see an escape path down through the floral jungle, but not dressed as she was in a hospital gown and bare feet. She opened a door at random and found a bathroom. She slipped inside, relieved herself and checked her appearance in the mirror.

She was not at all pleased by what the mirror showed her. The events of the past days had left their mark on her face and her hair. Her face looked narrow and pinched and her eyes seemed lifeless and sunk too far into their sockets. Her hair, which her mother had taught her to call "auburn" and which normally glowed and curled and brought her compliments, hung stringy and lifeless. She looked at her pale arms and legs. She belonged to a health club, for heaven's sake, she thought, she had spent months toning her muscles and hours lying on a tanning bed, and now she was horrified by the stick-like limbs protruding from the hospital gown. No wonder Alex Perenyi had left.

She tried another door and found what she had been looking for. The bedroom was tiny, and made more so by another example of the colorful wallpaper so favored by whoever owned the house. This one was a series of broad stripes in red, green and gold. The only furnishings were a narrow bed and a dresser, but on the bed was a small pile of laundry, Perenyi's laundry, Lizbeth concluded.

From the pile she selected a starched white lab coat, a tie which she fastened around her waist to keep the lab coat together, and a pair of black dress socks to take the place of shoes. As an afterthought she picked up a pair of white Jockey shorts. They would look ridiculous but she couldn't face the idea of going down the stairs and out onto the street without underwear. This she blamed on the nuns.

Now was the time to try the stairs. There were no signs of life below. Cautiously, testing each step for tell-tale creaks, Lizbeth began her descent into the regions of the cabbage rose wallpaper. At the curve of the first landing she stopped, frozen. Down below a door slammed, another door opened, loud voices drifted upwards.

"How could you let him go?"

Flora, Lizbeth thought, and she's hopping mad.

"We were finished with him. We didn't need him."

Lizbeth recognized the second speaker immediately, an angry and defensive Joe Ralko.

"I needed him," Flora said.

"Needed him for what?"

"We're not finished with the woman yet,"" Flora said. "We have to give her more of the drug."

"We'll give it to her ourselves."

"No, we must let the doctor do it. What if we give her too much?"

"What if we do?" Joe asked. "What difference does that make to you? I thought you wanted her dead? What about this blood feud you've been ranting on about?"

Lizbeth caught her breath. So it hadn't been a dream, Flora really had sworn vengeance for her cousin's death.

"I will take care of that when I'm ready," Flora said, "and in the meantime she must live. Where is the doctor?"

"Peter took him to the station," Joe said with an air of finality.

Lizbeth heard quick footsteps in the hall and the sound of a scuffle.

"Let me go," Flora screamed.

Lizbeth crawled to the edge of the landing and peered down through the banisters. Flora and Joe were two flights below her in the hallway locked in an angry embrace.

"Why are you so anxious to have him back?" Joe demanded. "

"We need him."

"You mean you need him."

"Don't be absurd!"

"Haven't you had what you want from him already?" Joe asked. "Don't think I haven't seen you looking at him, touching him—"

"No," Flora said.

"I'm not sharing you with anyone," Joe said.

"Who are you to talk?" Flora asked. "I saw the way you looked at that woman. I've seen you trying to protect her."

"She's nothing," Joe said. "It was years ago when we were kids. I don't feel anything for Lizbeth. You can do what you like with her."

Lizbeth felt a cold shiver run up her spine. I have to get out of here, she thought.

"And what about the doctor? You know he'll talk." Flora said.

"By the time anyone believes him, we'll be gone," Joe assured her.

Their grappling had turned from angry to passionate and Joe's voice had dropped to the low persuasive whisper that Lizbeth had remembered for years.

"I won't share you."

"Will you leave all this behind?" Flora asked.

"I'm coming with you to Belgrade," Joe said. "I can't wait. I've been stuck here for far too long. You've woken me up Flora, you've woken us all up."

"But first we must take care of the prince," Flora said.

Joe laughed. "First we take care of ourselves."

His hands slid down and grasped the taut curves of Flora's backside. He pulled her closely against him. She moved her hips, grinding against him and making him groan.

Joe broke the embrace and led her toward the stairs. Lizbeth shrank back. They stopped at the first landing and she moved forward to look down on them again. She felt unclean and voyeuristic looking down on their twining arms and listening to the moist sucking sound of their kisses.

Her bird's eye view showed her that Flora's amazing silver hair was a work of nature with no dark roots. Joe, on the other hand, was getting a little thin on top. It was strange to think of the number of years that had passed since Lizbeth had wound her fingers into that once thick black hair, years that had thinned it out to reveal the vulnerable pink scalp.

Joe's hands moved to the front of Flora's shirt and busied themselves with the buttons.

"Your sister —" Flora protested.

"Gone;" said Joe, "I heard her leave."

"Does she know anything?"

Joe shrugged his shoulders. "She doesn't care."

Flora stopped him as he tried to ease her blouse off her shoulders. "What if she has told Stefan?"

Lizbeth sat back and enjoyed the feeling of relief at hearing Stefan's name. He was still close by; she had only to find him. All she needed now was for Flora and Joe to get off the stairs and out of her way. Unfortunately she wouldn't put it past Joe to conclude his business with Flora right there on the landing among the cabbage roses.

"She hasn't told him," Joe said, "or he'd be beating down the door by now. Stop worrying."

Flora released his hands and allowed her blouse to fall to the floor.

Not on the landing, Lizbeth thought, please, not on the landing.

Apparently Flora had no wish to be ravaged on the carpet. "Come on," she whispered, grabbing Joe's hand and leading him towards an open doorway. He followed her obediently and the door closed behind them.

Five minutes, Lizbeth thought cynically, or ten at the most. Unless Joe had changed his style, he'd be ready to explode by the time they reached the bed and five minutes later he'd be ready to leave. He never did waste much time talking after it was all over.

She hurried down the stairs, making no sound on the thick

carpet. The flooring in the hallway was made of uneven oak timbers, slippery and treacherous for her feet in Alex Perenyi's black socks. She shuffled as fast as she could to the front door, opened it, and stepped out onto the street.

She paused for a moment, looking around and trying to find her bearings. The house was at the end of a short cul-de-sac and she could see a main road just a few yards away. She hurried down the steps, along the sidewalk, made a hasty right turn and found herself on a busy street where she had to pause to get her breath, amazed at how weak she felt. She found that Perenyi's shorts weren't such a good fit after all and that she would need to either hold them up or lose them, and she preferred not to lose them. Clutching her ill-fitting underwear, she moved carefully along the street.

The crowd of pedestrians on the sidewalk thickened as she travelled and soon she saw that she was approaching the downtown shopping district. She looked up again, trying to get her bearings. The sun was high, mid-afternoon, she thought. The scent of sea which hung in the air was almost drowned by the fumes from the traffic as buses and cars swept past.

Lizbeth moved determinedly onward, trying to blend with the crowd. One or two people glanced at her and glanced away again. She knew that she made a strange figure, but she had not forgotten the legendary British acceptance of eccentrics. However strange she might look no one would be so rude as to stare.

Resisting the urge to look behind her, she allowed herself to be swept up into the crowd as it surged along the sidewalk. Soon she was on a shopping street lined with department stores.. She continued to clutch her underwear and hurry along on her stockinged feet. She cast a sidelong glance at the shop window displays. If only she had a few dollars, or pounds, she thought, she could make herself look like everyone else instead of looking like a refugee from a medical experiment.

She began to form a plan. She rejected it several times and tried to come up with alternatives, but she knew that she really had only one course of action open to her. She stood for a moment in the doorway of the Marks and Spencer Department Store. She knew where she was, Marks and Spencer had always stood exactly on this spot. She knew where she was going. She set off confidently and within a couple of minutes was at the taxi stand outside the train station.

She thought again about her plan. Her mother had family farther north in the high mountains of Snowdonia, but she hardly knew them and they had not exchanged so much as a Christmas card since she left for the States. The girls she had known in the convent were probably living somewhere around Swansea but she had no idea where. No, there was really only one person she could go to but she was very unsure of her welcome.

She padded to the head of the line of taxis. The cab driver snoozed behind his newspaper. Lizbeth rapped on the window. He looked up and assessed her with shrewd Celtic eyes.

"Newton," she said.

"Hop in, love."

Lizbeth opened the door.

"Got any luggage?"

"No."

"Train was early, was it?"

Lizbeth looked around and realized there were no passengers coming out of the station. "I didn't come on the train," she said, climbing into the back of the taxi before the driver had the chance to notice that his passenger had no handbag, no shoes, and very strange clothes.

The driver reached out and flicked off his sign. "Newton," he said, confirming.

"Dell Close, top of the hill."

He eased out into the traffic.

His route took them back along the path Lizbeth had taken and within a few minutes they were passing the top of the cul-de-sac and Lizbeth could see the house where she had been held. The double decker bus in front of them halted at a bus stop and the taxi driver stopped behind it.

The taxi started forward again and Lizbeth saw Flora on

the sidewalk outside the house. She was looking anxiously to the right and to the left along the road. A few hundred feet away Joe was doing the same thing. Lizbeth smiled grimly and slid down in the seat, hiding herself from view.

With their brief lovemaking behind them, Flora and Joe had obviously gone to check on their captive and found her missing. Where, she wondered, would they start looking for her? Would they come to the same conclusion that she had come to, that there was only one place for her to go?

The taxi driver cleared the downtown traffic and pulled out onto the wide promenade fronting the curve of Swansea Bay. The waters of the bay sparkled in the afternoon sunlight, and across the bay the chimneys and cooling towers of the Port Talbot steel works caught the light.

The tide was out, revealing acres of mud flats and a small army of people digging for bait. A string of freighters lined up on the horizon, waiting for the tide to turn and sweep them into the Swansea Docks. The scene was immediately familiar to Lizbeth; nothing had changed in her years of absence.

They drove past the Star of the Sea Boarding House standing shoulder to shoulder with other converted Victorian houses and looking out on the bay through lace curtained windows. Lizbeth looked at it for a moment, remembering how much of her teenage life had centered around its big old kitchen and dark paneled public rooms.

Looking across from the house to the sea wall and the beach, Lizbeth saw the old men. They were lined up on a narrow strip of hard-packed sand, performing their maneuvers. Sprightly and upright, they seemed unaffected by age as they marched and turned in perfect unison.

Leaving the outskirts of the city behind, the taxi picked up speed. The lighthouse on Mumbles Head became visible, and later the crumbled Roman towers of Oystermouth castle. Soon the driver turned his vehicle inland, changing gears for the steep hill and the narrow road. Stone cottages crowded in on either side with cats watchful on the windowsills, and dogs snoozing on front steps.

Newton Village, Lizbeth thought. Home.

She looked nervously out of the rear window for any sign they were being followed. No, she thought, not yet, but eventually they'll guess where I'm going. Another right turn brought them past the big grey house where Grigo had lived with Viktor. She saw that it had been converted into a Retirement Home.

The driver, obviously familiar with the village, made several more turns onto a post-war development of small brick houses and finally into Dell Close.

"What number?" he asked.

"Twelve, it's on the right."

The taxi halted outside a white bungalow with a well-tended front yard. Roses peeped over the guardian brick wall and ivy climbed the gate posts.

"If you'll wait," Lizbeth said, "I'll get the money."

"You don't have it with you?"

For the first time the driver turned to look at her, no beating about the bush for him, not where money was involved.

"What are you up to?" he asked.

"Nothing," she said, "I work at the hospital, and I had some trouble."

The driver looked at her skeptically and then climbed out onto the sidewalk. He opened the door for her.

"I'll walk in with you, love, just to make sure."

Lizbeth fumbled with the gate. Last time she had passed through that gate she'd been holding the arm of an American soldier and shouting defiance at the man who stood in the doorway of the house and told her never to darken his door again. Well, here she was, darkening his door again.

She saw no signs of life in the bungalow but next door a lace curtain twitched, and across the street a man appeared in his front yard industriously picking dead blooms from his rose bushes. Again she looked around for signs of more malevolent watchers. They would come, she was quite certain of it.

She thought that the doorbell rang loudly enough to awake the dead. When its echoes faded away they were replaced by an ominous stillness. The only other sound was the wheezing breath of the cabdriver waiting at her side.

Somewhere within the bungalow a door slammed and footsteps approached. They sounded to Lizbeth as though they were advancing forever along a marble hall but that could not be, the bungalow was tiny, he had only to take a couple of paces from the back living room to the front door.

The door opened.

"Dad," Lizbeth said.

Jamie Price wore an old cardigan and grey slacks. His hair and eyebrows were snowy white, and broken veins gave his face a ruddy glow. He said nothing.

"Dad," Lizbeth said again, "it's me."

"Five pound twenty," said the cab driver.

Price looked at the man, and then at his daughter. Lizbeth was horribly aware of her limp hair, her stockinged feet, the oversized lab coat, and the way her hand clutched at the waistband of Perenyi's underwear.

"I didn't have any money," she said.

Her father finally spoke. "I always knew you'd come to a bad end."

"Five pound twenty," the cab driver repeated.

Price reached into the pocket of his slacks and produced a five pound note and a handful of change. The cab driver counted the money. There was no tip. He looked at Price and looked away again; there would be no tip.

For a moment the driver's hand rested on Lizbeth's shoulder. "Be careful, love," he said, and then he walked away and climbed into his taxi.

Lizbeth heard the taxi drive away.

Price barred the doorway. "I told you never to come here again.I told you that if you went away, you needn't bother to come back."

Something of the teenaged Lizbeth surfaced. She looked at

the angry old man who had done nothing for her but send her away. She hitched up her underwear and gathered the lab coat around her.

"I'm coming in," she said, "whether you like it or not."

CHAPTER SIX

Alex Perenyi awoke as the train pulled into Paddington Station. He flexed the fingers of his right hand experimentally and winced. Damn, he thought, I wonder what Peter would have done if he were really trying to hurt me. He consoled himself with the thought that he had done the right thing. If he had put up any further resistance to Peter's attempts to get him on the train, Peter would have followed through with this threat. Alex's hand would have been damaged beyond repair and his career would now be over.

He felt in his pocket for the money that Peter had given him. A hundred miles ago he had decided to do the only sensible thing and to take a taxi to the American Embassy, tell them who he was, and ask for their assistance. No problem.

And what else could he do, he asked himself. He had done what he could for Lizbeth Price and it was more than she deserved. Even after Peter had forced him aboard the Swansea to London Express he had given a passing thought to simply jumping off the train at the first opportunity and going back to make sure that she was alright. He had not, however, been prepared for the speed at which the train travelled. His only experiences of trains had been the long lines of freight cars he had seen crawling along Pennsylvania's railroad tracks. This train flashed through the bright afternoon like a speeding bullet. Houses and factories passed the windows in a blur of color followed by vistas of green fields, grazing animals, a wide river, a flash of ocean. The train never slowed, and it certainly never stopped.

Eventually he drifted into a light sleep and only awoke when the train pulled into the station.

Well, it could have been worse, he thought, he could have been in Paris or Rome and unable to read or speak the language. As it was, he had no trouble finding a taxi and telling the driver that he wanted to go to the American Embassy.

He soon discovered that finding the Embassy would be the easy part. Entering was a different story entirely. The clock in the entryway told him that the time was 5:30 and the mass exodus of staff told him that the day shift was heading home.

The half dozen marines who manned the exit were cheerfully bidding good night to everyone who left but they had no intention of allowing Alex to enter. His troubles started with the very first marine he encountered. After his initial muddled explanation that he had no passport, no identification at all and that he had been brought to the UK against his will, the marine lifted one cynical eyebrow and told him that the Consular Office would be open in the morning. He could apply there for a replacement passport.

"I was kidnapped," Alex insisted. "Look, I'm Alex Perenyi, Dr. Alex Perenyi, from Pittsburgh; someone has to be looking for me. If I could just see an Embassy official..."

"Not without an appointment."

"I don't have time for an appointment."

The marine remained stoically polite. "I'm sorry, sir, but without identification I can't let you in. Come back tomorrow and make an appointment."

"For God's sake," Alex exploded, "I'm an American citizen and I'm coming to you for help. Isn't that what you're supposed to do; help American citizens?"

"Unfortunately," said the marine, "you can offer me no proof of your citizenship...sir."

Alex noted that a small man in a dark suit had stopped to observe the argument. He looked like an Embassy worker, just leaving for the night. Alex spoke louder. "I'm an American citizen and I demand that you help me."

"We'll help you tomorrow," said the marine. "I'd advise you to leave now before we have to remove you and hand you over to the British police."

"I'm not a criminal," Alex insisted, "and I'm telling you, I've been kidnapped. Can't you at least look up my record? Perenyi, Alex Perenyi."

From the corner of his eye he saw the small man moving towards him.

"The consular officer can look up your records in the morning ...sir," said the marine. He laid a firm hand on Alex's shoulder.

"What do you expect me to do?" Alex demanded. "Am I supposed to sleep on the sidewalk? I have very important information."

The small man stepped forward, cutting off the rest of Alex's sentence. "How are you tonight, Brady?" he asked, looking up at the marine.

"I'm good, sir," the marine replied. "Can I help you with something?"

The small man took a deep breath and looked at Alex.

"I was just thinking," he said mildly, "that it wouldn't look very good for us if this man really is a US citizen and we send him out to sleep on the sidewalk."

"I didn't mean that literally, sir. I just meant he should come back and —"

"Of course you did," the small man said placatingly, "but suppose he has no money. I would assume that if he has lost his passport, then he's also lost his money, is that right, sir?"

"Not lost," said Alex, "I've been trying to tell this robot here that I've been —"

"Kidnapped," the marine said.

The small man smiled and nodded his head. "I agree it's not very likely, but let's give the poor guy the benefit of the doubt, shall we? Why don't you give him one of those vouchers we have for the hostel, can you do that?"

"I would have to charge it to your department," said the

marine.

"Fine, fine, charge away. I'll wait here while you go and write it up, and then I'll get him on his way." He turned to Alex. "It's just a couple of blocks."

The marine turned away and began tapping on a computer.
"What Department is it sir?" he asked.

"Diplomatic relations; European royalty."

Alex could hardly believe his luck. "That's why I'm here."

The small man silenced him with a look. "Not now," he said firmly. "Let's get you a voucher and get you settled."

A few moments later Alex stepped out into the heart of the golden evening clutching a printed voucher. It was, he reflected, his only possession.

The sidewalks of Grosvenor Square were thronged with people. The small man walked beside him and they moved with the crowd, flocking together like sheep and shuffling towards a sign for an Underground Station.

The small man tugged on his arm. "Just keep walking till you reach the Dog and Mermaid," he said, "I'll be in the Saloon Bar. Don't talk to anyone." He slipped away from Alex and disappeared into the crowd.

Alex bypassed the Underground Station and saw a sign up ahead. A garish picture of a large breasted young woman and a black Labrador proclaimed this to be the Dog and Mermaid.

He pushed his way inside and found himself in a dense mass of humanity over which hovered a haze of cigarette smoke and the odor of beer. He worked his way through the crowd around the bar, and into the next room under a sign that said Saloon Bar. The room was marginally less crowded and he spotted the small man sitting at a secluded booth with two glasses of beer in front of him.

"Thought you could probably use a drink," the small man said, as Alex dropped down into the seat. His high pitched voice sounded nervous and uncertain.

Alex looked at him while he took his first sip of warm

beer. He seemed very young, his shirt collar too large for his skinny neck, his eyes squinting through thick glasses.

"I'm Michael Oliver Ellington;" he said, "most people call me Moe,"

"Alex Perenyi," Alex said, "most people call me Doctor. What the hell is this cloak and dagger stuff about? Where's the hostel, I could use a shower?"

Moe Ellington cleared his throat, took another sip of beer, and swallowed nervously before he spoke.

"I have ascertained that a Dr. Alex Perenyi and a Lizbeth Olwyn Price are indeed missing from Northern General Hospital. On the night you were reported missing, several nurses were attacked and locked in a supply room, and blood was found in Miss Price's room. At the moment, Dr. Perenyi is the subject of quite an extensive manhunt. There is some thought that you are responsible for Miss Price's disappearance. That's what this is about, Doctor." He laid a final, angry emphasis on the word "doctor".

"What!" Alex roared. "Have they completely lost their minds?"

"One of the nurses, a Miss Jackie Corning, reported that you had shown an interest in Miss Price that was more than professional," Moe Ellington continued pedantically. "You had been visiting her in the middle of the night, holding personal conversations which was not your normal style and—"

"This is absurd," Alex interrupted. "What about the blood? That's not Lizbeth Price's blood, you know."

"Perhaps you had help."

Alex buried his head in his hands. "I don't believe this. I've done nothing. Isn't anyone going to help me?"

Moe leaned forward across the table and spoke softly and urgently.

"You're in trouble. At some point very soon that straw brained marine is going to turn in his report and someone on the night staff is going to read your name, which you unfortunately repeated several times."

"Because I'm an American citizen," Alex protested, "and my Embassy owes me shelter."

"I wouldn't insist on it," Moe replied. "What I would do is just drink your beer and listen to me very carefully."

Alex stared into the other man's face. "Who are you? Why do you want to help me?"

"Political ambition," Moe replied. "I'm at the bottom rung of the ladder, Doctor, and I've been at the bottom rung for years. You're my ticket to the top. The Embassy staff laughs at me. They think I have the silliest job in the Embassy, but when I overheard you talking to that marine, I understood. I'm the only person in that whole Embassy who would understand."

"Explain," Alex ordered, and Moe Ellington explained.

His diplomatic function was to maintain the link between the U.S. Government and Europe's ex-royals. When he first arrived in London he had done everything he could to find a different assignment. It was obvious that the ex-royals were thought of as no more than a joke. They existed in large numbers and included a Pretender to the throne of France, an ex-King of Greece, dozens of Russian exiles, and even an Italian king-in-waiting. These disenfranchised aristocrats gathered at funerals and weddings, and Moe gathered with them.

"I was confused at first," Moe said, "they all look alike, they really do, so I did some more reading and found out that they're all related and that's why they're all so tight with each other. They're all descendants of old Queen Victoria."

"I don't see what that has to do with anything," Alex said impatiently.

"You will," Moe assured him, and he continued with his explanation. No sooner had he taken up his position at the Embassy, Moe said, than the Berlin Wall fell, and the people of Eastern Europe surged westward to experience the joys of capitalism.

Moe's new royal friends perked up their ears, polished off their coronets, and began to wonder if they might one day go home again. For most of them that would mean returning to a home they had never seen and to palaces that had become Communist Party Headquarters. Still, they hoped against hope that they could reclaim their country estates and return to live among forelock-tugging peasants.

"Of course," Moe said, "they were only too happy to share their hopes and plans with this nice young American, so long as I was taking them to fine restaurants and picking up the tab."

Alex drained his beer glass and set it down on the table with a meaningful thud. He was hoping that Moe was good for another round, maybe several more rounds. Moe, however, had come to the meat of his story and would not be distracted.

"The Yugoslavian royals figured among my acquaintances," he declared, "and that, of course, is where you come in."

Alex looked at his empty glass. "Do I?"

Moe failed to take the hint. "Yugoslavia was one of those countries cobbled together by the great powers at the beginning of the last century, supposed to unite the Serbs, Croats, and Slovenes after the collapse of the Austro-Hungarian Empire. They put in a king, of course, someone who could unite all those different people. Basically they gave it to one of the European Royal Families, and told them to go ahead and make a dynasty for themselves, and make the people love them.

Then we had World War II and some very strange and questionable behavior by the Royals. They lost their thrones, and the Communists took over."

"Well, now the Communists are gone," Alex said, "so what does that mean?"

Moe nodded. "It means that it's open season on all forms of government in those countries. Do they want to be united, or not united, communist states, religious dictatorships, republics, democracies? Who can say? For want of any clear leadership, they're just fighting each other. It's all they know."

"I do read the newspapers," Alex said.

"So will you know that this is getting to be a real problem for NATO, and the UN, and for the President. What you will not know is that the answer to the problem may be contained in the memory of your patient, Miss Price."

"So she really does know something," Alex said.

"Oh yes. Your Miss Price is quite a valuable asset, or at least, what she knows is quite valuable, she herself seems to be rather unpredictable."

Alex had to acknowledge his mistake. "I didn't believe her. I thought it was all ridiculous, like a comic opera."

"Unlike most comic operas," Moe said, "this is one with missiles and land mines, and some very nasty stuff going on."

Alex opened his mouth to speak, but Moe interrupted him. "Let's get back to who is related to whom, and especially who is related to Miss Price. You see King Alexander of Yugoslavia married the daughter of the Queen of Romania and they had three children, Peter, Tomislav and Andrej."

"Are all these people really kings and princes?" Alex asked. "I've never heard of them."

"Once upon a time they had real status," Mo replied "and they still take themselves very seriously, but let me continue my story."

"Sorry."

"No problem. Eventually young Peter inherits the throne of Yugoslavia and becomes King Peter but there are those who think that young King Peter sold out to the Nazis in World War II. Although he got out of Yugoslavia alive and went to live in England, the deal with the Nazis cost him the support of many of his people. It's simple really, people who are about to be conquered need a warrior, a hero, someone larger than life and that was not King Peter. Instead they found one from another obscure side of the Royal Family. They found a man who was willing to fight the Nazis for the throne of Yugoslavia, even though his claim was tenuous at best; Prince Grigori."

Alex tried to interrupt, but Moe cut him off, eager to continue his explanation.

"This," he said, "is where your Miss Price comes into the picture. Prince Grigori was everything a hero should be:

charming, handsome, athletic, an expert swordsman, a champion sailor, and a legendary womanizer. Of course he was not actually King, but he caught the popular imagination. He was something straight out of Hollywood. He escaped from the Nazis by sailing the Royal Yacht out of Montenegro in the teeth of a howling gale on a night when no sensible man would put to sea. Even the German fleet was too sensible to leave port, so the prince got clean away."

Moe took another sip of beer. Alex waited.

"He brought the boat to Britain," Moe said, "with the aid of a crew made up of rebel officers of the Royal Guard led by Colonel Stefan Bubani."

"Stefan," Alex said, "that's who she's looking for! She's looking for Stefan."

"Also on board," Moe continued, "was a British naval officer who had been smuggled into Montenegro to help the prince escape, his name was Price, Jamie Price. Now do you see where we're going?"

"I'm beginning to," Alex said, "but it's her brother she's worried about. I still don't understand why—"

"Sex," said Moe, "it's always such a problem, isn't it?"

"Is it?"

"Or lack of it," Moe said, "or at least that's what Prince Grigori thought. He was used to getting what he wanted, whenever he wanted it because he was, after all, a national hero, but when he arrived in Britain he was just another exile, and not a really important one. Instead of finding him a place in London, the British government left him cooling his heels in Wales where Lt. Price had brought the boat ashore.

Very pious people, the Welsh, they sing a lot about love but they keep their daughters on a very tight rein, or at least they used to. But despite the tight reins the prince just helped himself to the nearest available woman."

Moe finished his beer and set the glass on the table. "Do you want another?" he asked.

Alex's need to know overcame his need for beer. "Not yet.

Justr get to the point."

"All right, all right," Moe said. "To cut a long story short, Prince Grigori helped himself to Lt. Price's fiancée and made her pregnant and the girl's parents forced the prince to marry her. She gave birth to a son, then the prince enlisted in the British Navy and was killed in the invasion of Normandy. Jamie Price came back from the wars and married the widow and Lizbeth Price is the result of that marriage."

Moe paused and smiled. "Was that short enough for you? Now do you want another beer?" he asked.

"Yes, but—"

"But what?"

"Why don't they know where the brother is?"

"That's a good question," Moe said. "'I'll be right back."

He collected the beer glasses and disappeared into the crowd around the bar. Alex sat alone and tried to relate what he had just heard to the woman he had left behind in Swansea. Before Moe had returned with the drinks, Alex had already decided that he had judged Lizbeth Price too harshly. She really did have a secret that was worth guarding.

Moe deposited two more glasses of beer on the table. "Drink up," he said, "you look as though you need to get a buzz on."

"I didn't believe her," Alex said. "I didn't take it seriously."

"Not even when they started shooting?" Moe asked.

"She started shooting," Alex corrected him. "I thought she was off her head."

"They smuggled you out of the country," Moe said. "They chartered a plane, they chartered a boat, how much more would it take to convince you they were serious?"

"I took them seriously," Alex admitted, "I just didn't take her seriously. I thought they'd turn out to be something official and she'd turn out to be a lunatic."

He looked into his beer and sighed. "I was also very angry," he added.

"Drink up," Moe said, "and we'll get out of here. We've

been here too long."

Alex realized that he had been so absorbed in what Moe was telling him that he had forgotten his own precarious position. He gulped down the rest of the beer and stood up. He felt unsteady on his feet and grabbed for the edge of the table. I shouldn't be drinking this stuff on an empty stomach, he thought.

"Where do you want to go?" Moe asked.

Alex shrugged his shoulders. "I don't know."

"I wouldn't advise the hostel;" said Moe, "they'll come for you there as soon as they put two and two together."

Alex shook his head. "I think I'd better go back to Wales. I don't think I should have left her on her own."

"Before we go back—" Moe started to say.

"We?"

"Yes, we. I'm coming with you. But before we go I think we should find out what we're really up against. Everything I've told you so far is pretty much common knowledge; you could have found it out from any historian, what we need to know are the things the historians don't know."

"Where the prince is," Alex suggested.

"First," said Moe, "we need to know why he disappeared. If we know why he's been hidden, we might be able to guess where he's been hidden. And I think I know just the person to ask. Straighten your tie, Doctor. We're going to visit royalty."

CHAPTER SEVEN

Countess Helena Iole lived in genteel poverty just south of the Thames, in the London Borough of Tooting.

Moe Ellington sat serenely in the cab during the fifteen minute journey from the Dog and Mermaid to Tooting Broadway but Alex travelled with his nose pressed to the window watching the streets of London pass by in the long golden evening, noticing that even at 9:30 at night the light of the sun still lingered, and the streets were alive with people. He kept a watchful eye on the crowd and wondered why they hadn't been followed.

Moe pulled Alex away from the window. "Relax, no one's watching me, so no one's watching you. Eventually someone will read the log book and discover that I signed you out to a hostel, then they'll go to the hostel and find you never registered. Then they'll try to find me. It will all take time, and they'll never think to come here."

The Countess' house was one of a terrace of shabby Regency townhouses. Her front door opened directly onto the sidewalk and nothing but a wrought iron trellis separated the Cuntess' estate from the rest of the world.

The front door was opened by an upright old man in a black suit shiny with wear.

"Michael Ellington, U.S. Embassy to see the Countess," Moe said, producing a business card from his breast pocket and handing it across to the ancient retainer.

"I'll see if she's in," the old man said.

"She's expecting us," Moe assured him.

"How does she know we're coming?" Alex asked.

"I phoned," Moe said, "from the pub."

"I'll see if she's in," the old man repeated. "If you will please wait in the hall."

They entered a narrow hall, papered a long time ago in red and gold. The old man doddered up the stairs and disappeared from view.

"This will take all night;" Alex said, "why don't we go on up? You said she's expecting us?"

"All they have left is their dignity," Moe replied "and if we take that away then they'll really be nothing, and believe me Alex, these people aren't nothing."

Moe looked around at the dilapidated hallway. "Countess Helena is the daughter of a Russian Grand Duke. She was born in the Winter Palace in St. Petersburg. She has never forgotten who she is, although everyone else has. She has an amazing memory, and she knows everything these people do. If anyone can help us, she can."

"When did you phone?" Alex asked.

"What?"

"When did you phone the Countess? You didn't phone while I was with you?"

"I phoned when I went to get the beer."

"So you were coming to see her with or without me?" Alex said.

"Yeah."

The silence became uncomfortable. Alex looked hopefully up the stairs. "What does she live on?" he asked.

"Believe it or not, she's still living on the proceeds from selling her mother's jewelry. The wealth was incredible, but there's not much left now. She's 92 years old, Alex, so it doesn't have to last her much longer."

The butler creaked his way down the stairs. Nudging Alex forward, Moe started up the stairs to meet the old man who seemed relieved not to have to come all the way down again.

"Will the Countess see us?" Moe asked.

"Yes, sir. Follow me. She is in the drawing room."

As they moved at a stately pace along the hallway, Alex found himself thinking impatiently about Lizbeth. Nine hours had passed since Peter and Joe had ushered him out of the house in Swansea, anything could have happened to Lizbeth in that time. She could have had an unfavorable reaction to the drug he'd administered, she could have had a return of her fever, or she could have reacted unfavorably to her first solid food. He didn't even want to think about what damage Joe or Flora could have inflicted in another attempt to get information from her.

Now that he knew a little more about the secret Lizbeth was guarding, he understood how high the stakes were, and how high the price that Lizbeth might have to pay.

The entered the drawing room.

"Mr. Ellington," said a beautifully modulated feminine voice. A silver haired woman sat regally upright in a faded velvet chair.

"Countess," Moe exclaimed, moving forward and bowing gracefully over the hand extended by Countess Helena. "May I present Dr. Alex Perenyi."

Alex stepped forward and found himself clutching a tiny ring-adorned hand and looking into a face of extreme age, highlighted by the most youthful and beautiful brown eyes he had ever seen.

"Ah, Doctor," said the Countess, speaking in beautiful, aristocratic English without a trace of a Russian accent, "you have brought us such a story. We are all grateful. Please, please sit down, just there on the sofa, my hearing is rather poor and I need you to sit close to me."

Alex found a place for himself on the spindle legged sofa, and Moe took a seat on the other side of the Countess. The Countess dismissed the serving man with a graceful wave of her hand and turned her attention to her visitors.

"These are exciting times," she said. "I'm glad to have

lived so long. Slowly but surely we are reclaiming the things that were stolen from us. I am not strong enough to travel to St. Petersburg, but at least I can rejoice in the fact that it's no longer called Leningrad. Ah, that man ... but you didn't come here to speak of
Russia, you have news of the Yugoslav prince?"

"Yes," said Moe, "I think we have news, but the news only gives rise to questions, Countess, and we thought that you would be the best person to answer our questions."

"Tell me what you know," the Countess ordered.

Alex looked around the room as Moe gave the Countess a brief version of the story of Alex's abduction from the United States. The room was crammed with furniture, most of which looked like priceless antiques. Every surface was cluttered with ornaments and objets d'art. Every inch of wall was hung with pictures or mirrors, every shelf was crammed with knick-knacks. All of this, Alex knew, would have barely furnished the smallest corner of the smallest room in the Winter Palace where Countess Helena was born.

"I see," said the Countess as Moe finished his story, "and now you're wondering why the prince disappeared, and why he hasn't been found."

"Do you know?" Alex asked.

"It is possible that I do. There was much talk, but it was a long time ago;the young man has been missing for 34 years." The old woman laughed. "I suppose I should not call him young; he is not young anymore."

"Is he still alive?" Alex asked.

"That is something I don't know.".

"Has anyone heard from him?" Moe asked.

The Countess raised her hands. "Gentlemen," she said, "you must let me tell my story in my own way. I am an old woman and set in my ways."

Alex and Moe each mumbled an apology, although Alex's was tinged with his rising impatience.

"There were many more of us a few years ago," the

Countess said, "but we've been dying off. I don't see too many people now, but once upon a time we met regularly. I knew the Yugoslavs, I knew them very well. We were all related, of course, through our descent from Queen Victoria. My husband, the late Count Iole, also had family connections with Serbia, and Montenegro, and so we knew Prince Grigori, the father of the man you're looking for."

The Countess smiled apologetically. "His behavior was absolutely disgraceful. I think the man really believed that the *droit de seigneur* still existed and that he had every right to ravish young women of the lower classes. In this case I blame the woman as much as the man. She was a passionate creature and quite extraordinarily beautiful. When one is beautiful one is allowed to behave like a trollop, you know. Beauty is its own excuse."

The Countess looked at Alex. "What of the daughter?" she asked. "Is she a beauty?"

Alex thought about the question for a moment. "I don't know," he said.

"Really?" the Countess asked.

Alex thought again and then nodded his head. "Yes," he said, "I think she is, but her personality gets in the way."

The Countess nodded as though his answer was not unexpected. "They married, of course," she said, "the Prince and the Welsh woman. The boy, your patient's half-brother, was born in wedlock."

"So he has the right to inherit?" Moe asked.

"If there is anything to inherit, he has as much right as any other member of his clan."

"What else do you know?" Alex asked.

"I don't know anything that Mr. Ellington couldn't tell you himself." She smiled at Moe. "Mr. Ellington has impressed us all with his knowledge of our affairs. Our daily comings and goings seem to be of immense interest to him."

Moe's pale face flushed in embarrassment. "We would be delighted if you'd tell us in your own words, Countess."

The Countess inclined her head graciously and continued. "When Prince Grigori escaped from the Nazis he brought certain loyal followers with him, on board the royal yacht. It's quite remarkable really; apparently the British protected them by making the yacht part of the Royal Navy. From what I've heard she's actually being preserved somewhere so they can use her again for his triumphal return. I can't imagine where it is, but I'm sure it can't be seaworthy after all this time."

She sighed deeply. "It would be nice to see it," she said, "one does miss pointless luxury, and she was a beautiful craft."

She sighed again, lost in the memory of former glories, and then she took up the story again in a quavering voice. "They set up their own court in that place in Wales where they were living. There was a small contingent of the Royal Guard, commanded by Colonel Bubani."

The Countess smiled. "The colonel was a charming man, such a brain, and such courage, and so young to be a colonel. When the prince finally took his commission in the British Navy most of the guard signed up with him, but he left a few of the older men behind to keep an eye on the child. There was also a tutor, Viktor something. I can't remember his last name, but he had been at school with the prince. He was a very strange man. I didn't care for him."

She paused for breath and then said "Even if Prince Grigori hadn't died in the War, it would have been impossible for him to return to Yugoslavia. It was impossible for any of us to return."

"The Communists." Moe said to Alex. "They moved in as soon as the Germans moved out."

"There was nowhere for us to go," the Countess said. "The war was over and we were still exiles."

"And the boy?" Alex prompted.

"Such a scandal," the Countess replied, "and such a mystery. After the prince died, the woman married her original fiancé. There was no love lost between the new husband and the tutor the prince had appointed for his son."

"Viktor," Alex prompted.

"Yes," said the Countess. "Viktor kept the boy separated from his mother. Of course that was not unusual; the boy was a teenager by then and a mother's influence is not the best thing for a boy of that age. There was an incident and the boy was blamed. I don't know what the incident was but it created a scandal. There was much talk over the dinner tables of our little clan, although no one knew what the boy was accused of doing. The police were involved, and there was talk of kidnapping. Viktor took the boy away. The mother knew where he had gone, but not the stepfather. Unfortunately Colonel Bubani was away, travelling in America, raising funds among the expatriates there and he knew nothing of what was happening until it was too late and the prince had simply disappeared and —"

"And when things died down, the mother took Lizbeth to visit her brother," Alex interrupted, finally seeing the story fall into shape.

"And on the way home," the Countess said, "the mother was killed, along with her two escorts."

"And no one else was left who knew where the boy was," Alex said.

The Countess nodded. "The girl was little more than a baby and she could not remember where they had been. Viktor and Grigori had vanished."

The old woman sighed. "I don't think the death of the mother was an accident. I don't think the little girl was supposed to survive either."

She gave Alex a very shrewd look. "I believe Viktor wanted them all dead. I believe he wanted to be free of all external influences on the boy. Something very nasty had happened in Wales and he didn't want it to happen again."

"And you have no idea what it was?" Moe asked.

The old woman sighed again. "The Royal families of Europe had many skeletons in their closets. For generations we had been marrying our cousins and our second cousins and the children were weak and given to strange perversions. I am not surprised that the people didn't want us anymore."

"So you don't know anything else?" Alex asked.

"Colonel Bubani returned from America and launched an extensive search for the young prince but with no success. Of course, the key to the secret was Lizbeth Price but she was a small child, and she apparently had no memory of where she had been and what she had seen. She was questioned by many people including the police. The scandal kept us occupied around our dinner tables for quite some time, but for many years now there has been nothing but silence."

"Until now," Alex said.

"The remnants of Prince Grigori's court are still waiting," said the Countess. "They're old now, and poor, but they're still together. If they could find their prince, I'm sure they would make every effort to give him to the throne, although I doubt they would succeed. But who can tell? Strange things are happening in Europe."

"And what about these other people," Alex asked, "the ones who have Lizbeth now, what do they want?"

"I don't know," said the Countess. "As I have told you, I am quite certain that the colonel and his companions would wish to restore the prince but as for these other people, I don't know. There is nothing left of the union that was once Yugoslavia. I suppose it is possible that a prince could return and be accepted by all the people and Yugoslavia could exist again. I imagine that would be a better state of affairs than the one they have at present with each little tribe at war with each other little tribe."

"Would they really accept a king?" Alex asked.

"The Spanish did," the Countess said, "and even the British did. Oliver Cromwell rid them of King Charles and they restored his son to the throne at the first opportunity. Stranger things have happened. I am naturally in favor of the restoration of the old order, but I have what you Americans call a 'vested interest'."

Alex smiled at the old woman, marveling at the sharpness of her wits and the clarity of her world view.

"Miss Price is being held by a young people," the Countess said, "and their views are not the same as mine. Maybe they have a reason for wanting the war to continue, or maybe they have found out something more about the young Grigori. It is possible they know the nature of his crime."

"But you don't?" Moe confirmed.

"Rumors," the Countess said, "it will serve no useful purpose to repeat them."

"There's one more thing," Alex said. "There is a woman involved in this and she seems much more threatening than any of the men. She's been saying something about Lizbeth having to pay for a blood debt."

The diamonds on the Countess's fingers flashed as she brought a hand hastily to her throat. "Is it a family matter?" she asked.

Alex nodded. "I guess so. Lizbeth killed a man in Pittsburgh and this woman is that man's cousin. The way she looks at Lizbeth is downright evil."

"And her name?" the Countess said.

"Flora Balka."

"Balka," the old woman said softly, "it is not a name that I recognize but Prince Grigori spread his seed far and wide. You must understand that Grigori Gruda's Welsh son is not the only person having a claim to the Yugoslav throne. This woman may well represent the interests of another party. As for the blood debt, it is an old custom. If a member of one's family is killed, the death must be avenged. It is usually the men who do this thing, but these days I suppose a woman might feel the same way. The blood debt must be paid. Miss Price must give her life, or the life of a member of her family. It is the way of these people and not to be taken lightly. I think that Miss Price will be in need of your protection."

"Is there anything else you can tell us," Alex asked, "anything at all?"

"I have shared with you everything I choose to share."

The countess turned her eyes away from Alex as though

resisting the temptation to tell him more.

Moe stepped forward and bowed over the old lady's hand again. "Thank you, Countess. We'll leave now."

Countess Helena closed her eyes and sat back in her chair. "Yes," she said, "you may leave now."

Alex surprised himself by bowing as he left the room but outside on the street modern reality crowded in on him and he wondered if he really could believe the old lady's story of palace intrigues, mysterious crimes, and royal blood feuds.

While Moe concentrated on finding a taxi, Alex considered what he knew of the wars in Bosnia, Serbia, and Croatia. He knew little except for the images drawn from his TV screen of blue helmeted UN Peacekeepers, huddled civilians, and fierce men with rifles and tanks. The thought that Lizbeth Price might hold the key to ending such a conflict seemed absurd and yet everything he had heard seemed to confirm its truth.

Moe finally succeeded in gaining the attention of a cruising cab driver which put an end to Alex's thoughts of distant warfare.

"Where to?" the cab driver asked, and Alex realized that he had no idea where they might go next. Once again his fate was in the hands of someone else.

"Eaton Park Square," Moe said.

The taxi moved smoothly through the fading twilight and Alex, exhausted by the events of the day, drifted into sleep. He awoke to hear Moe cursing.

"Shit, they're watching my house."

Alex sat up suddenly, grasping for reality. "Who?" he croaked.

"The Embassy."

Moe leaned forward and tapped the cab driver's shoulder. "Pull over here."

The taxi pulled over. Moe paid the driver and pushed Alex out onto the sidewalk. The sun had finally set but the street was brightly lit with gas lamps. A chill had crept over the evening, and Alex shivered as he stood coatless in the evening air.

"Over there," Moe said, "that's my house, and that's an

Embassy car."

"So I see," said Alex, thinking that the long, sleek black Cadillac with the diplomatic plates could hardly have come from anywhere else. "They're not exactly inconspicuous. What do they want?"

"I think it means they believe at least some of your story, and they've come looking for me to confirm it."

"You?"

"I'm the expert," Moe said. "I don't suppose anyone expected me to get my moment in the sun, but I guess this is it. I just happened to be in the right place at the right time."

"No," Alex said, "you're not turning me over to them; I'm not going to let you."

He turned and started off at a shambling run along the sidewalk. He was more tired than he had ever been in his life and his legs would barely carry him but he tried to put as much distance as possible between himself and the Americans. Suddenly he was grasped from behind in a grip of amazing strength. He jerked to a halt, gasping for breath.

"Calm down, Doc," Moe said.

Alex looked down on the little man who had somehow maneuvered him into an unbreakable arm hold. "I've got to get to her," he said.

Moe tightened his grip and wrenched Alex's arm upward. For the second time that day Alex felt like an incompetent weakling.

"Stand still," Moe said.

Alex stood still.

"Now listen carefully," Moe whispered, "and don't do anything else to draw attention to yourself. We're going to walk away from here, nice and quietly. Away from the Cadillac, Doctor, not towards the Cadillac. Do I make myself clear?"

"Why?" Alex asked.

Moe loosened his grip slightly and began to steer Alex toward a narrow alleyway which lay between two of the Victorian houses.

"I'm no more interested in talking to them than you are," he said. "If I turn you over they're going to bring out the heavies and I'm not going to get a chance."

Alex stumbled as he entered the dark alley but Moe held him upright. For such a small man he has remarkable strength, Alex thought, or perhaps I'm unusually weak.

"On the other hand," Moe continued, "if I could bring them the prince, or better yet, a solution to the problem—"

"That should take you a couple of steps up the ladder," Alex agreed.

"Sure would."

Alex struggled against the hand on his shoulder. "Okay, I understand. Now let me go."

"My car is in a garage one block over," Moe said. "There's no garage with the house and I don't like to leave it on the street. I don't think the Embassy knows about it. If we're lucky they're only watching the house."

Alex and Moe scuttled along a dark alleyway and came out in the adjoining square. Moe led the way to a block of garages set at the end of a side street and opened a padlocked door.

"I don't take the car to work," he said, "no point in trying to drive around Central London."

He pulled the door open. Inside Alex saw the faint outline of a black car. Without turning on any lights, Moe guided Alex into the rear seat and instructed him to keep down, then he slid behind the driver's seat, started the engine and drove the car quietly out of the garage.

Alex stayed down in the back seat, not looking out. He felt the car make innumerable turns and twists and saw the reflection of street lights flashing by. Finally the ride smoothed out and Alex sat up to find that he was being driven at high speed along a four lane expressway, apparently on the wrong side of the road.

"Where are we going?" he asked.

"West," said Moe. "We just picked up the M4. We're on our way to Wales."

Alex hauled himself over onto the front seat, and settled

down next to Moe. "And then?" he asked.

"I thought we'd start with the old soldiers, the Royal Guard; they should know a thing or two."

"And you know where to find them?"

"I know where to start," said Moe, "which is more than you do. You look like death, doctor. Lie down and go to sleep. I'll wake you when we get there."

Alex awoke to find a pale dawn lighting the sky and Moe still driving at high speed on a now deserted highway. The clock on the dashboard told him the time was 4 a.m.

"Feel better?" Moe asked.

Alex nodded. "Where are we?"

"Still on the M4. We'll be crossing the Severn Bridge in a couple of minutes and then you'll be back in Wales."

"Is it really only 4 a.m.?" Alex asked. "How come it's so light?"

"We're a long way north. You get used to it, but it's pretty grim in the winter when the sun sets at 3:30. There's a rest area up ahead, could you use a cup of coffee?"

"Sure could," Alex replied, "and something to eat." He hesitated. "I hate to say this, but, well... I don't have any money. I don't have anything, not even a coat, or a toothbrush, or..."

"I have it covered," Moe said.

"I'm going to owe you."

"If we pull this off, you won't owe me a thing," Moe assured him, "and if we don't pull it off, what you owe me will be irrelevant, 'cause I'll be in Leavenworth or somewhere like that."

He looked at Alex and smiled. "Just joking."

He slowed the car and pulled off the highway into an almost deserted parking lot surrounding a motorway service complex.

Alex stepped out into the chill, clean morning air and breathed deeply, sensing a hint of the ocean in the damp air. He turned to look back at the automobile.

"What is it?" he asked.

"Rover 2000," Moe replied. "Nice car. Goes like a bat out

of hell."

"I noticed."

The restaurant area was uncrowded, not surprising considering the early hour. Moe purchased a toothbrush and disposable razor. He handed his purchases to Alex, pointed the way to the rest rooms, and told him he'd meet him in the coffee shop.

A few minutes later, wide awake and looking slightly less rumpled, Alex stood in the doorway of the restaurant. Moe was seated at a booth, drinking from a thick white coffee cup. Alex assumed that he would have to buy his own coffee with the small change left from the money that Peter had given him, and headed towards the counter.

He looked over his shoulder, telegraphing resentment to Moe because surely the little man could have bought him a cup of coffee. Alone at the table, Moe made an unimpressive figure with his narrow shoulders and thinning hair, but Alex remembered the strength of his grip and the speed of his decisions and wondered about him. He wondered why there was only one coffee cup.

Two police officers brushed past Alex as he stood in the doorway and he instinctively shrank away from the contact. They were tall young men in navy blue sweaters and flat caps with checkered bands. Apart from the night sticks hanging from their belts, they appeared to be unarmed. They walked among the scattered travelers, pausing to ask a question at each table. Their path brought them inevitably towards Moe Ellington, and Alex saw Moe look up, watching their approach. Moe and Alex locked eyes across the restaurant. Moe nodded almost imperceptibly, and took something from his pocket. He lifted the coffee cup and saucer, set something beneath it, and replaced the cup and saucer.

The policemen approached and stopped at Moe's table. Alex strained to listen above the muted clatter from the kitchen and the low hum of voices.

"... your car, Sir?"

"Yes, officer."

"... identification."

Moe produced his wallet, and offered his identification.

"Your embassy..... very urgent .... with us ...."

Moe rose to his feet smiling affably. Alex could hear him quite clearly.

"Some sort of crisis?" he asked.

"I don't know, sir. I only know that they are very anxious to find you."

Moe grinned. "I'm impressed; they've never put out an APB on me before."

"Sir?"

"All Points Bulletin; I guess you call it something else."

"Yes, sir. If you would come with us, we'll escort you to your car and make sure you get pointed in the right direction."

"Of course, of course," said Moe. "I suppose I should get myself one of those new mobile phones and then they wouldn't have to send the police to hunt me down. Have you told them you found me?"

"We'll call it in from the car, sir""

"I'm sure you will," Moe agreed. "Well, let's get going. If my Embassy is in such a hell of hurry to get its hands on me we'd better not keep them waiting."

Trailed by his two escorts, Moe strode past Alex without so much as a glance in his direction. Alex watched with an ever-increasing sense of hopelessness as the three men moved through the restaurant lobby and out of the building.

He stood for a few moments, looking at the table where Moe had been sitting. Now he knew why Alex had not bought another cup of coffee. Two cups of coffee would arouse suspicion. He slid into the deserted booth trying to shake off the immobility of fear. He stared at Moe's cup and saucer. The saucer sat crookedly on the table as though there were something underneath. He picked up the saucer and smiled. "Quick thinking, Moe," he said softly.

Moe had left him an American Express card and something else, a slip of paper. Alex read the neat printing. "Star of the Sea." He pocketed the card and the paper. Star of the Sea.

He knew where to go. He looked around the restaurant and the bland faces of the few travelers. The question was how to get there.

CHAPTER EIGHT

Gregory Gibbons awoke reluctantly. Sun streamed through his windows bringing glowing life to the oriental rugs spread across his bedroom floor. Birds sang in the trees that screened his bedroom from the road. He stretched his arms and legs and felt the soreness of his muscles, so little digging and yet his body ached. He was not, he thought, designed by God for manual labor.

"A king should have servants" Viktor said.

Gibbons sat upright in the bed. "So you're still here," he said.

"Always," Viktor replied, "but you can't leave me in my bedroom forever. I'm beginning to smell."

Gibbons sniffed the morning air and detected a faint odor of decay.

"You have to do something about me," Viktor said.

"I'm going to," Gibbons assured him. "I'm going to get someone to help me."

"Dangerous;" Viktor warned, "very dangerous! Remember the last time."

"That was years ago," Gibbons said, "I was a boy. I'll do better this time."

"I would advise against it."

"Be quiet," Gibbons snapped, "I don't want to hear another word from you."

To his surprise, Viktor's voice disappeared and the air was

once again filled with the sound of the birds in the eaves. Gibbons stretched carefully and thought about the day ahead. So many little chores to do, but this would be the last day for chores. After today, someone would perform those small services for him.

Gibbons wondered if the boy would be a quick learner. No, he thought, I mustn't rush him. If I rush him I'll frighten him. I don't want to frighten him.

He rose from his bed, and draped himself in a magnificent Chinese silk dressing robe. The colors of the robe had been dimmed by the passing of many years and the belt, which had tied so easily around the waist of a fifteen year old boy, strained to accommodate the same waist thirty years later, but it was still magnificent. It was, Gregory thought, one of the very few items he possessed that had been handed down from his father.

In the hallway the smell of decay was much stronger. Gibbons paused at the closed door of Viktor's bedroom and tried to gather together the shreds of his common sense. He knew that he had to stop thinking about the boy and start thinking about Viktor. He had to go back up the garden and dig around among the bones until he had a hole that was big enough. But where had they come from? Where had all the bones come from?

"They're going to look for him," Viktor said.

"I know that," Gibbons replied, "I'm not stupid."

"You're not practical."

"Kings don't have to be practical. Kings have to be magnificent."

With the smell of decay threatening to overwhelm him, Gibbons hurried into the kitchen and flung open the windows. He opened the refrigerator and took out a package of bacon and a couple of eggs. He set the frying pan on the stove.

"See," he said, "I'm being practical, I'm cooking."

"Very good," said Viktor.

He cracked the eggs into a basin and scrambled them with a fork.

"I have it all worked out. I'll take him away somewhere with me. We won't stay here where anyone can find us; we'll go away."

He set the bacon in the pan and turned on the burner. Slowly the smell of frying bacon overcame the smell of Viktor.

"I only wanted someone to play with," he said.

"I know."

"They thought it was something bad, but it wasn't."

"I know."

"I just wanted to talk to him. I wanted to know what it was like to go to school and sit in a classroom with other children. I wanted to know how to ride a bicycle. I wanted him to play cricket with me. I wanted to be like other children."

"You're not like other children," Viktor reminded him.

"I'm a king," Gibbons said. "I have a land across the ocean."

"And you have me to look after you," said Viktor.

"I don't want you."

"You will."

As Alex stood up to go outside, a large group of people crowded through the doorway, heading for the restrooms. He slipped between them and made his way out into the parking lot. Perhaps he could hitch a ride. Was that even legal in the UK? He had no idea. Once outside he saw a large bus idling at the curb, the interior lit with a welcoming orange glow. That explained the people crowding into the restaurant. He walked around to the front of the bus where a digital sign read "Port Talbot and Swansea". He found himself thanking a God he had ceased to believe in and approached the door of the bus. It slid open welcomingly and Alex put his foot on the first step.

"Ticket?" said a low voice from the driver's seat.

"I want to buy one," Alex said.

"Not here, mate, this ain't a bus stop."

"You stopped," Alex argued, "doesn't that make it a bus stop?"

"We're express from Heathrow. No stopping."

"You stopped," Alex repeated stubbornly.

"Rest Stop," said the driver. "You can't board here."

"I need to get to Swansea," Alex pleaded, "and you're going to Swansea."

"We're non-stop," the driver insisted.

"Well, is there another bus that's not non-stop?" Alex asked.

The driver shook his head. "Don't think so. Local buses don't come up the M4, you'd have to go into town."

"How far is town?" Alex asked.

The driver shrugged again. "Don't know. I just drive this route. Heathrow to Swansea, three bloody times a day, that's all I know mate. Step aside please, there's people trying to board."

Alex wondered if he could board unnoticed with the horde of returning passengers, but it wasn't going to happen. The driver checked the passengers' tickets one at a time and kept a beady eye on Alex. Finally the doors swung closed and the bus pulled away.

Alex surveyed the parking lot. A couple of huge semis idled in the far reaches of the asphalt along with three or four shiny family saloons. The only other vehicle was a tiny old mini-car with a surf board strapped to the roof. The board was longer than the car itself. As he watched a young man, hardly older than a boy, came bouncing through the restaurant doors humming to himself.

He has to be American, Alex thought looking at what appeared to be a California surfer with long baggy shorts, a luminous green sweatshirt, long stringy blonde hair, and a string of beads around his neck.

Alex approached him cautiously. "Hi," he said.

"Hello mate," the surfer replied.

Okay, so not an American.

"I was wondering…" Alex said uncertainly.

"You wanna lift?" the boy asked.

"A lift? Oh a ride. Yes, if you're going to Swansea or anywhere near."

"Going right through Swansea and out the other side," the

boy said. "Yeah, I'll take you. You an American?"

Alex nodded. "Yes. I'm sorry, I seem to be stranded here."

"No problem," the surfer said, "happens to me all the time. You know, I run out of petrol, run out of money, get kicked out by a chick, it's all part of life, man."

The surfer philosophy was delivered in a strange sing-song accent and was barely comprehensible.

They approached the tiny car together. "Austin Mini," the boy said, "she's getting on a bit, but she'll make the trip."

He cleared the front seat, tossing all the items onto the tiny back seat, and then gestured for Alex to climb in. It took some effort for Alex to squeeze his tall frame through the door and get himself seated on the passenger seat. He felt as though he was sitting about six inches above the pavement, a fact that was confirmed when the car lurched forward and the surfer peeled joyously out of the parking lot.

As the sun rose behind them, they drove west, through a countryside of green hills dotted with white sheep. They crossed an enormous bridge and Alex saw a sign welcoming him to Wales. He noticed that all the road signs had become bi-lingual, in English and some other language with a plethora of consonants and very few vowels. He assumed it was Welsh. Soon purple mountains appeared on the northern horizon, and he caught glimpses of ocean to the south.

The motorway carried them westward past ruined castles and steep, heathered hillsides.

The surfer was talkative, plying Alex with questions about American lifestyles, fashions, and phrases. Alex told the kid that he was a doctor and not from California but the boy seemed eager to glean anything at all that Alex could teach him about anything American, and to feed it back to him in his own language of Welsh and English, combined with Beach Boys, and Chicago gangster. All conversation was carried on above the Mini's crackling radio, emitting a constant stream of Golden Oldies.

"I didn't expect to find surfers here," Alex commented.

"The Gower beaches got the best surf in Europe," the boy

said. "I'm on my college surfing team."

Alex remembered the temperature of the water when he had jumped off the launch that had brought him ashore. It now seemed that was a lifetime ago.

"Isn't the water too cold?" he asked.

The boy shook his head. "Not in a wet suit," he said, "I can surf all year round in a wet suit." He smiled and pulled back the sleeve of his sweat shirt revealing a sickly white arm that contrasted with his tanned, brown hand. "But you get lines," he said.

On the outskirts of Swansea the surfer turned the radio down a couple of notches, much to Alex's relief. It was a pleasure not to be assaulted with golden oldies and the surfer's sing-along and drum-on-the-dashboard accompaniment.

"Okay, this is Swansea; where to, dude?" the boy asked.

"Do you know a hotel called The Star of the Sea?" Alex asked.

"Sure do, man."

"Is it on your way?"

"Sure is. I'm on my way out to the Gower, got to go right past it."

The surfer flicked his bleached hair out of his eyes and looked at Alex long enough to make Alex wish he would look at the road, they were, after all, driving at over 90 miles per hour.

"I shouldn't think it was your kind of scene," the surfer finally said.

"I was given the name by a friend."

"It's pretty grotty," the surfer assured him.

Alex had no idea whether this constituted a compliment or an insult to the Star of the Sea. "I'll give it a try," he said.

"I knew a chick who lived there," the surfer volunteered.

"Oh yes?"

"Bronwyn, her name was. We took a couple of classes together at the Polytechnic. We went out a couple of times. She was okay, but her family was real weird."

"You met them?" Alex asked.

"You couldn't really call it meeting. I mean, I went in there a couple of times to pick her up and her brother was there, but he was always yelling about something or another. That's not my scene you know, man, I don't go for yelling."

"So there aren't any parents?" Alex asked.

"No, just Bronwyn and her brother and all these real old foreign geezers. Now, they were interesting, I mean, sitting around talking about what things will be like come the revolution."

"They're planning a revolution?" said Alex, amazed.

"Shouldn't think so," said the surfer, "I mean, not seriously, but they're always talking about getting their country back. I'm not sure what country it is," he added.

"And you didn't like the brother?"

The surfer shook his head. "Creepy dude. Bronwyn does all the work, and this brother is always in some back room holding meetings. I couldn't take it. I gotta be free, you know, man; I can't be dating some chick who can't get to the beach 'cause she's got to make dinner for some revolutionary old geezers."

"Of course not," Alex agreed.

"So you gonna stay there or what?" the surfer asked.

"Maybe," Alex said, "if I like it."

"Whatever."

The surfer shrugged his shoulders, turned up the volume, and joined in on the final chorus of "California Dreaming". That was followed by the nine o'clock news, to which Alex listened intently. He concentrated on the beautifully modulated BBC voice, wondering if he might hear his own name. There was news from Eastern Europe, all of it bad. Another fledgling democracy had collapsed and its leaders had fled, leaving the citizens fighting each other in the streets. A cease-fire had failed to last the night. The newscaster moved on to other things and the broadcast ended without any mention of a manhunt for a missing American doctor.

Alex looked out of the car window at the morning traffic

and thought about the missing prince. Could he really be the answer to the whole mess?

"Here you are, dude," the surfer said, bringing the Mini to a shuddering halt.

Alex unfolded himself from the front seat.

"Thanks a lot."

"No trouble, dude."

Alex stood at the side of the road and watched the faded red mini rattle away westward. He envied the boy his freedom. The sun was shining, seagulls soared overhead, and somewhere ahead of him the surf was up. Alex thought that he had never been that young, or that carefree.

The boy had deposited him on a wide sidewalk which ran along the top of a sea wall. On one side of him the wall dropped away to a sandy beach and a wide sweep of bay. The shore was lined with buildings, and across the bay he could see industrial chimneys pumping steam into the blue sky. He turned to look across the street at a row of Victorian houses standing shoulder to shoulder, facing the ocean. He read the signs lettered above their doorways; High Tide Guest House, Swansea Bay Private Hotel, Star of the Sea.

So here he was, he thought, but it had taken him almost five hours, anything could have happened in five hours.

A glass walled bus shelter offered Alex some shelter from the cool morning breeze, and he used the opportunity to stare at the front of the Star of the Sea hotel. The building was four stories high but very narrow, with bay windows on either side of a red front door. A striped awning sheltered the door and steps led down to the sidewalk. As Alex watched the front door opened. He shrank back into the bus shelter.

A group of maybe a dozen old men gathered on the front steps, several of them appeared to be lighting pipes, several more smoked cigarettes. A cloud of smoke soon gathered above their heads and drifted away in the light air.

When all of the pipes and all of the cigarettes were burning satisfactorily, the group moved as one down the steps and onto the sidewalk. They turned and set off in the direction of the town. Alex saw that one or two of them carried brown paper shopping bags and another wheeled a pull-along shopping bag such as Alex had seen old ladies using in the States. Watching them Alex was moved to pity for the remnant of the Royal Guard.

A bus pulled up at the bus shelter and discharged a passenger, a young girl in blue jeans, a tight tank top and a wealth of body jewelry. She was chewing on a wad of gum and carrying a bag of groceries. The girl looked at him curiously from under a veil of mascara-coated eyelashes. Alex looked away and the girl crossed the street and went up the front steps into the Star of the Sea.

Bronwyn? Alex wondered.

The bus driver looked down from his cab, "Are you getting on, boyo?" he asked.

Alex shook his head in refusal.

"Right."

The bus pulled away.

Alex waited a few more moments and then crossed the street. He had no idea what he was going to do, but he was going to do something. The young woman was in the house, he knew that much, and if he encountered her he would ask her outright if she knew where Joe Ralko might be found. Perhaps she would assume that he was part of Joe's revolutionary brotherhood. On the other hand, if he was lucky, she'd be in the back somewhere watching soap operas and he might be free to look around. And what, he asked himself, was he looking for? A clue, he thought, some hint of where Lizbeth was being held.

He climbed the front steps and opened the door cautiously. The small, dark hallway, which he assumed served as a reception area, was unoccupied, and furnished with a desk and a chair, fronted by a battered wooden counter. A broad staircase led upstairs, and a door to the right revealed a dining room. A swinging door at the back probably led to the kitchen. To the left he saw a deserted TV lounge where a collection of threadbare armchairs and sofas faced a wide-screen TV.

The desk seemed to be the obvious place to start. Alex slipped behind the counter and saw a telephone, a date book, and a message pad. His heart pounded. He checked the message pad. No messages. He opened a drawer and saw a pile of pink paper slips; messages. The writing was hard to decipher, but surely this one had "Joe" written in the top left-hand corner.

"It's the doctor, isn't it?"

Alex dropped the message and looked up. The girl was looking at him over the top of the counter. Her black hair dropped forward shadowing her pale young face, but Joe thought there was something astonishingly familiar about her features.

"I recognized you when I got off the bus."

Alex stood open mouthed, the message slip in his hand. The girl removed the slip from his fingers and put it back into the drawer.

"I can explain," he said.

"Don't bother, mate. I know who you bloody well are. I'd have to be stupid not to know who you are, but I couldn't make up my mind about you, could I? Well, don't look at me like that, like I'm something the cat dragged in, I'm Bronwyn Ralko and I'm not half as bleeding stupid as my brother thinks I am."

She chewed her gum for a moment and then said, "I know everything about you, except your name."

"Alex Perenyi."

The girl laughed. "Your name's about as strange as mine," she remarked. "So, Alex Perenyi, how did you escape? You have bloody escaped, haven't you?"

"They put me on the London train; I came back."

"For her?"

"I suppose so."

"She's not here."

"They were keeping us in another house," Alex said. "Do you know where it is?"

"I might," Bronwyn replied, "but it wouldn't do you any good, she's not there, either."

Alex felt his heart sinking. "What's happened?" he

demanded.

In the back of the house a door slammed.

"Watch out, mate, someone's coming," Bronwyn said.

Alex looked at the girl, pleading silently. She hesitated momentarily and then slipped across the hall and opened a closet door.

"In here," she whispered, and when Alex hesitated she pushed him urgently. "Get in the bloody cupboard."

Alex found himself among a rack of musty overcoats. Bronwyn left the door open a fraction of an inch. Light filtered in, and sound.

"Hi," he heard Bronwyn say breezily.

"Get out!" Alex recognized Joe's voice. "We need to use the phone."

"I'm not bloody stopping you," Bronwyn responded.

"Go and get lunch or something, and clean up your language will you," Bronwyn's brother commanded.

"It's not bloody lunch time."

"Well, just go away and make yourself busy. Where are all the old men?"

"How the hell should I know, I'm not their nursemaid? I expect they went shopping, it's pension day."

"Get out, Bronwyn," Joe repeated.

"I know what you're up to," Bronwyn said tauntingly.

Alex heard Flora for the first time, "Get out, little girl," the woman said, and her tone was cold.

"And if I don't bleeding want to?"

"What you want is of no interest to me, little girl." Flora's remark was followed by a moment of silence, and then a small gasp.

"Don't be long," Bronwyn said at length, in a small but determined voice. "I have things to do."

Alex eased the door open another inch and was rewarded by a clear view across the lobby to where Joe and Flora stood by the desk. Flora's hand rested on the telephone.

"Do you have to call them?" Joe asked.

"I have wasted too much time already on your amateur games," Flora replied. "When I came here I expected to find something more professional. I would never have allowed the woman to be brought here if I had known—"

"But I found her for you," Joe protested.

"And now you have lost her."

Lost her, Alex thought, what does he mean? How could they have lost her?

"We'll find her again," Joe said. "There aren't very many places for her to go."

Flora sniffed disdainfully. "She has gone to Bubani."

"She doesn't know where he is," Joe replied.

Flora sniffed again. "She's more resourceful than you are, Joe. No doubt she'll find out where he is."

"She didn't even have any clothes."

Flora lifted the phone. "We're not going over this again," she said. "You have had all night to find her and you have come up with nothing. We must move on. We must act on what we already know. I must call my people in London."

"And tell them what?" Joe demanded.

"That Gruda was hidden in a village within a day's drive of here, where there is a public house called the Dragon. My friends will contact the breweries, and obtain a list of pubs. We must act fast, Joe. If the woman has gone to Bubani, he will know what we know, and he will act."

"Flora!" Joe pleaded, "I've worked for this all my life..."

"And what a pointless life it has been," Flora said, "hiding away in this comfortable town, with nothing but talk."

"The time wasn't right," Joe protested.

"For people like you the time is never right," Flora snapped. "I don't know how I could have wasted so much of my time with you. I don't know if you can be allowed to serve the new administration, you are such pathetic amateurs. My friends in London laugh at you. They have been tested in blood."

"Wait a minute, wait a minute," Joe said. "I've thought of something Lizzie said. I should have realized it before."

"A clue?" said Flora disparagingly.

"Listen to me, please," Joe pleaded, "we don't have to go to anyone else. We can find him."

"How?"

"Do you remember me asking her about the name of the church?"

"She didn't know the name of the church," Flora said.

"And why not?"

"Because there was something obscuring her view of the sign. She couldn't read the name""

"Exactly," said Joe triumphantly, "she couldn't read the name because there were two big holly bushes planted in front of the signboard."

"This is your big clue, that the church has two holly bushes?"

"No, no, she was more specific than that. The signboard was at the side of the road, with the two bushes beside it, and they followed the road up a steep hill and out of the village."

"So?"

Crouching in the coat closet, Alex echoed Flora's question. So?

"It's a marker, an old West Country tradition." Joe said, "Two holly bushes side by side at the edge of the road is more than a coincidence. In the old days, when most people couldn't read, they would plant holly bushes at the bottom of a hill to show how steep the hill was, and how many horses a carter would need to get up it."

Alex was amazed that Joe Ralko would be aware of this trivial information.

"It's one of those dumb things we learned at school," Joe said, "and that one stuck."

Flora was silent but Alex could see that she was smiling.

"If there were two bushes being used as a road marker, and that's a West Country tradition, then the church Lizzie saw was somewhere in the West Country," Joe said. "That narrows it down a lot. We know we're looking for a pub called the Dragon, next to a church, and at the foot of a steep hill, and it's somewhere in Devon or Cornwall."

"What is Devon or Cornwall?"

"The two western counties of England," Joe said. "On a clear day, you can look across the Bristol Channel from here and see the Devon coast."

"So," said Flora, "we have narrowed our search. I still must call my friends."

"We don't need them," Joe pleaded. "We can look in a guide book. It won't take long now that we know where to look."

"And you have such a guide book?"

Alex felt a brief flash of sympathy for Joe Ralko as he heard him mumble that they could get a guide book from the library and heard Flora's scornful response.

"I can arrange it," Joe said. "We'll be ready to go as soon as we know the name of the village."

Flora said nothing, but she moved away from the telephone on the desk.

"Peter!" Joe yelled. "Milos!"

Two men came from the back of the house. Alex recognized the hulking figure of Peter, the man who had taken him to the station. Milos matched Peter in height and probably exceeded him in weight.

"We're going to need a car," Joe said, "a fast one, and no questions asked."

Milos rubbed his hands together in delight. "A Jag," he suggested.

"Whatever you can find."

"We can find a Jag," Peter assured him.

"Discreetly," Joe said, but Peter and Milos were already on their way out the front door in a rush of huge feet.

Joe raised his voice again. For a moment, at least, he was commander of his forces, and he knew what to do.

"Bronwyn!" Joe shouted.

"We don't need her," said Flora.

"I have to borrow something," said Joe.

Bronwyn arrived through the kitchen door. She was wiping her hands on a tea towel as though she had been busy at the sink although Alex was quite sure the girl had been listening at the door. Flora's malevolent glance indicated that she had the same suspicions.

"I need your library card," Joe said.

Bronwyn laughed out loud, and Flora sighed deeply.

"I lost mine," Joe said. "Come on, hurry up, this is important."

Bronwyn was enjoying herself. "Don't tell me your little revolution's going to fail because you don't have a bleeding library card," she said.

"Shut up and give it to me."

"She knows too much," Flora said.

Bronwyn opened a desk drawer, pulled out her purse, and offered Joe a card.

"I'm going out," Joe said, "and I won't be back. Take care of things."

"What do you mean, you won't be back?" Bronwyn demanded.

"I mean what I say; I won't be back."

Bronwyn looked at her brother for a long time. "I don't know what she's told you," she said eventually, indicating Flora with a scornful tilt of her head, "but I'd have thought you'd be better off to side with him. If he's going to be king or emperor or whatever, wouldn't you want to be on his side?"

Joe snatched the card from his sister's hand. "Maybe you don't care about our family name," he said, "but I do. One day, when you find out what he really is, you'll thank me for removing this stain from our family's honor."

"Well, it's very nice of you, I'm sure, to keep the stains off our family name but what kind of bleeding name is it? What's so great about being called Ralko? It's a bloody stupid name, if you ask me?"

"The name has value in the old country," Joe said.

"So what? Who cares about the old country? And anyhow,

how is this Gruda bloke going to mess up our family name, his name isn't Ralko?"

"He's our cousin," Joe said. "I thought you knew that."

"No," said Bronwyn, "no one told me."

"Well, you know now."

"Does that mean we're royalty?" Bronwyn asked. "Am I some sort of princess?"

"Of course not," Joe snapped. "Grow up, Bronwyn."

"The Queen's cousins are all royal," Bronwyn insisted.

"Being related to Grigori Gruda is not like being related to the Queen of England," Joe said.

"Come, enough of this nonsense," said Flora, imperiously, "we must go."

"Remember," Bronwyn taunted, "no loud talking in the Reading Room."

Whatever reply Flora planned to make was interrupted by the opening of the front door. Alex pushed the closet door open another couple of inches to see who had arrived.

"Hey Bronwyn, how are you doing, dude?" asked the voice that Alex had listened to for hour upon hour in the early morning.

"Chris?" Bronwyn said.

The surfer strolled into view, brightening the hallway with his neon sweat shirt and floral shorts.

"I thought I'd check up on the doc," Chris said. "He seemed sort of lost, you know, travelling like that without even a coat, so I thought I'd make sure he was okay."

"Doctor?" Flora asked. "What doctor?"

CHAPTER NINE

Alex shrank back among the coats, his heart pounding. It seemed to him that Bronwyn took forever to answer the question and once again he cursed his helplessness. Just a week ago he had been Dr. Alex Perenyi, respected surgeon. When he spoke, people listened. When he snapped his fingers, nurses ran to do his bidding, and when he delivered his diagnosis, patients nodded their agreement and submitted themselves to his knife. Since then he had been forcibly removed from his own domain. He has endured one indignity after another. Now he was being held at the whim of a pouting eighteen-year old girl and all because he had gone into the hospital in the middle of the night to check on the condition of his patient. That's where it had begun and he had no idea where it would end.

"Joe," Bronwyn said, suddenly polite, "you remember Chris Evans, don't you?"

"Hi, dude," Chris offered cheerfully, "have I come at a bad time?"

"What doctor?" Flora repeated.

"And this is Joe's friend Flora," Bronwyn said coolly. "Flora's foreign, and she doesn't understand good manners."

"Oh," said Chris.

"Poor old Doc," Bronwyn continued, "I saw the poor bugger, but I don't think he saw me. I don't think he knew he'd lost his coat; I mean, he was out of it, way out of it."

Chris made a puzzled grunting noise which Alex felt

inclined to echo.

"Did you ever meet Doc," Bronwyn continued brightly, "he took some classes with us, and I brought him home here a couple of times? Did you meet him, Joe?"

"No," said Joe briefly.

"His old Mum died in London," Bronwyn said, "and he was really out of it. He said he was going to her funeral, and he didn't have his coat or luggage or anything. Where did you see him, Chris?"

"Oh," Chris said, "I saw him ... uh ... at the station."

"Shouldn't you be going, Flora?" Bronwyn asked. "Don't you have to go to the library? Surely you want to be finished when the boys get back here with that Jaguar. I don't suppose you want them to leave it parked on the street out there, won't it be kind of *hot* out there?"

"Shut up, Bronwyn," Joe said. "Come on, Flora, let's go."

"Why do you put up with her?" Flora asked.

"Because she's my sister," Joe replied. "You know how it is with family."

Alex heard the front door slam. For a long moment he heard nothing but silence, and then Chris spoke.

"Hey dude," he heard Chris say, "what was that all about?"

"That was bloody close, that's what that was," Bronwyn replied. "You were bloody great, Chris; you caught on right away, didn't you?"

"No problem," Chris said. "I mean, I'm cool. Where is he?"

"In the coat cupboard," Bronwyn said.

She flung open the door and Alex emerged gratefully into the light and air.

"Dude," said Chris.

Alex made a mental note to teach Chris some new words.

"Thanks," Alex said to Bronwyn. "Thanks very much. I wasn't sure you were going to help me."

"Neither was I," Bronwyn replied, "but then, well, I

realized what Joe was saying, Grigori Gruda, the prince, he's our cousin."

"So it's the family protection thing," Alex said. "You people sure have a strong sense of family."

"What family protection thing?" Bronwyn asked. "I don't give tuppence about my family. What's Joe to me? Nothing. It's me I bloody care about. I mean, if Gruda is going to be king, and I'm his cousin, then I'm going to be somebody too. I'm tired of being nobody, and I'm not going to let that bitch Flora take away my chance."

Bronwyn shook her dark hair out of her eyes and looked inquiringly at Alex.

"Do you know the story? Do you know what I'm talking about?"

"Yes I do," Alex said. "I found out about it at the Embassy."

"I don't," Chris said, "but that's cool, I never know what's going on."

Bronwyn laughed, and the laugh transformed her from a harpie to a pretty young girl.

"Come on, Chris," she said, "you're not really as daft as you look. You can't fool me."

"Whatever," Chris replied, easily.

"I'll tell you about it on the way," Bronwyn said. "We don't have long, even that thick-as-mud brother of mine is going to find his way round the library eventually, and it won't take Milos more than five minutes to steal the car he wants. We have to get out of here."

"Where will we go?" Alex asked.

"To see Uncle Stefan," Bronwyn said, "Colonel Bubani."

"You know where he is?"

"Of course I bloody do," Bronwyn turned to Chris. "Can we all get in your car, or is it full of junk?"

"I'll throw the junk out," Chris said magnanimously

A few moments later Alex stood on the sidewalk and watched as Chris tossed the contents of the rear seat of his car into a municipal garbage can.

When a space had been cleared Bronwyn slid into the rear seat, and Alex, once again, folded himself into the front seat. Chris started the engine and looked up into his rearview mirror.

"Wow," he said, "is that the car your brother's waiting for?"

Bronwyn turned in her seat and Alex looked into the wing mirror. A sleek black Cadillac slid into a parking space a couple of yards behind them.

"They wouldn't ..." Bronwyn said.

"They didn't," Alex confirmed. "That's a U.S. Embassy car."

"Cool," Chris said. "Look at the size of that thin. Are they friends of yours, Doc?"

"I doubt it," Alex replied, "and I don't want to hang around here and find out. Get going."

Chris slammed the car into gear and the Mini struggled forward. Alex kept an eye on the rearview mirror. He saw the doors of the Cadillac opening. Men in suits climbed out onto the sidewalk. They were large men, in dark suits and a little man was with them; Moe Ellington.

"Wait," he said to Chris, and then thought better of it. "No, sorry, go ahead. Let's get out of here."

Alex had suddenly lost his trust of the little American. Moe was ambitious. Moe would do anything to get ahead, and Moe had three Embassy staffers with him whom he would certainly like to impress. Alex decided he felt safer with Bronwyn Ralko and Chris Evans than he did with Moe Ellington and the men in suits.

As the Mini rattled off at all of 20 miles per hour, Alex kept an eye on the side mirror. The men in suits were crossing the street. They never even glanced at the old red car with the neon surfboard strapped to the roof.

"Okay," said Alex.

"Cool," said Chris.

Golden oldies blasted from the radio but Chris reached out

and turned the volume way down as Bronwyn slid forward in her seat, and started to tell Chris the long story of the missing prince. Alex relaxed and watched the scenery sliding by.

They left the city behind them and followed the shoreline of a wide bay. A couple of miles ahead of him, on a hilltop, he saw the ruins of a great castle, and a rocky promontory adorned with a lighthouse. Between the castle and the lighthouse, a village spread itself up the slopes of the hill. Alex listened with one ear to Bronwyn's explanation and Chris's response, which consisted of interjecting the word "cool" every couple of seconds.

Alex learned little from Bronwyn's explanation, although her telling of the story was far more colorful than Moe's, and far more personal. She had grown up amongst the remnants of the Royal Guard. Her father had taken part in the escape from Montenegro, and the voyage to Britain. The story of the prince was something Bronwyn had learned early in life but she hadn't given it much thought until Flora Balka arrived on the scene.

Chris interrupted to ask where they were going.

"Just keep driving," Bronwyn said.

Alex turned in his seat. "Tell me about Flora," he said.

"Why do men always want to know about bloody Flora?" Bronwyn asked.

"I don't," said Chris. "I thought she was scary."

"So did I," Alex admitted, "but she's the one in charge, isn't she?"

"Oh yeah," Bronwyn said, "I mean, Joe had been running the movement for years, not that they'd done much, in fact they'd done bugger all if you ask me. They hadn't found the prince, and they didn't have the balls to go over to Serbia or Bosnia and join in the fight, so it was all pretty much of a joke."

"Until Flora came," Alex said.

"You're right about that," Bronwyn agreed, "I don't know where Joe found her, although I suppose really she found him. Anyway, all of a sudden Flora's got Joe and his stupid committee running around looking for the prince; seriously looking for him and not just playing around. She says he has to be found just to make sure."

"Make sure of what?" Alex asked.

"That's what I asked, but no one tells me anything. So she keeps digging and digging and then the old uncles start telling her to mind her own business. She's giving them the evil eye and they're giving it right back to her. The uncles came to me and told me I must never, ever, tell her anything about that stupid old boat of theirs, like I care about their boat; it would probably sink like a stone at the first splash of water."

"Do they still have that old thing?" Chris asked.

"Oh yeah," Bronwyn replied, "it's their great big royal treasure. Anyway, somehow or another Flora the magnificent digs up some old scandal that's been buried for years and now my brother, whose been a royalist all his life, suddenly wants to find the prince and kill him."

"Cool," Chris said. "Any idea why?"

"I asked the uncles, but they can be tight mouthed little old buggers when they want to be. They kept telling Joe to get rid of her, but he wasn't thinking with his head, if you know what I mean. All he wanted was to get into her knickers, and that's what he's been doing, morning, noon and night. Every time she wants something she lets him have a poke, it's bloody sickening. She's after something of her own that one is, and it's not Joe."

"I can see how Joe could be persuaded," Alex said.

"Then," Bronwyn said, "that American woman phoned and said she'd remembered something, and all hell broke loose around here."

Chris slowed the car as they approached a traffic light. They were now directly under the walls of the ruined castle and Alex looked up at the ragged stone arches and blind windows silhouetted against the blue sky. When he looked down again his head was spinning and he grasped the door handle for support.

"You all right, dude?" Chris asked.

Alex nodded, and lost his balance again.

"You look bloody awful," Bronwyn said.

He could hear her but he didn't want to open his eyes to

see her, he was too busy clutching the door handle.

"Is he okay?" Chris asked.

Bronwyn's voice came from far away. "Don't bloody faint," she said.

Alex shook his head, trying to clear the fog from his brain. What was the matter with him, he wondered. The answer was simple and quite obvious once he gave it a moment's thought.

"I think I'm just tired and hungry," he said.

"Is that all?" Bronwyn asked.

"I think so," Alex mumbled. "I don't think I ate anything yesterday or maybe the day before. I had some coffee this morning, early. I think that's all I've had."

"You men are all the bloody same." Bronwyn said, "You don't have an ounce of common sense, you'd sooner lie down and die than admit you're hungry."

"I don't have time to eat," Alex said.

"You don't have time to pass out." Bronwyn insisted. "We'll have to find him some food, Chris."

"Cool," said Chris.

"Shut up," Alex growled. "don't say that word again."

"See what I mean," Bronwyn said, "definitely hungry. Where can we feed him?"

"We don't have time," Alex protested.

Bronwyn leaned back in her seat. "Shut up," she said.

"You got any money?" Chris asked.

"No," said Bronwyn, "but I'm sure he has. He's a doctor, they always have money."

"Not kidnapped doctors who've been abducted with nothing but the clothes they stand up in and a stethoscope," Alex muttered.

"Cool," said Chris, and then "Sorry, dude."

Alex couldn't help smiling. The boy was like a half-trained puppy, he thought, anxious to please and with no idea how irritating he was.

"I have an American Express card," Alex offered. "It's not mine, but I think it would be really cool if I used it anyway."

Chris pulled the car over to the curb and he and Bronwyn discussed where they might use an American Express card while Alex slumped in the seat with his eyes closed. They were right of course; he really couldn't go on much longer without food.

Finally Christ and Bronwyn settled on something called The Beach Hut, and they rattled on into the village.

A series of sharp turns led them through narrow streets lined with pastel colored cottages and out onto the waterfront of a tiny bay. High rocky cliffs surrounded a semi-circle of sandy beach. The Beach Hut occupied a narrow strip of land between the parking lot and the crowded area where sun bathers lay stretched out on deck chairs under a watery sun.

Alex allowed himself to be led into the restaurant and settled into a chair. Chris and Bronwyn seemed to know the waiter, and Chris discussed the state of the surf with him while Bronwyn ordered herself a cheese sandwich. They looked at Alex. He asked for a hamburger.

"Do you eat meat?" Chris asked, looking as though Alex had said that he ate small children.

"Don't you?" Alex replied.

"We don't serve animal flesh," the waiter said.

"Okay, okay, I'll have a cheese sandwich. Do you serve coffee?"

"Espresso, Cappuccino, or regular?"

"Regular," Alex replied, and closed his eyes again, barely listening to the conversation buzzing around his head. When it arrived, the cheese sandwich was remarkably good, made with a sharply flavored white cheese and spread with a sweet brown relish. The coffee was strong and satisfying. Alex sat up and started to take notice.

"That's better," said Bronwyn. "Now all we need to do is get you some clothes."

"I don't need clothes," Alex responded. "I need to get out of here."

"Doc," Chris said, "you need some clothes."

"What's wrong with what I have?"

Chris hesitated, and looked down at the table. "Well you see, Doc... I mean, I'm not big on washing, not showers and stuff, but I go in the sea every day, and ... well, you smell, Doc."

Alex thought back over the last 48 hours and then nodded his head. It was a long time since his body had seen soap and water.

"They sell clothes in here," Bronwyn said, "and they have washbasins in the restrooms. You could give yourself a quick splash."

"All right, let's get on with it."

Alex hurried to the racks and selected the least offensive of the garments; a navy blue sweat suit, and white sneakers. Beside him an elderly man held up a similar outfit in pink.

"It's not for me," the old man said.

"Of course not," Alex responded.

"For my daughter."

Alex nodded.

"She has nothing to wear," the old man continued. "All these years, and then she comes to me empty handed. What am I supposed to do?"

Alex took his purchases to the counter and slid Moe Ellington's American Express Card across to the cashier. The girl accepted it without a moment's hesitation.

The old man interrupted the transaction by inquiring whether the Beach Hut sold women's underwear.

"No," the cashier replied, turning away to swipe the credit card through a card reader.

"Something, anything she could wear," the old man pleaded. "She doesn't have anything."

The cashier rolled her eyes upwards. Alex heard the credit card reader dialing in a number and the hum of distant electronic communication. From the corner of his eye he could see Chris and Bronwyn waiting by the doorway. Time was wasting.

"Anything," the old man repeated.

"A two piece bathing suit," the cashier suggested, "over there."

"Yes, of course, thank you."

Still holding the pink sweat suit, the old man hurried away to the bathing suit racks.

"Poor old thing," said the cashier, "I didn't know he was that way. He lives up the top of the hill and comes in here for his coffee. He's never done anything like this before."

She smiled brightly and handed Alex his purchases. She read the name on the credit card. "Thank you, Mr. Ellington, enjoy your stay."

As Alex headed for the men's room, he saw the cashier step out from behind the counter and go to the aid of the old man.

He had just completed a rudimentary wash and was relishing the comfort of his new clothes when Bronwyn tapped on the door of the men's room.

"Hurry up."

He opened the door and Bronwyn grabbed his hand. She pulled him out of the shop and pointed to a steep path that led up the cliff face to the road above.

"Up there."

"Why? Where's the car?"

"They phoned. Hurry up. Chris has taken the car. He'll meet us at the corner. Of course they probably can't get here this quickly, but it's better to be safe than sorry, isn't it? Come on. Can't you go any faster?"

Alex resisted her urgent tugging. "Who phoned?"

"The Americans, I suppose. While you were in the men's room the phone rang. I think it was someone saying that you were using a stolen credit card."

Alex started up the cliff, moving as fast as his tired legs would carry him. So Moe Ellington had turned him in. As soon as the number came through the credit company they contacted the Embassy. God, how could he have been so stupid?"

Anger lent wings to his feet, and he scrambled to the top of the cliff with Bronwyn close behind him.

"Over there," Bronwyn said, pointing to the red Mini waiting in a side street.

Alex settled into the front seat. "Go," he said to Chris.

"Okay, dude." Chris slammed the little car into gear. ""Where to?" he asked.

"St. Caerog," Bronwyn replied.

"Oh, cool," said Chris, "the surf's up at St. Caerog."

"To hell with the surf," Alex snarled.

"Stefan Bubani lives at St. Caerog," Bronwyn said.

Alex turned in his seat, trying to look out of the tiny rear window as the car made its laborious way up the hillside. When they crested the hill, he was able to look back and see the tiny bay spread below him, with the colorful dots of beach umbrellas and the white walls of The Beach Hut. He could also see a large black car pulling into the parking lot.

"Go!" he urged Chris.

"I'm bloody going!" Chris replied.

All three of them kept their eyes on the rearview mirror as they headed across the windswept moors. Glimpses of ocean came and went through the driver's side window.

"Do they know about Uncle Stefan?" Bronwyn asked.

Alex told her that they did, and that he was sure they knew where the old Serbian colonel lived. He lapsed into anxious silence, thinking about the speed of the black Cadillac and the leisurely pace of the Mini.

Chris was hunched over the steering wheel, urging the car forward with his body. Alex felt sorry for the boy. All he had wanted was the sun and the surf, and look at him now, he thought. Alex wondered how long it would be before Chris could think of this particular experience as "cool."

Chris flung the car into a narrow side road bounded by high hedges. They splashed across a ford, turned a sharp corner, and came out into the center of a tiny village. A grey stone chapel dominated the central square displaying a faded sign reading "St. Caerog Parish Church".

"Where to?" Chris asked.

"By the Lifeboat Station," Bronwyn replied.

"Cool," Chris said, and Alex breathed a sigh of relief. The

boy's personality was still intact.

"There it is!"

Bronwyn pointed to a building perched precariously on the cliff fifty feet above the bay. A wide cement launch ramp ran from the building, down the cliff face and out into the deep water.

"What is it?" Alex asked.

"The St. Caerog Lifeboat Station," Bronwyn replied. "Don't you know anything?"

Alex shook his head. "Not about the sea," he said.

"It's for rescues," she said. "You know, ships in distress and all that sort of thing."

A couple of cottages huddled beside the Lifeboat Station and overlooked a wide sweep of windswept bay. The sun which had brightened their morning had gone behind the bank of clouds that had begun to gather ominously on the western horizon. Great rolling waves crashed onto the sandy beach, which was deserted except for a pack of dogs roaming along the water's edge. Beyond the rollers, where the ocean moved in great, grey swells, Alex saw two surfers, kneeling on their surfboards and waiting their moment.

"Where's his house?" Alex asked.

"Down there," Bronwyn said, pointing to the second of the cottages. "This is as close as we can get in the car."

A barrier reading *Royal National Lifeboat Institute Official Vehicles Only* barred the road. Beyond the barrier lay a path which looked fit only for mountain goats, but it appeared to be the only path to the Lifeboat Station and the cottages. Chris climbed out of his seat and stood a moment, staring down at the beach. Alex could see that every fiber of the boy's body yearned towards the great crashing waves.

"Come on, Chris," Bronwyn said, "aren't you coming with us?"

Chris turned away from view. "Okay, dude," he said easily.

Alex climbed out of the car and found himself buffeted by a strong, gusty wind. He was glad of the sweat suit and zipped it up to the neck. They skirted the barrier and headed down the path.

Something huge swept low over Alex's head, and he was momentarily in its shadow. "

What the hell!" he exclaimed, ducking nervously and wondering if Moe had somehow managed to bring in aerial reinforcements.

"Derek Hughes," Chris said cheerfully, and Alex recovered his wits in time to see a hang glider lazily descending towards the beach. The flyer landed easily on the wet sand and was greeted by the pack of dogs.

"You're all crazy," Alex said, looking around at the rugged wilderness surrounding him, the grinning boy at his side, the distant surfers on the heaving ocean, and the hang glider pilot who was throwing stones for the pack of prancing dogs.

He wondered what he would find in the tiny cottage clinging so precariously to the cliff. It seemed an unlikely place from which to plot a revolution.

CHAPTER TEN

The interior of Colonel Stefan Bubani's cottage confirmed Alex's worst suspicions. The revolution was in deep trouble.

The colonel himself was an impressive enough figure, a grey-haired upright man with a skin tanned brown by wind and weather. His face, adorned with a bristling moustache, was intelligent and hawk-like, dominated by lively brown eyes. His handshake was firm, and when he hugged Bronwyn he lifted her off her feet.

It was the equipment that worried Alex. The main room of the cottage drew its light from a picture window framing a view of the ocean. In front of the window a trestle table housed Stefan's command post. Alex identified a WWII vintage shortwave radio, a manual typewriter, a CB radio, and an old black rotary phone.
The most up-to-date piece of equipment in the room appeared to be the television, and even that was more than twenty years old.

"So," the old colonel said, in almost perfect English, "you bring me news. I knew it, I knew it. These old bones of mine have been telling me for days that something is happening. Tell me everything."

He seated himself bolt upright in a straight backed chair. "Begin," he said.

Bronwyn launched into her story, glancing occasionally at Alex for confirmation. Chris wandered over to the table and looked longingly out of the window at the breaking waves. His fingers wandered idly to the knobs of the radio and suddenly the equipment emitted a burst of static.

"Leave that alone, boy!" the colonel barked.

"Sorry," Chris said.

"That radio is my ear on the world, with it I know everything that is happening."

Alex made his own mental inventory of all the things the colonel couldn't find out from his radio, which included fax transmissions, e-mail, and cellular phone calls. The list was endless.

"So, little one," the colonel said to Bronwyn, "we must find this place before your brother does."

"Do you know why Joe's turned against you?" Bronwyn asked.

The colonel waved a dismissive hand. "Some old gossip. He is a fool to believe such nonsense. My family has served the royal family for three generations, and we know better than to believe these slanders."

"But there must be something behind it," Bronwyn persisted. "They sent the prince away. Why did they send him away?"

"It was done in secret," the colonel said. "They didn't consult me. It was the old man, Viktor, the prince's tutor. I never liked him and I never trusted him. But this is ancient history, child. Now we can begin again. We must find Lizbeth Price. She'll share her secret with me."

"Do you have any idea where to look?" Alex asked.

"I can think of a few places," the colonel said. "I must call out the troops."

The colonel had no trumpet with which to summon his troops, only a telephone. He spoke urgently and at length in a language that Alex had never heard before. He replaced the receiver and rubbed his hands together in satisfaction.

"They will look for her," he said, "and then they will come here."

"Who?" Alex asked, with a growing suspicion that he wasn't going to like the answer.

His suspicion was correct. Colonel Bubani had alerted his

old comrades in arms. The contingent of old men who Alex had seen trundling their shopping carts into town was now on full alert and searching for Lizbeth.

The colonel crossed the room and stood next to Chris, looking at the ocean.

"Great surf," Chris said.

"But unfortunately a storm approaches," the colonel said. "This will make our journey difficult."

"Where you going, dude?" Chris asked.

The colonel raised a querying eyebrow.

"I think Chris watches a lot of American television," Alex said, "but it's a good question, Colonel. Where are you going?"

"As soon as we find him, we'll be taking the prince home."

"Here?" Alex asked.

"Home," the colonel repeated, "to his own country."

"To Serbia?" Bronwyn asked.

"To Yugoslavia," the colonel replied.

Christ shook his head. "It's gone, man. There's no more Yugoslavia."

"And look what we have in its place; endless wars!" the colonel snapped. "With the prince on his throne the people can be reunited."

"Cool," Chris said helpfully, "but what if they don't want to be reunited?"

"You think they prefer war?" Bubani asked. "Don't be ridiculous, young man.:

"How will you get him out of the country?" Alex asked.

The colonel turned away from the window. "The way we came in. We still have our ship."

"Uncle Stefan," Bronwyn exclaimed, "you don't mean the Defiant?"

"Of course I do."

"But, Uncle, it's so old, and there's a storm coming."

"She brought us here through a storm. The sea is no different now than it was fifty years ago."

"Do you really have a ship?" Chris asked.

The colonel smiled proudly. "Come," he said, "I will show you. Wait here, Bronwyn, in case the phone rings. She's already seen the Defiant," he added.

"Many times," Bronwyn confirmed.

Alex noted that her vocabulary had improved considerably in front of the old man, and she had abandoned her chewing gum. Without the ceaseless chomping and the repetitive swearing, Alex thought she was quite a pleasant kid.

The colonel took a bunch of keys from a hook by the front door and led his visitors out onto the cliff path. Alex noted that the wind had acquired a cold edge and had increased in velocity. The bright sunny morning had given way to a chilly and threatening afternoon.

Bubani unlocked the side door of the Lifeboat Station and led them into the boathouse. The interior of the building was enormous. The lifeboat towered above them, poised at the head of its ramp and ready for launching. The scene reminded Alex of the fire stations of his childhood; yellow slickers hung from pegs on the wall, with rubber boots lined up neatly below them.

"Why isn't there someone here?" Alex asked.

"They're all volunteers," Chris said. "They call them when they need them."

"Over here," the colonel called.

Alex edged around the stern of the lifeboat, and stopped in amazement. Now he understood why this building had seemed too large to house just one lifeboat. Another boat stood poised above another ramp, but this was no lifeboat, this boat was a wooden-hulled sailboat some seventy feet in length. Her name was written on her stern in gold letters "HMS Defiant".

"Oh wow," Chris said. "Oh wow!"

"What is this?" Alex asked. He was no sailor, and certainly no connoisseur of vintage sailboats, but he knew that this one was a beauty.

"The royal yacht," Stefan said. "The ship that brought us here."

"How did you manage to keep her?"

"A courtesy of King George VI. Officially the Defiant is a ship of the Royal Navy."

"HMS Defiant," said Chris. "Her Majesty's Ship. Cool!"

"She's carried on the official records," the colonel said, "and kept here with the permission of the Admiralty, but she is still ours."

"And you brought her here all those years ago?" Alex asked.

"Under the nose of the Nazis," Bubani replied.

He rested a hand on the varnished oak planks. "It was a hell of a voyage."

"Bad weather?" Chris asked.

"That was the least of the problems," Bubani replied. "The Prince was not an easy man. He was accustomed to taking command and very unwilling to take advice from anyone. He did not like the man the British navy had put on board."

"You mean Lizbeth's father?" Alex asked.

The colonel nodded his head. "They hated each other from the very beginning. Prince Grigori was a man of the world, Lieutenant Price was not. Price carried a Bible with him and the prince carried a bottle of brandy. I have always suspected that Prince Grigori's interest in Olwyn was brought about mainly by a strong desire to annoy Lt. Price, and he certainly succeeded."

Bubani patted the Defiant's graceful hull. "I spent the entire voyage praying that the Defiant would bring us safely ashore before our two commanders killed each other."

A worried frown creased Chris's face. "How long since she's been in the water?"

"A few years," Bubani admitted. "We had her out for the 40th Anniversary of D-day."

"That's more than a few years," Chris said. "She'll have dried out."

"She'll be fine," Bubani said. "I've always looked after her. Her batteries are charged, her water tanks are full, and she's fully provisioned. We keep ourselves ready."

A voice called out from the other side of the lifeboat.

"Uncle Stefan, are you in here?"

"Over here, Bronwyn," Bubani called back.

Bronwyn came around the stern of the lifeboat. "The uncles phoned," she said. "They've seen something."

"What have they seen?" Bubani asked.

"It was Uncle Paul. He said that they've been watching Jamie Price's house. They didn't actually see Lizbeth but they talked to a couple of the neighbors who said that old Mr. Price had a woman in his house."

"Just as I thought," said Bubani.

"She arrived in a taxi yesterday afternoon," Bronwyn continued, "and, according to the neighbors, she hasn't been seen since. They said that Mr. Price had gone out this morning but he's home again now, so Uncle Paul thinks they're both inside."

Alex didn't like Bronwyn's news. He was relieved that Lizbeth was at her father's house, but why hadn't she come out again? Was she sick, he wondered?

"Does Lizbeth's father know where you live?" Alex asked the colonel.

"He knows," the colonel said, and turned back to Bronwyn, "What else?" he asked.

"Flora and Joe are back at the Star of the Sea. Uncle Luc thinks they found what they were looking for at the library because they're waiting very impatiently for Milos to get back with the car."

"So they're ahead of us," said Bubani.

"They will be when Milos gets back," Bronwyn confirmed.

The colonel sighed impatiently. "We need little Lizzie."

"She's not so little," Bronwyn commented.

"Have you seen her?" Alex asked.

"Sure, I have," said Bronwyn, "didn't I tell you? I took her some food after you left. We had a conversation, sort of."

"Did she eat the food?" Alex demanded.

Bronwyn shrugged. "Some of it. Does it matter? It was fish and chips."

"Fish and chips," Alex groaned, "that's not what you give

to someone who's recovering from abdominal surgery."

"Flora said to give it to her."

"I'm pretty much convinced that Flora's trying to kill her," Alex said. "We have to find her, Colonel; she needs a doctor."

"We'll go back to the house," said the colonel, "and I will make arrangements."

Alex found little comfort in the colonel's promise. He imagined that Lizbeth would not take kindly to being kidnapped yet again, this time from her father's house.

They emerged from the boathouse to find that the wind had changed direction and was blowing hard from the north, driving dark clouds across the face of the sun.

"Surf's up," Chris said, looking longingly at the beach.

A group of surfers had collected at the edge of the waves, surrounded as always by a pack of dogs. The sounds of their voices and the barking of the dogs were carried upward on the wind and Chris listened enviously.

Louder than the noise from the beach was the noise coming from the village, where a confrontation was taking place. Alex heard car horns, raised voices, and revving engines.

"Do you think it's anything to do with us?" he asked.

"I don't know," Chris said, "you wanna look?"

Alex said that he'd look. Bronwyn and Bubani went on ahead to the cottage, and Chris and Alex hurried up the trail to the road.

The noise grew louder as they approached. Rounding the corner of a dry stone wall, they had a clear view of the village square where a large black car had come to a halt nose-to-nose with a bright green South Wales Transport bus. The engines of both vehicles were still running, and the bus contributed clouds of black diesel smoke to the general confusion.

"Come on, dude," Chris said, motioning Alex forward into the churchyard where he concealed himself behind a gravestone and watched the scene with an amused smile.

Having recognized the black car, Alex was not able to share in his amusement, but he crept forward and crouched beside Chris. With a volley of Welsh curses, the bus driver lumbered from his cab to confront the other driver. The Americans stayed in their car with the windows firmly closed.

The bus driver rapped on the window. "What's the matter with your eyes?" he shouted.

The window descended a few inches and Alex caught sight of a blond crew cut and sun glasses.

"Didn't you see me stop?" the bus driver demanded.

A slip of paper was offered through the window. The bus driver looked at it skeptically. "What's this, boyo?" he asked.

The man in the car said something.

"That's what you think," the bus driver declared. "Let me tell you, boyo, the god-damned President of the god-damned United States himself wouldn't have god-damned immunity, not if he hit a god-damned South Wales Transport bus."

"Now there's gratitude for you," Chris said to Alex, "and after America won the war for us."

Alex looked at him quickly to see if he was serious. His expression was unreadable.

"We'd better get back," Alex said. "It's no coincidence that an Embassy car is here. They're here to watch the colonel."

"And doing it so inconspicuously," Chris commented.

Alex had no idea what to make of this unexpected outbreak of sarcasm and decided to blame it on the fact that the surf was up and Chris wasn't at the beach.

The altercation in the village square showed signs of ending. Alex and Chris slipped quietly away, and were inside Bubani's cottage in time to see the Cadillac round the corner and park at the head of the trail. The back door opened and a man emerged. Moe Ellington, with the wind whipping his sparse hair, walked to the barrier and looked down the path to the cottage. After a long moment he turned and climbed back into the car, settling down to wait.

Gregory Gibbons woke suddenly from a troubled sleep.

He was irritated to find that he had fallen asleep in his armchair at such an important time. Of course, he had worked hard all day and he had been feeling quite tired. He had spent a couple of hours with the check books trying to find out how much money he had. Viktor had always been very careful with money.

In addition to the checking account, there was a savings account and quite a sizeable portfolio of stocks and bonds. They were all in the name of Gregory Gibbons so there should be no difficulty in obtaining sufficient cash.

"Sufficient for what?" Viktor asked.

"So that I can get away from here," Gibbons replied. "They'll be looking for the boy. I'll have to take him away. And, of course there is the matter of the bones in the garden and the fact that you are beginning to smell."

"What else would you expect?" Viktor asked. "How long have I been dead?"

"About a week."

"And you're just going to leave me there?"

"I don't like digging."

"There were a lot of things I didn't like doing but I did them in order to keep you hidden," Viktor said.

"I don't want to think about you," Gibbons told him. "I want to think about the boy. He'll be here any minute so go away and leave me alone."

Gibbons went into his bedroom and pulled a long hooked pole from under the bed. He reached up with the pole, opened a trapdoor set in the ceiling and pulled down the foldaway attic stairs. He climbed up into the attic and looked around. Everything was ready.

He glanced out of the window towards the ocean and saw dark clouds gathering in the west. Across the Bristol Channel in Wales it would already be raining, and the rain might well arrive in Dragons Green before sunset. At this moment, however, the sun was still shining and that meant the paper boy would be making his rounds on time.

As if in answer to Gibbons' wish, the doorbell rang.

"Paper boy," a voice called through the letter box.

"Coming," said Gibbons. He hurried down the attic steps, crossed the hall and opened the front door. There he was, with his friendly young face.

"One pound ninety two," the boy said.

He had dropped his bicycle on the front lawn, not bothering with the kick stand. The back wheel was still spinning. Gibbons noticed every detail.

"Come in, I'll get my wallet."

The boy stepped fearlessly across the threshold.

"Close the door, we don't want to let the flies in."

He heard the door close with a satisfying thud.

He smiled at the boy. "Can you change a fiver?"

"Easy." The boy reached an eager hand into the pocket of his grimy shorts. "You're the last on my rounds so I've got lots of money."

Gibbons laughed. "You should be careful who you say that to; someone might want to rob you."

The boy looked surprised.

"Not me," Gibbons added hastily, "but you can't be too careful. The world's full of crazy people, you know."

"Oh, I know," the boy agreed. He wrinkled his nose. "It smells funny in here."

"I'm having trouble with the drains," Gibbons said. "I'll have to get the plumber in to fix them."

He handed the boy a five pound note and waited while the boy sorted through his change with plump fingers. Their hands met briefly in the exchange of coins.

"I expect you have to take the money straight back to the shop, don't you?" Gibbons commented. "I don't suppose you like to carry it around with you."

"I'll take it tomorrow," the boy said. "I'm going down to the beach at Darundel Bay tonight. I'm going to take the short cut from the back of your house."

"He's not expected back," Gibbons said to Viktor.

"He might be meeting one of his friends," Viktor warned.

"I'm sure he has friends."

"You going to meet a girl?" Gibbons asked, trying to assume a conspiratorial smile.

The boy blushed. "Of course not. I heard that a Japanese freighter went aground on the rocks out by Foley Light and that there's all sorts of interesting stuff washing ashore at high tide."

"Ah," said Gibbons, "beachcombing, an honorable profession. Does your mother know you're going?"

The boy nodded. "She gave me some sandwiches; cheese and pickle."

"Very nice," said Gibbons, "but wait a minute, I think I have something you can add to your feast. Wait just there, I'll be right back."

"Okay."

The boy waited, jingling the coins in his pockets and wrinkling his nose at the unpleasant smell which filled the bungalow.

In the sunlit kitchen Gregory Gibbons picked up the length of rope he had prepared. The boy would not be missed for hours, and even then his mother would say that he'd gone beachcombing at Darundel Bay. He smiled triumphantly as the idea came to him that later, after dark, he would take the boy's bike over to Darundel Bay and he'd leave it on the beach. No, better still, he'd throw it off the cliff. They'll think he's drowned, he thought. They won't even look for him.

"This is not a good idea," Viktor said.

"I have to have someone," Gibbons replied. He turned towards the hallway, holding the rope behind his back.

"Grigori!" Viktor called loudly in the back of Gibbons brain.

"What?"

"Have you ever thought you might be insane?"

"I am not insane," Gibbons replied. "I am royal and don't you forget it."

Alex was amazed to learn that Uncle Paul and Uncle Luc could be reached on their car phone. The technology was new, and Alex knew of no one among his friends who yet possessed a mobile phone. Nothing he had seen of the old men or of Bubani had led him to think they would possess a car, let alone a car phone, but Colonel Bubani had dialed a number and was talking to his troops who were following Jamie Price's car.

"He has Lizzie with him," Bubani told Alex, who was hovering anxiously at his elbow, "and it looks as though they're headed towards the Gower. I think he's bringing her here."

"Not with Moe and his goons waiting on the doorstep," Alex protested.

"Hey," said Chris, "if they wanted us, they'd just bust in here, wouldn't they? I mean, that's what they do in the movies?"

"He's right," Bronwyn agreed.

"I know he is," Alex said.

He couldn't imagine why the Americans were waiting in the car instead of pounding on the colonel's door.

"I am under Royal patronage," Bubani said. "They won't dare touch me, or any of my men, there would be diplomatic hell to pay. No, they're waiting for you or Lizzie."

"So what do we do?" Alex demanded. "How's Miss Price going to get in here with them waiting on your doorstep?"

"We will need a diversion," said the colonel. He spoke rapid Serbian into the telephone and then hung up. "Luc will force Lt. Price to pull over and then they will wait until I tell them it is safe to proceed. I have established a rendezvous with my other men. They will arrive here together."

Although Alex was impressed by how much the colonel had achieved in one telephone call, two things still weighed heavily on his mind. First the colonel and his men were well into their seventies, if not eighties, and not really equipped to grapple with the Embassy heavies. The second problem was Lizbeth Price's health. Could she run; could she even walk?

The colonel rose from his seat and paced the floor, rubbing his hands together. "So now we need a diversion," he said.

"When will they be here?" Alex asked.

"About twenty-five minutes from Newton to here," said Chris.

Since he had seen the American car, the young surfer had undergone a transformation. No one had been "dude" and nothing had been "cool". He sat in a dark corner of the room without so much as a glance at the ocean.

"They will call when they are all assembled. Lizzie, the Lieutenant, and my men, and we will make our diversion," said Bubani.

"What diversion?" Alex asked.

The colonel said nothing, continuing his restless pacing of the floor. All three of them watched him. At last the old soldier snapped his fingers.

"We will launch the lifeboat."

"What?" Chris shouted. "Don't be stupid, you can't launch the lifeboat."

Bubani continued as though Chris had not even spoken. "The Americans will be forced by the police to move their car because the volunteers will be arriving in their own vehicles. They may even tow your little car, young man, but I am sure you will be able to recover it."

"This is ridiculous," Chris said.

The colonel continued undaunted.

"The village is full of tourists, and they will come running to see the lifeboat launched. There will be chaos and confusion, and in the chaos my men will bring Lizzie here. The Americans will see nothing."

Chris was on his feet, confronting the colonel. "You can't launch the lifeboat," he repeated. "Don't you understand it's a crime?"

"And what is the punishment?" asked Bubani.

"The punishment is something you carry with yourself for the rest of your life," Chris said. His voice was passionate, and his face was flushed under its tan. "What will happen if you launch that lifeboat on some wild goose chase and then something happens where someone really needs the boat? Look at the weather out there, it's going to be a bad night. What if there really is a ship in trouble? What are you going to do then? How are you going to live with yourself?"

"I already live with lives on my conscience," Bubani said.

"So do I," said Chris, "and I'm not adding more lives to it."

Bronwyn reached out and took the boy's hand. "It's all right," she said.

"No it's not," Chris replied. "He can't do this."

Alex looked at the passion on the boy's face. There was something going on here, something more than a dispassionate objection to raising a false alarm. Had Chris done it himself? Alex wondered. Sometime in his careless teens, had Chris launched the lifeboat with fatal consequences?

"You don't have to actually launch the boat," Bronwyn said.

"We need a diversion," Bubani argued.

"We can make the diversion," said Bronwyn, "without putting anyone at risk. All we have to do is turn on the siren at the Lifeboat Station. We can do that, can't we, Uncle, you have a key, don't you?"

Alex listened in fascination to Bronwyn's plan. She reminded him of someone, he thought, but he couldn't place the resemblance.

She presented her plan with confidence and logic. Normally the lifeboat was launched in response to a signal received by the Coast Guard, and relayed by radio to the Coxswain of the Lifeboat. The Coxswain would hurry to the Lifeboat Station and alert the volunteer crew, all of whom lived and worked close to the village, by sounding the siren. He would also telephone them or alert them with a beeper, but Bronwyn was convinced that the siren alone would be enough to start a chain reaction.

"They'll all come rushing over here," she said, "but they won't launch the boat, because there'll be no Coast Guard signal telling them where the trouble is." She looked at Chris. "When you and your friends pulled that stupid stunt of yours, you sent the Coast Guard a signal, didn't you?"

So, Alex thought, that's it, once bitten, twice shy.

Bronwyn flicked back her dark hair and smiled. "I'll go down and set off the alarm," she volunteered, "on my own. There's no need for anyone else to be involved. Enough said."

They sat together, waiting for the phone to ring. Finally Alex ventured an opinion.

"Colonel, I know I'm a newcomer to this situation, but do you really think that anything you're doing can truly affect the situation over there?"

"Of course it can't," said Bronwyn, "I've been trying to tell them that for years, but they don't listen."

"You underestimate us," said Bubani, "and you underestimate our prince. If he is half the man his father was—"

"What if he's not?" Bronwyn interrupted.

"You've been listening to your brother and that Balka woman and her communistic propaganda. We shall have our prince, and we shall have our country back," the colonel declared.

Bronwyn shrugged her shoulders. "Whatever! I'm just doing this for a lark, that's all."

"It's not a lark," Alex said.

The phone rang. The colonel listened and then turned and pointed a commanding finger. The old men were assembled. They were on the outskirts of the village and they had Lizbeth Price and her father.

"Leave the cars," Bronwyn said, "and walk in. Can the woman walk that far?"

"Can she?" Alex asked as the colonel waited for an answer from the caller.

The colonel nodded his head. "She can."

"Okay", said Bronwyn, "tell them to wait in the in the graveyard, and make their way into the cottage when the confusion starts."

Another ten minutes crawled by before Bronwyn slipped out the back door of the cottage and made her way to the Lifeboat

Station along a narrow trail which was sheltered from the view of the watchers in the Cadillac. Alex kept his eyes on the American car; nobody and nothing moved.

Bronwyn ducked into the door of the lifeboat station and moments later the wailing of a siren sounded, drowning the sound of the wind and the ever-present roar of the breaking waves.

Alex saw activity in the black car. Moe came out into the open again, together with three large companions in matching dark suits, sunglasses and short haircuts.

The quartet was standing outside the car and staring helplessly at the wailing siren mounted on the roof of the lifeboat station when the first police car arrived. The wind whipped away the sound of their voices, but Alex could see that Moe was no match for the two Welsh policemen. Within seconds, the four Americans had returned to their car, slammed the doors and driven slowly away.

The police officers looked at Chris's car, and then looked over the edge of the cliff.

"Stupid gits," Bronwyn said, coming breathlessly through the back door, "they think it's Chris down on the beach."

Alex looked at her in relief. "You're back," he said, unnecessarily.

"I wasn't going to hang around and get bloody caught," Bronwyn said. "It's not going to take them long to find out there's no real alarm.

The first tourists arrived on foot at the same time as the first crewman arrived in his car. Within a couple of minutes the scene at the head of the trail was one of complete chaos. Tourists with cameras milled around inadequately controlled by the two police officers, while crewmen's cars pulled into the parking lot and the volunteers hurried into the building. Overhead the siren continued to wail.

The crowd increased steadily and Alex finally spotted a contingent of elderly men filtering in among the tourists. In the midst of the group was a woman in a bright pink sweat suit. He breathed a sigh of relief; Lizbeth!

The old men regrouped at the head of the trail. Far from being an invalid supported on anyone's arm, Lizbeth seemed to be very much in charge. She took the lead as the little party headed down the trail.

The wailing of the siren ceased abruptly. Alex saw the crew of the lifeboat streaming back out of the boathouse. "False Alarm," he heard them shout.

The crowd of tourists turned away. "False alarm," they said to each other, putting their cameras back into their pockets and bags. The lifeboat crew started back up the trail, passing the hurrying contingent of old men, each group looking curiously at the other.

Lizbeth was first through the door. She fell into Stefan Bubani's welcoming embrace.

"Ah, little Lizzie," he said, "I knew that one day you would remember."

The old men crowded in behind Lizbeth, filling the tiny room with a chatter of foreign language. They were uniformly thin and browned by years of exposure to the sun and wind and, although they varied in height, they all had the same thick thatches of grey hair and bristling moustaches. Each and every one of them wore highly polished brown boots and light, rainproof anoraks. Last into the room was the tall, white haired man whom Alex had already seen at The Beach Hut buying the very pink sweat suit that Lizbeth was now wearing.

"Colonel," said Lizbeth's father.

Bubani nodded. "Lieutenant."

"I have brought her to you," Price continued, "what you do now is your own business."

"Dad..." Lizbeth said.

"I won't be involved," her father insisted.

Bubani moved to block the door. "Lieutenant, please, stay a few more minutes, We don't want to draw attention to ourselves, and if you leave questions will be asked."

Price said nothing, but he moved away from the door and

stood looking out of the window, turning his back on everyone.

"All right, young Bronwyn," said one of the old men, "where's our lunch?"

"Sorry Uncle Paul, no lunch today."

Alex waited for Lizbeth to catch sight of him. What would she do, he wondered, would she forgive him his desertion of her? She looked up and their eyes met. Her mouth opened in surprise and she said nothing. Alex moved forward, realizing that he was experiencing a pleasure in seeing her which was way beyond anything required of a doctor-patient relationship.

"Dr. Perenyi," she said at last.

"Miss Price."

No, he thought, that was wrong, he should have called her Lizbeth. She'd asked him to call her by her first name.

"I thought you went to London," she said.

"They weren't very interested in my story, or at least, not at first and I didn't think they'd reach you in time to help you. I see that you were able to help yourself."

"I didn't expect you to come back," Lizbeth said. "You didn't have to."

"Well," Alex said, "you are my patient."

The smile that had been hovering around the corners of Lizbeth's mouth died. "Don't worry about me, Doctor, I'm fine."

"I understand you've been eating solid food," Alex said. He could have kicked himself as soon as the words were out of his mouth. He didn't want to know about what she'd been eating, he wanted to know if he was forgiven.

"Bronwyn Ralko brought me fish and chips."

"And how was that?" Alex asked, doggedly sticking to his medical questions.

"Cold and greasy."

"I don't mean the taste. I'm talking about the after effects, Miss Price. I reconnected the lower intestine, and really, this was too soon for solid food; I need to know if the bowels are ...."

His words died away. Of course he needed to know about the bowels, but not now. Why on earth was he asking her about her bowels here in a room full of people who had gone suddenly quiet?

"My bowels are perfectly fine, doctor," Lizbeth replied.

"No they're not," her father said, turning to Alex. "Are you the doctor?"

"Yes, sir."

"Aye, well, she's had a hard time," said Price. "I didn't want her in my house, but I couldn't throw her out, not when she couldn't walk, couldn't even stand up."

"Dad!" Lizbeth complained.

"I didn't want to keep her," the old man complained, "so when I found out what the trouble was I gave her prune juice. That does the trick. Prunes always do the trick, don't need fancy medicines, just some prune juice. After that I couldn't get her out of the toilet."

"Dad," Lizbeth wailed again, "stop talking about it. I didn't come here to talk about my... my ... insides."

"Bowels," said Price.

"Doesn't anyone want to know what I've remembered?" Lizbeth demanded.

"Tell me," said Bubani, simply.

Lizbeth sat down in Bubani's desk chair and waited until every eye was upon her. "Dragons Green," she said.

"Dragons Green!" Bubani said. "Ah yes, Dragons Green."

"Ah yes! What's that supposed to mean?" Bronwyn asked.

"It means that I shall look it up."

"On what?" Bronwyn asked, "I don't see a computer; can you phone someone?"

"I could call in to the college computer," Chris offered.

"I shall look it up in my Road Atlas."

The colonel rummaged around among the books on his desk and produced a battered old atlas.

"But that's out of date," Bronwyn protested.

"I expect the village has been there for a thousand years," said Bubani, "and it will be in my atlas. Ah, here it is."

He held the open book out for their inspection. "Right

under our noses."

Chris studied the map. "You can see it on a clear day," he said.

"So close we should have smelled him," Price growled and turned away in disgust.

"I'll thank you not to speak that way of our prince," Bubani said.

"He's the son of the father," said Price, "and he'll go the way of the father."

'Show me where it is," Lizbeth said stepping between the two old men. Bubani took her arm and led her to the window. He gestured with a bony finger.

"Dragons Green, Devon," he said, "straight across the water there, as the crow flies, two miles inland from Darundel Bay. On a clear day you'd be able to see the church steeple. He was under our noses all the time."

"She could stand at the window and see it," Price muttered.

"Who could?" asked Lizbeth.

"Your mother," said Price.

"You mean you've known where he was all along?" Lizbeth asked.

"No," said Price. "If I'd known where he was, I'd have taken care of him years ago."

"Don't say that, Dad," said Lizbeth.

Price went to the front door of the cottage and opened it slightly. "They killed your mother," he said to Lizbeth, "and I've never forgiven them for it. If you're not careful, they'll kill you."

He went out, slamming the door behind him.

Alex saw Lizbeth square her shoulders as she turned away from the door. Her eyes were very bright, but her mouth was set in a determined line.

"Forget about him," she said. "Tell me what you're going to do now."

Bubani replied as though the answer was a foregone conclusion. "We're going to take the prince home to Belgrade."

The old men raised a ragged cheer. Surprisingly Bronwyn joined them, her face alight with unexpected enthusiasm. Chris emerged from the dark mood that had overwhelmed him and started to smile.

Alex looked at Lizbeth. Their eyes met, and he saw a flash of fear.

"How will you do it?" she asked.

"HMS Defiant," Bubani replied.

The old men cheered again.

Alex looked out the window at the wind-whipped sea. Dark clouds scudded across the sky, and rain splattered against the glass. The surfers had come ashore and were standing in a loose group on the beach and even the dogs had abandoned their frenzied rush in and out of the waves.

Alex thought of the old boat, poised for flight, and tried to imagine how it would fare on that unwelcoming ocean.

"How would you get there?" he asked.

"Easy," said Chris.

He unrolled a map and spread it out on the table. With a suntanned finger he traced a route southwest into the Atlantic, across the Bay of Biscay and along the coast of Portugal. His finger paused at Lisbon, paused again at Gibraltar and then turned eastward into the Mediterranean. He traced a long path to the foot of Italy, and then turned northward into the Adriatic, and on to Montenegro.

"It's a hell of a long way," Alex said.

"Sailors do it all the time," Chris said. "It's a piece of cake."

"In weather like this?" Alex asked.

"The weather won't stay like this," Chris assured him. "It'll clear up in a day or so, and then they can go."

"Do you think they'll wait a day or two?"

Bubani answered the question himself. "We sail tonight," he said.

His men raised another cheer, and Chris and Alex looked at each other hopelessly.

CHAPTER ELEVEN

The old men were clustered around the charts, talking in their own language. Alex saw Lizbeth sink down into an easy chair and went to her side.

"Are you sure you're all right?" he asked.

"I seem to recall that you discharged me from your care," she said. "I'm no longer your patient. If and when I ever get home you can send me a bill, but in the meantime I'm not answering any more questions about my stomach, my bowels, or any other part of my body."

"Would it help if I apologized?" Alex asked.

"For drugging me?"

"I had no right. It was an abuse of my responsibility as your physician, but I really thought it would make things easier for you."

"You didn't believe me, did you?" she asked

"It's quite a fantastic story."

"And it's not over yet."

Alex gestured to the old men. "What are they going to do?"

"Crazy as it may sound, they're going to launch the Defiant, sail across to Dragons Green and —"

"Tonight?"

"It's not far. Ferry boats cross from here to the Devonshire coast all summer. With a wind like this they'll be there in four or five hours. It's faster than going by road."

"Are you going with them?" Alex asked.

"I'll go as far as Dragons Green. I want to see my brother."

"Then I'll go with you," Alex found himself saying.

She looked at him directly with her interesting hazel eyes. "You haven't been invited. Go home, Doctor."

"I want to help," Alex said. "You may need a doctor; all these men are pretty old; who knows what might happen to them? And ... I ... er ..."

"You what?"

"I don't know how to get home. Things are kind of complicated at the Embassy."

"And I thought you were worried about me," she said.

She turned her head away but he had already detected an unexpected quiver in her bottom lip and a sudden brightness in her eyes.

He caught hold of her arm and turned her to face him. "I am worried about you," he said. "You're not as tough as you think you are."

"I'm not tough at all," she said. "It's all an act. Actually I'm scared to death."

"So am I," Alex admitted.

Whatever she may have wanted to say next was interrupted by a loud rapping at the door which sent the old men scurrying to roll up the charts.

The rapping came again, and a voice shouted "Are you in there, Colonel? This is the police!"

Bubani hurried to the front door. "We have done nothing," he said softly to his followers. "We have nothing to fear."

He opened the door and welcomed the two blue-uniformed officers as though they were old and dear friends. "Constable Rhys, Constable Meredith, how are you today?"

The two policemen stepped into the already crowded room and looked around in surprise. "Having a party, Colonel?" one of them asked.

"A national holiday, Constable Rhys," said Bubani.

"I see," said Rhys.

Meredith ignored Bubani and looked at Chris. "Changed your nationality, have you?" he asked. "You given up being Welsh, young Evans?"

"Yeah, that's right," Chris mumbled.

"He came with me," said Bronwyn.

"And you are?"

"Bronwyn Ralko. These are my uncles."

"Well," said Meredith, "we've nothing against you, Miss, but your boyfriend will have to come with us."

"What has he done?" Bubani demanded.

"We've had a false lifeboat alarm," Constable Meredith said, "and that's a very serious matter."

"Of course it is," Bubani agreed.

"You may not know it, sir," Meredith said, "but young Mr. Evans has done this before."

"I didn't do it this time."

"So what are you doing here?" Meredith asked.

"Surf's up," Chris replied.

"Don't give me that," Meredith said. "I've been down to the beach to talk to your friends, and they haven't seen you this afternoon. You haven't even got your feet wet. Just you come along with us."

"Is he under arrest?" Bubani asked.

"He's helping us with our inquiries," Meredith said.

Although he muttered something under his breath about Gestapo tactics and police states, Chris allowed himself to be led outside. He offered no excuse, and said nothing about Bronwyn, or Bubani, or all the things that were happening in the cottage.

As he passed Alex he said softly, "I'll give them an hour, and then I'll talk."

Bubani followed Meredith to the door. "Constable," he said, "I wonder if you would do me a favor."

"I'll try," said the Constable, "you know we always do our best for you, Colonel; diplomatic courtesy and all that sort of thing."

"There is an American car..." said Bubani.

"I saw it," said Meredith, "damned great black thing, taking up half the road, full of big military looking blokes. They weren't happy when we moved them on."

167

"We all know how Americans are," Bubani said, and Alex decided to keep very quiet and say nothing.

"What do you want me to do with them?" Meredith asked. "I can't run them out of town like they do in the movies. This isn't Tombstone."

"If you could just keep the parking area clear a little longer," Bubani suggested, "they're interrupting our national celebrations, and if you could stop them from parking up there I think we could finish what we have to do."

"We could keep them busy for quite a while," Rhys offered. "They hit a South Wales Transport Bus. I think we could ask them a few questions about that."

"They've been waving their bloody diplomatic passports at us," said Meredith, "so we can't keep them forever, but we'll do the best we can."

As soon as the police officers had departed, taking Chris with them, Bubani and his men broke into frenzied activity. Bronwyn made a couple of attempts to ask her uncles what they planned to do about Chris but she received no answers. Eventually she gave up asking and joined in the preparations.

Bubani's plan had been ready for many years, this much was obvious. From closets and cupboards came boxes and bundles. Bubani disconnected the radio and dropped it into a box. He handed plastic containers to his men and they filled them with fresh water.

"There's food and fuel on the boat," he said.

His men lined up and Bubani unlocked a cupboard and passed out World War Two vintage rifles. The old men took them, handling them with practiced ease.

"So now," said Bubani, "we are ready."

"I'm coming with you," said Lizbeth

"Of course."

"So am I," said Bronwyn.

"There's no need," Bubani responded.

"I can help," said Bronwyn, "really I can, and I don't want the uncles to go without me. I mean, what am I going to do without my uncles?"

She smiled happily at the old men, and they smiled back, showing their strong white teeth. Alex might have believed her if he hadn't already known her true motives.

Alex tried to add his own name to the crew lists. "I'm coming with you. I'm a doctor, I can help. Some of your men don't look ... well, let's just say they're getting on in years."

"You don't have to come," Lizbeth argued, "we can take care of ourselves."

Bubani solved the problem by thrusting a cardboard box into Alex's arms.

"We go," he said.

"We go," the men repeated, and the last remnant of the Royalist Forces of Yugoslavia marched out of the cottage door and along the cliff path.

Bubani activated a hydraulic lift and the great door of the boathouse swung upwards and away, leaving the bow of HMS Defiant exposed to the ocean.

The old men swarmed aboard. Alex followed Lizbeth up the boarding ladder and for the first time in his life stood on the deck of a sailing vessel. Around him on the oak deck lay an array of neatly coiled ropes. Double doors, now flung open, led to an enclosed steering station dominated by a carved oak wheel. A companionway led from the steering station down into the interior of the ship where the soldiers busied themselves storing the provisions.

Alex returned to the deck and moved forward. The twin masts appeared to be on pivots so that they could be raised as soon as The Defiant was out of the boathouse. Bubani organized the unwrapping of the sail covers, and soon red canvas sails were revealed, ready to be hauled up as soon as the masts were raised.

As Alex returned to the stern he looked through an open hatch and was relieved to see another of the old men connecting a modern twelve volt battery and priming a large and efficient-looking engine. Looking out at the fast approaching night, and hearing the crashing of the waves, he felt safer knowing that they would not be relying entirely on the red canvas sails.

Thinking of engines, the smell of gasoline, and the rolling waves, reminded him of his miserable journey from Ireland. He wouldn't be much use to Lizbeth or anyone else if he spent this entire trip with his head in a bucket.

Lizbeth came and stood beside him. She touched his arm. "She's a wonderful boat," she said, "I used to go out in her when I was a kid."

"She's old," Alex countered.

"That doesn't matter with sailing ships. This boat will take on anything the sea will throw at her, and speaking of throwing, or throwing up ....."

"I'll be okay," Alex said.

"It's not a night for weak stomachs." Lizbeth replied. "Let me see if Uncle Stefan has anything."

Uncle Stefan had pills, but he didn't have them with him as he did not expect that any of his men would become seasick. The pills were back in the cottage, in the bathroom cabinet. Alex looked again at the heaving waves and hesitated.

"Go and get them," Lizbeth said, "you'll be no use without them."

"Hurry," said Bubani. "Everyone is aboard and we must be gone before the Americans return."

Alex climbed back down the ladder. The sun was setting rapidly behind the storm clouds and the light of the day was dying. On board HMS Defiant the red and green navigation lights were lit and a warm yellow light shone from the cabin windows. She was ready to go.

He stumbled back along the path in the gathering darkness. Bubani had left no lights burning in his cottage and Alex hesitated to turn them on. He groped through the darkness to the bathroom, and turned on only the light above the medicine cabinet. He found an array of medicine containers and paused to read the labels, surprised at what he found.

If his prescriptions were to be believed, Bubani, so energetic and upright, was a sick man. Heart, Alex thought,

The Serbian Solution

probably angina, and rheumatism. Why hadn't the colonel taken the medicines with him? Did he think that seeing the prince would cure him of these ills? Alex scooped up the containers, and then located a packet of Dramamine. He swallowed two of the pills and washed them down with water from the bathroom tap, and then he turned off the bathroom light and went out through the front door.

The wind from the gathering storm caught him full in the face and cut through his lightweight sweat suit. He spared a moment to hope that Bubani had a supply of jackets or coats on board HMS Defiant to protect him from the cold north wind.

He looked up once and thought that he saw the dark outline of a car at the trail head. He hurried forward, wondering if the Americans had returned and hoping that they had not. How strange, he thought, that the very people he had thought of as rescuers, now appeared as enemies.

He was within fifty feet of the boathouse when he was grabbed from behind in an all too familiar grip. Moe Ellington, he thought, angrily.

The newspaper boy had a mother. Gregory hadn't really thought about the possibility of an over-anxious mother searching for the boy so soon, but here she was. She was plump like her son, and fair haired, and she was standing on his doorstep. The porch light revealed that she was a pretty woman in her late thirties, but the prettiness of her face was marred by the look of almost hysterical anguish which contorted her features.

"Have you seen my Jim?" she asked.

"Jim?" Gregory repeated, and then, "Oh, you mean young Jim who delivers the newspapers?"

"Yes, that's him. It's after dark and he hasn't come home." "Oh dear, you must be very worried."

"I am, I am." Tears trickled down the woman's plump

face. "You was last on his rounds Mr. Gibbons, and I wondered if you'd seen him. He's a good boy, and he knows not to stay out after dark."

Gregory was distracted by thoughts of his own mother. Had she ever cried over him, he wondered. No, of course she hadn't. She had simply climbed into that big grey car and driven away. She had never thought about him again.

"I'm so worried," the woman said.

"Don't get involved," Viktor warned.

"She's really upset," Gibbons told him.

"It's too late now. You can't go back on what you've done. Talk to her sensibly, Grigori."

Gregory looked the woman in the eye. "He came here," he said, "but that was several hours ago. He said something about going to Darundel Bay. He said you'd given him permission and some cheese and pickle sandwiches."

"I did, I did," said the anguished woman.

"I'm sure he's forgotten about the time."

Jim's mother sniffed unhappily. "But it's starting to rain."

Gregory looked knowingly at the sky. "We're in for a storm. I do hope that Jim understands how dangerous the tides can be at Darundel Bay."

"Very clever," Viktor whispered.

Gregory's suggestion was rewarded by renewed sobbing from the boy's mother, and he was satisfied that he had planted an idea in her mind.

"Do you think I should call the police?" she asked.

"She's a weak woman," Viktor said. "She can't make up her mind but you can do it for her. Tell her what to do. She's used to being told what to do."

"I hate to make a fuss," the woman added.

"I'd give him a few more minutes," Gregory said. "Boys will be boys, you know."

The woman nodded her head. "I suppose you're right. I'm probably making a fuss about nothing. I'm overprotective, that's what he says, and he does have lights on his bicycle."

"He's probably on his way home now," said Gregory encouragingly. "You should go home and wait for him."

He smiled easily, but his mind was racing. The bicycle was leaning against the back wall of the house. Thank heaven she'd come to the front door or she would have seen it. What would she do now? She'd go home and wait for a while but then what would she do? In another hour, or maybe only half an hour, she'd be on the phone to the police, asking them to look for her boy and then the police would come here and ask what time young Jim had left to go to Darundel Bay.

"Didn't you know the police would come?" Viktor asked.

"I'll take care of it," Gregory promised him.

"The bicycle has to go," Viktor said.

"I know."

"Get rid of her."

"All right."

"Good night," he said to the weeping woman, not actually slamming the door in the woman's face but closing it nonetheless.

He went to the back door. He should take the bicycle now. He should pick it up and carry it across the heath to the top of the cliffs and hurl it into the sea. But the boy was upstairs; he was quiet, of course, because of the tape over his mouth, but he would be frightened. Gregory didn't want him to be frightened, he wanted him to be happy. He wanted them both to be happy.

He climbed up to the attic. Jim lay on a mattress on the floor. His hands and feet were bound with rope and his mouth was taped. His eyes were bright and fierce with anger. Gregory was a little afraid of him. He made a cautious approach to the child, reached out a tentative hand and eased the tape from his mouth.

"Was that my Mum?" Jim asked immediately.

Gregory nodded.

"She won't give up till she finds me," he said confidently, "and when she does, do you know what she's going to do to you?"

"She won't find you," Gregory said. "My mother never

found me."

"Your house stinks," Jim said.

"I'm sorry."

'You stink."

"I don't."

"Yes you do, you're a stinking old pervert."

"I'm not. I'm not a pervert."

"Yes you are," Jim insisted.

"No, no," Gregory said, "I just want you to stay with me. We'll have a good time. We can go anywhere we want to go, I have money and—"

"I don't want your stinking money."

"Just think what we can do," Gregory pleaded. "We can have fun, we can play—"

"Go play with yourself," Jim shouted.

"Shut him up," said Viktor. "Keep him quiet."

With considerable effort, Gregory managed to subdue the squirming boy and re-tape his mouth.

"This isn't going to work," he said to Viktor.

"That's what I told you last time," Viktor said. "Do I have to fix it for you again?"

"Yes," said Gregory, "I think you should fix it."

Alex fought against the arm that imprisoned him. "Get the hell off me!" he shouted, twisting furiously in Moe Ellington's grip.

In London Moe had held him easily, but in London he'd been tired and hungry and very unsure of himself; now he felt like a different man, and he managed to free himself and confront Ellington face to face.

"Don't do anything foolish," said Moe. "Look behind you."

Alex turned to see two large men coming down the trail

towards him, guns drawn.

"Stand still," an American voice barked.

Alex raised his hands.

"Where is she?" Moe asked.

They don't know, Alex thought. They've only just returned, and they don't know that Lizbeth, Bubani, and the old men are in the boathouse.

"What the hell's the matter with you?" Alex shouted. "How come you turned me in? I thought you wanted to help me."

"I wanted to help myself," said Moe. "They picked me up and I had to do something. Where is she, doctor?"

Launch the boat, Alex said to himself. Launch the boat and get out of here.

"Wait here, Ellington," said one of the gunmen. "Frasier, go check the cottage."

The other man went on down the path to Bubani's cottage.

"CIA?" Alex asked.

Moe nodded his head. "It's national security now."

"You mean they believed you?"

"Not completely, but they're willing to listen."

Lights came on at the cottage windows, breaking through the encroaching darkness. The wind roared in their ears, blanketing any sound from the boathouse.

Launch the boat! Alex urged silently. Get out of here!

Alex tried to keep Moe's attention focused on him and not on the boathouse. "I supposed you found me from the American Express card. I should have run you up a bigger bill."

"One navy blue sweat suit." Moe replied. "In addition to watching for you to use the card, we put a tail on Joe Ralko."

In the excitement of the past hour Alex had forgotten about Joe and Flora.

"Where is he?"

"He's heading southeast on the M4 in a stolen Jaguar. He and his friends are not very good car thieves, and if it wasn't for our request to the British police they'd have been picked up already. However, the British bobbies are co-operating and we're all waiting to see where they're going. I don't suppose you'd like to tell me and save us all a lot of time, would you?"

"Go to hell!" said Alex.

Moe grinned. "You've really changed your tune."

"So have you," Alex said.

Frasier came out of the cottage, leaving the lights burning. "No one there," he called, "but they've not been gone long."

"Damn!" said the other man.

Frasier came back up the path. He was a large young man in a dark suit. His blond hair was cropped so short that it barely ruffled in the wind.

He stood in front of Alex. "Are you Alex Perenyi?"

"Go to hell," said Alex yet again, surprised to find that his vocabulary was deserting him.

"Talk to us, doctor," Frasier urged, "and it'll go easier for you."

Alex shivered in the biting wind.

"There's nothing for you here. I was looking for Colonel Bubani, but he's not at home. I'll talk to you, but not out here. Can we at least get out of the wind?"

Frasier took a step closer. "Of course he's not at home. They got away during the lifeboat drill, didn't they?"

Alex shrugged his shoulders.

Frasier seemed ready to force an answer out of Alex, but he was stopped by a sudden explosion of sound. A loud, rumbling noise came from the boathouse. Alex felt a sense of disappointment. He had wanted to be on board and that was not going to happen; not now.

Timbers creaked as the old boat slid down the greased rails. The three men forgot about Alex and raced to the edge of the cliff, with Alex close behind them. They were in time to see the dark shape of HMS Defiant hurtle down the ramp and plunge into the bay, sending up clouds of spray. She rolled dramatically, swayed, and then came upright, riding the waves. Alex heard the motor kick immediately into life.

The moon appeared between the ragged clouds and lit the

scene. Men swarmed the deck, winch handles turned, ropes were pulled, and slowly the two masts were raised upright. The red canvas sails spread themselves before the howling north wind and the Defiant heeled over and buried her rails in the waves.

The four Americans watched in amazement as Prince Grigori's royal yacht established a south-westerly heading and raced for the horizon.

"Where the hell's she going?" Moe demanded.

"Home," said Alex.

CHAPTER TWELVE

Lizbeth knew she should feel triumphant. She had maneuvered the doctor off the boat, and they had set sail without him. However, there was little room for triumph amid the sheer excitement of being at sea again.

HMS Defiant plunged bow first into the breaking waves and walls of water crashed over the foredeck where the uncles struggled to raise the sails. Bubani stood at the wheel, his face set into a grimace of concentration. Lizbeth forced herself to be silent. She would ask later, but now she must let Bubani get on with his work.

She went down the companionway into the saloon and found Bronwyn perched on the edge of a seat, clinging to one of the oak grab rails. Lizbeth braced herself against the rolling of the boat and made her way to a seat beside the pale-faced girl.

"What the hell are they doing?" Bronwyn screamed. "Do they know what the hell they're doing?"

Lizbeth forced herself to smile. "You can trust the uncles; they know how to do everything, don't they?"

"They only think they know everything," Bronwyn wailed. "God, what's going on out there?"

"We'll ride better when the sails are up and the course is laid in," Lizbeth reassured her.

"What the hell do you know about it?" Bronwyn stared at Lizbeth angrily. "This is all your fault. We're going to drown and it's all your bloody fault."

On the other side of the cabin a locker door flew open, spilling boxes and cans onto the floor. The cans rolled from side to side, and the door of the locker alternately swung open and then crashed shut. The cabin filled with noise. With an instinct formed by a childhood of training, Lizbeth moved easily about the cabin, returning the provisions to the locker. She closed the door and latched it.

Bronwyn watched her with envious eyes. "You're not even bloody scared, are you?" she asked.

Lizbeth shook her head. "It's too late to be scared. I found that out years ago. Once you're actually at sea, you just have to deal with whatever the weather throws at you. There's no point in hiding your head and screaming."

"I'm not screaming," Bronwyn said.

"And you're not hiding your head," Lizbeth said. "You're doing just fine."

HMS Defiant heeled over leaving the two women clinging to the grab rails to keep themselves from being hurled to the floor.

"Over the other side," Lizbeth ordered.

They scuttled across the cabin to the padded seats below the portholes. Here the force of gravity pulled them down into their seats, and they were able to stay in place without effort. The noise outside quieted and died away. The thudding of the engine was suddenly silenced, and the rhythm of the ship settled down.

"We're on course," said Lizbeth, "with the sails set."

As if to confirm her statement, the companionway door was opened and the uncles descended to the cabin chattering loudly in their own language and shaking water from their coats and hats.

"Where's our supper, Bronwyn?" asked Uncle Paul.

"In one of those cupboard things," Bronwyn replied, but she managed a weak smile.

"Come," said Uncle Paul, "I'll show you how to light the stove."

"I'm not bloody cooking." Bronwyn protested. "I didn't come here to cook."

Uncle Paul, the largest of the men and the uncle Lizbeth remembered best from her childhood, laughed heartily. "What did you come for?" he asked.

"Well," said Bronwyn, "I thought that ... well, Joe told me that we're related to the prince, and I thought that .... I thought that, if he's a prince, then I must be a ..."

"Princess," concluded Uncle Paul. "Princess Bronwyn." He laughed again. "Why not? Sit down, Princess Bronwyn, and I will make your food."

Lizbeth left Bronwyn to the teasing of her uncles, and climbed up to the pilot house where Bubani remained alone at the wheel. HMS Defiant was riding well, pointing high into the wind with her lee rail buried in the white water. Waves crashed across her foredeck and Lizbeth hoped that no one would be ordered forward, for such a sea could sweep a man off his feet and carry him away. On a night such as this there would be no point in turning back to look for a man overboard, he would be lost from sight immediately among the mountainous waves.

The lights of the city were no more than a glow in the darkness behind them, and the lights of the opposite shore were not yet visible. They were surrounded by a velvety darkness, and the only reality was the warm glow of light from the cabin and the flickering blue lights of the navigation instruments.

"I'm glad you left without the doctor," Lizbeth said.

Bubani kept his eye on the horizon. "The Americans were back. I saw their car. I couldn't wait any longer."

"He's probably gone with them and told them everything" Lizbeth grumbled.

"That's a shame," Bubani replied. "We could have used him. We need a younger man on board."

"He's no sailor," Lizbeth said.

"Perhaps not, but I think he's intelligent. He was smart enough to find his way back from London." Bubani smiled. And he found you."

"Yes he did, didn't he?" said Lizbeth, and, to her own surprise, she too smiled.

HMS Defiant made her way out into the Bristol Channel. An hour into the voyage they spotted a flashing navigation buoy and laid in a course toward the Devonshire coast. The north wind which had been their adversary on the old course now became their friend as they ran before it with their red canvas sails spread. The boat settled down onto an even keel and an atmosphere of peace settled over the old boat. The wind steadied, no longer attacking them in sudden, furious gusts, but the sky behind them remained ominously dark and cloudy.

Lizbeth gave herself up to the long-forgotten pleasure of night sailing. Despite the urgency of their journey and the threat of the storm, she reveled in the joy of being aboard a sailing vessel at sea. She appreciated the way HMS Defiant handled the waves, sinking down into the troughs and then rising again, shaking the water from her foredeck and surging forward. The only sound was the wind whistling through the old rope rigging and the creaking of the hull.

"Here," said Bubani, "take the wheel."

Lizbeth stepped forward, eager to take control. She touched the wheel and felt the ship as a living thing beneath her. Bubani gave her their compass heading and then went below, leaving her alone.

Lizbeth looked away from the compass and set her course by the stars. She forgot about the ache in her side. She forgot about Alex Perenyi, and she even forgot about her brother. Out here in the lonely night watch, she found her thoughts turning to memories of her father. When she was no more than ten years old he'd brought her out into these waters and taught her to sail and to navigate, and never to be afraid, because fear was a waste of time.

"Oh, Dad," she said to herself, "where did it all go wrong?"

Through all her childhood years he'd been such a good father and everything he had done was for her protection, or so he said. Even though she'd cried and complained when he stopped her from visiting her old Uncle Stefan, he'd acted in her best interests. The Royalists were upsetting her with their constant questions, their hypnotists, their therapists and all of their other attempts to unlock her memories.

No, she admitted to herself, there had been nothing wrong between them until Joe Ralko came on the scene and her father responded by sending her to boarding school. But school walls and vigilant nuns had failed miserably to keep Lizbeth and Joe apart. Whatever did I see in Joe, she wondered, because whatever it was, it's not there now.

Lizbeth looked up at the stars to check her course, but the stars were no longer visible. The dark clouds had closed in again. HMS Defiant was practically flying before the wind, but Lizbeth was having trouble holding her heading, which meant that the wind direction was changing. As the storm built around them, the winds were becoming more and more westerly.

The steering grew heavy and she strained to hold the boat on course as the wind tried to capture the spread of canvas and turn the boat toward itself. Lizbeth knew that she should call Bubani and the uncles up on deck. To maintain their heading they would have to shorten their sails and for safety's sake they should hoist their storm sails. Who would go forward? Lizbeth wondered. The uncles were all too old and unfit for the task of fighting heavy wet canvas on a heaving deck.

She looked at her watch and realized that she had been alone on watch for more than an hour. She was surprised that Bubani had not at least come up to check on her. She rang the bell beside the steering station to bring the new watch on deck. Bubani came up from below with a grim expression on his face.

"Should we shorten sail," Lizbeth asked, "before the wind gets any stronger?"

Bubani shook his head. "It's a race between us in this boat, those Americans on the land, and that traitorous Ralko boy. We'll not win by shortening sail."

"But I can't keep my heading," Lizbeth said. "I'm being blown off course."

"Do the best you can," said Bubani. "I have other things to

think of. We're taking on water down below."

"Taking on water!" Lizbeth exclaimed with an unintentional squeak in her voice.

"We were bound to," Bubani said. "Her timbers have dried out but with luck it will only be temporary, until the timbers swell. For now it's all hands to the pumps. I can't send anyone to help you. Keep her on course as best you can."

He ducked down below, leaving Lizbeth alone in the windblown darkness. All hands to the pumps, she thought. Twelve uncles, Bronwyn, and Bubani, all handling the pumps, that sounded like one hell of a leak.

HMS Defiant plunged on through the darkness with Lizbeth praying for the first light of dawn in the sky and a glimpse of land ahead. She battled to hold the wheel steady but she knew she was losing the fight. Slowly but surely the wind was winning, and HMS Defiant was being blown off course. She rang the bell again. Uncle Paul came up this time.. He had taken off his jacket and rolled up his shirt sleeves and he looked exhausted.

"We have to shorten sail," Lizbeth said. "I know Uncle Stafan won't like it, but we have to do it."

Uncle Paul nodded. "I'll go forward."

"Not on your own."

"It's all hands to the pumps down there. I have to go alone."

"But you can't do it by yourself," Lizbeth protested.

The old man looked forward at the wave swept foredeck and up at the billowing sails and admitted defeat.

"You're right. I can't do it alone. Just sail any course you can," he said, "we'll find out where we are at daybreak, by then we should have sealed the leaks."

As they crested a wave Lizbeth caught sight of a light on the horizon. She watched it intently, losing it in each wave trough and rediscovering it at each crest. A lighthouse, she thought, or a lighted buoy. She imagined an enormous buoy chained to the seabed and draped in seaweed, rolling and tossing in the passing waves, with its bell clanging out a warning and its flashing beam of light cutting through the darkness to warn sailors of the rocks ahead.

Of course, she thought, it could be a channel marker, or this could be a welcoming light beckoning her into harbor, if only she knew where she was, if only someone would come up and help her. She reached forward again to ring the bell. A hand closed over hers.

"We don't need them, Lizzie," said a familiar voice in her ear. "We can do this by ourselves."

"Dad?" Lizbeth whispered, convinced that she was dreaming, although the hand covering her own felt warm and real.

"That's the Foley Light," her father said, moving forward into the dim light shed by the navigation instruments. "It marks the Darundel Rocks. We'll need to drop the sails and start the engine."

"Dad," Lizbeth repeated.

"There's no time to waste," her father said. "We'll be on the rocks before we know where we are. Go below and get Bubani."

"They're manning the pumps," said Lizbeth. "We're leaking."

"I'm not surprised," said Price. "You can't leave a wooden boat like this to dry out and then expect it not to leak." He looked up at the sails. "I'm surprised the sails are holding out. I don't doubt they've rotted and they'll be torn to shreds in no time. Go below, Lizzie, and get Bubani. Tell him he can choose between sinking slowly or sinking very fast when we hit the Darundel Rocks""

Lizbeth looked at her father one more time to make sure that he wasn't a figment of her imagination, and then she went below.

The scene which greeted her below decks was one of barely controlled chaos. The main saloon, which had been such a cozy retreat, was now a soggy mess with a shallow layer of water sloshing across the floorboards. The hatches covering the bilges had been taken off and several uncles labored at the manual bilge pumps.

Looking forward, Lizbeth could see that the uncles were also manning the forward pumps. In their search for the pump handles they had thrown open lockers and cupboards and the contents had spilled out around the cabin. Cans had escaped from the lockers again and they rolled back and forth across the floor. Plates and cups had crashed down into the galley, and books had fallen from their shelves. Lizbeth's sense of order was affronted by the scene and she found herself picking up and re-stowing stores as she made her way forward towards Bubani.

"We need you on deck," she said to the colonel.

He barely looked up from his pumping. "I can't come now. Do the best you can."

Lizbeth grabbed his arm and he reluctantly stopped pumping and looked at her.

"It's all hands to the pumps," he said desperately, and then he realized that she had abandoned the wheel. "Lizzie," he said, "get back on deck. Don't leave the wheel."

"The wheel," she said, with a hint of pride, "is in the hands of the Royal Navy."

The old colonel looked at her in amazement. "Have we been boarded?" he asked.

"Come and see."

"I can't leave the pump. We're barely keeping ahead of the water. I've two men working with the caulking guns but I don't know if they'll do any good. She's separating badly."

Lizbeth looked up and saw Bronwyn huddling pale-faced in the corner of the cabin.

"Get over here and work this pump," Lizbeth ordered.

The girl shook her head mutely and continued to cling to the bunk, her face a picture of terror.

"Come on," Lizbeth urged, "it's a waste of time being afraid." She could hear the echo of her own father in the words and thought of the old man up there alone on the deck.

"We're going to sink," Bronwyn whispered.

"Don't be stupid!" Lizbeth snapped. "Get off that bunk and get over here. A great healthy girl like you should at least be able to work a pump. Come on Bronwyn, get up and help!"

"Just shut up," Bronwyn said, her face reverting to a childish pout. "If it wasn't for you, we wouldn't be in this mess."

The two women looked at each other across the bent form of the old colonel who continued to pump steadily, wielding the long brass handle of the bilge pump. Lizbeth could see Joe's features in the stubborn set of his sister's mouth, but the fear in her eyes owed nothing to her brother.

"Come on," Lizbeth urged, "Uncle Stefan needs to come up on deck with me. You have to help us, Bronwyn."

"You think everyone has to help you," Bronwyn replied, her voice rising to an ugly whine. "You're just like Flora, always giving orders and pushing people around. Well, no one pushes me around, when we get to Yugoslavia I'm going to be a princess and you're not going to be anything. You'll just be my brother's old cast-off girlfriend that he doesn't want any more."

Lizbeth shoved her way past Bubani and made a grab for the girl. Bronwyn retreated to the corner of the bunk and Lizbeth's grasping hand found only her lank, dark hair. Lizbeth pulled and the girl yelled. Lizbeth pulled again and her quarry came screaming out of the bunk.

"I don't care what you think of me, my girl," she said, realizing that she sounded exactly like one of the nuns she had so despised, "but you'll never get to your kingdom unless you put your hand to this pump."

Bubani released the pump handle and stood upright.

"I don't know how to do it," Bronwyn wailed, her eyes wide with a mixture of fear and anger.

"Don't tell me you're as stupid as your brother," Lizbeth said. "Even Joe wouldn't be too stupid to work a pump handle."

Bronwyn grasped the handle.

Got you! Lizbeth thought. "Pump," she said.

The girl pumped.

Lizbeth turned to Bubani. "Up on deck," she said.

To her amazement the old colonel obeyed her order and gave her a mocking salute. Lizbeth started to follow him and then hesitated, turning back to Bronwyn. The girl was working the pump handle steadily backward and forward, and a little color was returning to her cheeks.

"We'll be dropping the sails," Lizbeth said with as much confidence as she could muster. She had no idea how this could be accomplished by two old men and a convalescent woman, in such a boat, and such a sea but now was not the time to show fear.

"Why?" Bronwyn demanded. "Why do you want to drop them? Where are you going to drop them?"

"We're just lowering them to the deck. We don't need them anymore."

"Okay."

"In order to drop the sails," Lizbeth continued, "we will have to bring the boat up into the wind."

"So?"

"It'll get very noisy, the sails will flap and the ropes will be banging around on the deck but don't worry about it, it's not as bad as it sounds."

Bronwyn nodded, and even managed a faint smile. "I'll stay here and pump," she promised.

Lizbeth followed Bubani up the steering station. A faint daylight had begun to creep up from behind the eastern horizon, although it made little progress against the low, dark rain clouds. What little light there was showed them a grey sea, and a grey sky, and ahead of them a dark land mass. The beacon on the Darundel Rocks continued to send out its warning flashes. The light was much closer now, dead ahead on the bow.

Bubani and Price eyed each other across the sheltered enclosure of the pilot house. They had started the engine and Bubani had taken over the wheel, straining every muscle in a vain effort to keep off the rocks. Price had spread a chart out across the chart table and he studied it with fixed concentration.

"Do you want me to go forward?" Lizbeth asked, feeling that she was quite literally between the Devil and the deep blue sea. She could ignore the ache in her side and go forward onto the pitching foredeck to fight the wet, flapping canvas, but she doubted she had the strength to win the fight. Alternatively, she could remain in the stern, fighting the wheel and watch the two old men as they risked their lives on the foredeck.

"You take the wheel," Bubani said, "the foredeck is men's work."

"You're too old for men's work," Lizbeth wanted to say, but she couldn't. She moved forward and took hold of the oak wheel.

"Bring her up into wind," her father said.

Lizbeth spun the wheel until the bow of HMS Defiant pointed directly into the west wind. Their forward motion stopped abruptly and HMS Defiant reared and plunged like a tethered bronco. The red sails started to flap, and loose ropes writhed on the deck like demented snakes. Bubani and Price left the shelter of the pilot house and started forward across the wave swept deck. Lizbeth held the bow resolutely into the wind and watched them helplessly.

Gregory sat alone in the malodorous dark. He had been sitting for hours. Viktor wasn't speaking to him. Viktor wasn't telling him what to do. He had to think of something for himself.

Jim's mother would surely have called the police by now. They would come to see him and they would ask questions. He would have to take the boy away before they came. He blanched at the thought of trying to wrestle Jim into the car, the boy was so strong and so angry, and he didn't seem to understand what an honor it would be to serve a prince.

Of course he doesn't, Gregory thought, I haven't told him who I am. I have to tell him who I am. That's what went wrong last time. I didn't tell that other boy who I was.

He rose unsteadily to his feet. Jim had given him a couple

of good kicks in the shins and kneed him in the crotch. He hesitated at the foot of the attic steps, there was no sound from upstairs so maybe the little monster had gone to sleep. Gregory rubbed his bruised shins, there was something to be said for letting sleeping dogs lie. He would dispose of the bicycle first and then he would come back and tackle Jim. Yes, that's what he would do.

He reached under the bed for the hooked pole and very carefully folded the steps and closed the trapdoor. He went quietly to the front door and opened it. A gust of fresh air blew into the house stirring the stinking air. The first grey glimmers of dawn were lighting the sky and the rain was coming down like a ragged curtain.

He took his storm coat and cloth cap from their peg in the hallway and pulled on his muddy gardening boots.

"I have a plan," he said to Viktor.

Viktor ignored him.

Gregory hurried out into the backyard without locking the doors behind him. The hour was early yet and there were no passing motorists to see him moving around. He wheeled the bicycle up the slope of the backyard and hefted it over the stone wall which separated his property from the open moors. Looking behind him, he was pleased to see that the wind and the rain immediately obliterated his tracks.

Still wheeling the boy's bicycle, he trudged across the open grassland towards the cliffs above Darundel Bay. The boy would have cycled along the stony trail, but Gregory kept off the path, and forced his way forward across the hummocky ground. The moorlands were deserted, no rabbits crossed his path and no skylarks sang above his head. Even the seagulls were grounded by the storm.

Gregory wondered if a police car would be able to negotiate the bicycle trail and turned his head constantly to make sure that he wasn't being observed. What explanation could he offer, he wondered, for being in possession of Jim's bicycle? He sighed deeply at the workings of fate. He was a prince, and yet he had to offer explanations. He was quite certain that such explanations had never been required of his ancestors. According to Viktor they had been undisputed lords of all they surveyed.

At last he came to the edge of the cliff and looked down at the waves crashing on the rocks far below him. The village of Darundel lay to his right, invisible from where he stood. He was quite certain that the village would be waking soon. Of course, if Jim's mother really believed that her son had gone to Darundel Bay, then the village may well have been awake all night as the police came and went with their sirens and their spotlights searching for signs of the boy. High tide had coincided with the rising of the sun, and the police would have a few hours to wait before the tide turned and went out exposing the rocks, and allowing them to continue their search. By that time Gregory would have taken Jim away, and the bicycle would have been dashed to pieces on rocks below him.

He lifted the bicycle and tossed it far out, watching with satisfaction as it fell straight and true towards the sea below. The waves devoured it easily and it was gone from sight, leaving no trace.

"I've taken care of it," he said to Viktor.

Viktor ignored him.

"You don't think I can do anything for myself, do you?" Gregory asked.

"There's something out there," Viktor said.

Gregory lifted his eyes to the horizon and saw a boat with red sails struggling a mile or so offshore where the bulk of the Darundel Rocks heaved themselves out of the ocean and the Foley Buoy clanged out its warning bell.

Pity the poor sailors at a time like this, he said to himself, echoing the expression he had heard his mother use on wild winter nights. For a moment he could see her seated at the piano in the parlor of the big house, playing hymns. For such a storm as this, he thought, his mother would have played "For Those in Peril on the Sea." He looked at the distant yacht, and the looming rocks, and sang softly to himself, "Eternal Father, strong to save, whose arm doth rule the bounding waves. Oh hear us when we cry to thee, for those in peril on the sea."

The yacht seemed to be making no forward progress, her bow was pointed into the west wind and her sails flapped helplessly. He fancied that she was being carried sideways by the current towards the rocks, the same rocks that had claimed the Japanese freighter only two days earlier.

"She's taking one hell of a beating" he said to Viktor, and he wondered if the skipper was down below sending out distress signals. He scanned the rigging for the sight of a flag to tell him her nationality but she was too far offshore for him to see. There was, however, something familiar about her shape.

He stared at her in disbelief.

"Viktor!"

"I know," Viktor said.

"Is it?"

"Yes!" said Viktor.

"Yes!" Gregory shouted aloud into the storm. "Yes!" he shouted to the crew of his father's yacht. "I'm here!" he shouted. "I am ready!"

"No you're not," said Viktor.

"Oh God!" Gregory said, "I'm not ready."

His heart was pounding. He turned away from the cliff and began to jog inland. He must go to meet them, he thought, they mustn't come to his home. He guessed that they were trying to make a landfall at Darundel. If they managed to stay off the rocks, they would be in harbor within an hour.

He sent up a swift prayer to Viktor's powerful, angry God, and another to his mother's merciful God, and ran homeward through the early morning.

CHAPTER THIRTEEN

The curtain of rain parted and Lizbeth saw the Japanese freighter on the port bow. The huge ship had been driven headfirst onto the Darundel Rocks and lay partially submerged with its bow pointed to the heavens, while waves broke over the stern.

She longed to turn the wheel and steer clear of the menace but she couldn't, not yet. Her father and the colonel were still on the foredeck and she still had to hold HMS Defiant into the wind.

"Hurry up!" she screamed, although she knew they could hear nothing over the noise of the flapping sails and whipping ropes.

The main sail had been lowered and jammed through a hatch to add to the chaos in the cabin below. The forward sail was halfway down and writhing like a thing possessed. The two old men had been struggling with it for some five minutes and making no progress. From her remote vantage point Lizbeth could see what the old men couldn't see, that the sail halyard was caught in the rigging and the sail could not be lowered any further. She rang the bell to bring the watch on deck but no one came up from the cabin. And who would come, she asked herself, none of the old soldiers were capable of shinning up the rigging and freeing the sail?

As if in answer to her question she saw Stefan start cautiously up the ratlines. My God, she thought, he'll never make it.

With her heart in her mouth, she watched the old man struggle in the rigging. She could see that he had a knife and was slashing at the halyard that held up the sail. Again and again his arm rose and fell, and then the mass of red canvas collapsed onto the foredeck. Bubani rested, clinging to the mast.

The curtain of rain parted again and she saw the freighter so close on her port quarter that she could almost touch it. Dead ahead lay the towering shape of the Foley Light, the red metal buoy rolling with each passing wave, sending out its warning light and clanging its huge old bell. Behind the buoy loomed the foothills of the Darundel Rocks, black and shining, washed clean of seaweed.

Lizbeth looked forward. Bubani still rested halfway up the mast.

"Sorry, Uncle," she said.

She pushed the engine throttle forward and spun the wheel, turning HMS Defiant away from certain collision.

As the boat turned to her new heading, the sea crashed broadside against the Defiant's hull. Her masts swung in an arc against the grey sky and Bubani fell from the rigging like a ripe apple. He crashed to the deck, landing on the canvas of the sail.
Lizbeth clung tightly to the wheel, trying not to think of what she had done. She continued to hold a heading away from the rocks and the wrecked freighter, and found that she had to keep the engine at full throttle to keep from being dragged back by the tide and the current. She headed for open water, praying that someone, anyone, preferably her father, would come soon and tell her what to do.

He came at last, panting and exhausted, dragging Bubani. She watched him helplessly as he inched towards her, pulling the other man a short distance at a time and then stopping to get his breath. She rang the bell again but still no one came. She could only imagine the chaos below. At long last Price stumbled into the pilot house. His face was grey with exhaustion, and his breath came in loud, hungry gasps.

"Dad," Lizbeth gasped.

He turned from her to haul Bubani into safety. The colonel was conscious. His face was a mask of pain, but his eyes were very bright and determined.

"Uncle," Lizbeth said, "I had to do it ... the rocks."

"I know," Bubani gasped.

"Where are you hurt?"

"His leg," said Price, "broken, I should think."

The colonel pulled himself up to a sitting position. "Head for shore, Lizzie," he said.

"Just like that, is it," said Price, using a peculiarly Welsh sentence construction that Lizbeth hadn't heard in years, "and what about the rocks, there are rocks all through here? You sit quiet there and I'll get the chart."

He paused and looked his old rival up and down. "On second thoughts, I think you'd better get below and find out what's going on down there. Find out why no one's so much as poked their head out of the cabin."

Lizbeth nodded her head in agreement. "I keep ringing the watch bell," she said, "but no one comes."

Bubani dragged himself towards the companionway steps.

"Do you need a hand?" Price asked.

"Not from you," Bubani snapped back. He maneuvered himself into an upright position at the top of the steps and lowered himself down until his head disappeared from view.

Price unrolled a chart and set it out on the chart table. He studied it for a long moment, and then gave Lizbeth a heading. She spun the wheel, bringing the boat onto its correct course and leaving the Darundel Rocks safely behind them.

They rode in silence for a few minutes and then Lizbeth ventured a question.

"Dad, how did you get on board?"

"I came aboard before you did. I knew well enough what that old fool had in mind. I can read him like a book. I came on board and hid myself up forward in the lazaret, alongside the anchor chain. I knew you were in trouble when I found myself in water up to my ankles, that's when I came out here."

Lizbeth hesitated a long moment before asking her next question. "Why?"

The answer was not the one she had hoped for. "He's going to find that demon seed," said Price, "and I intend to find him first."

"Oh Dad," Lizbeth groaned, "that was so many years ago, can't you forget it?"

"Forget it?" her father shouted. "How can I forget it?"

His eyes, which until then had been calm and wise, began to take on the fanatical gleam which Lizbeth remembered so well. His love of the sea and his concern for the ship had calmed him for a while, but now he was back to being the obsessed man she had escaped from years ago.

"He took your mother from me," he said.

Lizbeth kept her eyes on the shore ahead and listened to the familiar ranting.

"Olwyn was my woman, and he took her. From the minute I mentioned her name he planned to take her, but she meant nothing to him, just another pretty face, another willing body in his bed."

"Don't talk about her like that," Lizbeth said. "She was my mother."

"And you've turned out just like her," Price replied. "I tried to stop you. I tried to keep you from them, but you went over to them, didn't you, you went over to them just like your mother did?"

"I was a kid," Lizbeth protested. "I didn't know any better."

"Born wild, just like your mother, just like your grandmother."

"My grandmother;" Lizbeth said, "what does my grandmother have to do with this?"

"I went to see them," Price said. "I went up north to see them."

"My mother's family?"

"Yes, your mother's family; I told them what you were

doing. I told them you were running around like a cat in heat—"

"Dad!"

"That's what I told them and I told them it was their fault. It didn't come from my side of the family."

"You told them that?"

"Yes," said Price.

"What did they do?"

"They attacked me. The men banded together and attacked me and they broke my nose."

Lizbeth tried to imagine what her grandparents must have thought when her father turned up on their doorstep and raged at them like a demented holy man. No wonder there had been no more Christmas cards.

She sighed and fell silent, waiting for her father to run through the familiar litany of her sins. She was wild, she was rebellious, and she was promiscuous. It served no purpose to tell him Joe Ralko had been the only one, and that she had already paid over and over again for that particular mistake. While she waited she steeled herself to ask the one question that only he could answer. She used to think that she didn't need to know but now that she was here, now that she had seen Joe again, she couldn't avoid the question any longer. He father finally fell silent.

"Dad," she said, "will you answer a question for me?"

"About them?" he asked.

"Indirectly," she replied. "It's an important question, and I want the truth."

"I always tell the truth," Price boasted.

"Tell me about my child," Lizbeth said.

She kept her eyes on the sea ahead and waited for his answer. In the eighteen years since she had left Wales, she had never quite forgotten the baby taken so abruptly from her while she was unconscious from the C-Section. The fact of the child's birth was always with her; always noted on her medical records; always evident in the faded white scar across her abdomen. Now, suddenly, she had to know.

"Devil spawn," said Price.

Lizbeth maintained her composure. "Don't start that, Dad, don't start with the Bible and the sins. I'm a grown woman, and I'm entitled to a simple answer to a simple question, was it a boy or a girl?"

"A girl."

Suddenly Lizbeth had a face for her child. Through all the empty years the child had been a mystery to her and she had not been able to comfort herself with images of her baby's childhood or teen years because she couldn't give it a body or a face, but now she could; she could give it her own body, and her own face. It, she, was a girl.

"Thanks, Dad," Lizbeth said.

Price reached into a locker beside the chart table and pulled out a pair of binoculars.

"He hasn't moved a thing," he said. "Everything is just where it used to be."

"At least he bought new charts," Lizbeth said.

"I'm not sure about that." Price raised the binoculars and looking steadily towards the shore. "According to that chart there should be a sea wall up ahead, but I don't see it." He lowered the binoculars. "Stay on this heading; I'm going below to talk to Bubani."

Lizbeth was once again left alone at the wheel as her father descended the companionway into the cabin. The morning was now as light as it was going to get with the sun completely obscured by layers of dark cloud. The land ahead was easily visible with house lights twinkling and car headlights moving along the rain soaked roads.

Turning to look behind her she could see the light of the Darundel Buoy flashing its warning, and the dark bulk of the freighter perched precariously on the rocks, waiting to slide off into the unwelcoming waters.

At last, dead ahead and right where her father said it would be, she saw the harbor wall. She rang the watch bell and immediately her father appeared on deck, followed by Bronwyn and Uncle Paul.

Price took note of the wall, consulted the chart again, and then moved to take the wheel. "I'll bring her in," he said.

Lizbeth stepped gratefully aside, and immediately became aware that she was cold, wet, and exhausted. The pain in her side was a dull ache that she had lived with for so long it was no longer a matter of consequence, but there was some relief in sitting down.

"How are things below?" she asked.

"We have controlled the leaks," said Uncle Paul. "I think the timbers have swollen; it was only a matter of time."

"And pumping," said Bronwyn. "I'm sick of bloody pumping."

"And Uncle Stefan?" Lizbeth asked.

"He is lying down," said Paul.

"And groaning a bit," Bronwyn added. "His leg looks bloody horrible."

Price turned to look at Bronwyn. "Must you use such language?" he asked.

"There's nothing wrong with my language," Bronwyn protested, "and how the hell did you get on board?"

Price continued to stare at her with such a look of disapproval on his face that she eventually turned away. "Your mother would be ashamed of you," he said.

"My mother is none of your bloody business," Bronwyn retorted.

The argument was stopped in its tracks by a couple of coughs from the engine.

"Where's the fuel gauge?" Price demanded.

"There isn't one," said Paul, "even the engine was an afterthought. The colonel had it installed after the voyage from Montenegro."

The engine had picked up speed again and was running smoothly, but they had all heard its warning and waited with pounding hearts for the next hesitation. Lizbeth imagined the motor dying and HMS Defiant carried helplessly with the outgoing tide, back towards the rocks.

"Jesus Christ," said Bronwyn, and was rewarded with another reprimand from Lizbeth's father.

HMS Defiant rounded the Darundel harbor wall and motored into calmer waters. The engine coughed again, and once again recovered.

Lizbeth had never visited Darundel, but she thought that she had never in her life been so anxious to arrive somewhere.

Darundel was a small fishing port surrounded by the high Devonshire hills. Stone cottages clustered around a semi-circular harbor where a fleet of fishing trawlers lay at anchor in the protected waters. A stone jetty reached out into the harbor, and Price prepared to bring HMS Defiant alongside. Paul called down into the cabin and the uncles, looking very much the worse for wear, swarmed up onto the deck.

"Stand by the lines," Price shouted.

On the foredeck, several of the uncles pushed aside the heavy folds of the collapsed foresail and began to work on the bow lines. Paul moved to the stern to handle the stern lines. Several figures appeared on the jetty, clearly visible in their yellow oil skins. Price brought HMS Defiant around in a wide circling motion and nudged her gently up to the jetty. Paul, with amazing agility for a man of his age, leaped ashore. On the foredeck, another uncle heaved a line to one of the waiting dock workers. The engine sputtered again, and died.

"Too close for comfort," Price muttered.

An oil-skinned figure approached them along the jetty, and, although his face was invisible under the hood of his raincoat, Lizbeth knew what he must be thinking, "What was this old wreck of a boat, where had she come from, and who were all these old men?"

When the official finally spoke, it was with such a heavy Devonshire accent that Lizbeth had trouble deciphering his words.

"Ye can't leave she here;" he said, or words to that effect, "this here's an official mooring. Ye'll have to take she to Yacht Club."

"Tie her off," Price shouted to Paul, ignoring the official.

The man leaned even further forward, pushing back his hood to reveal an official cap trimmed with gold braid.

"Be ye foreigners?" he asked. "Do ye speak English?"

"Aye" said Price, "we speak English. I'll be obliged if you'll tie her off forward."

"Ye can't stay here," the official repeated, "there's too much a doing today. Police business," he added.

Looking toward the houses, Lizbeth could indeed see the flashing lights of several police cars.

Price leaned over the ship's rail and looked the official in the face. "We're a ship of the line," he said.

"No, you're not."

"Royal Navy," Price confirmed. "HMS Defiant. Are you the Harbor Master?"

The man nodded his head, and took several steps backwards to look at the stern of the battered old yacht where HMS Defiant was painted in gold lettering, and the blue naval ensign fluttered damply.

"We weren't expecting ye," he said.

"Of course not," Price said, as if that was explanation enough.

The harbormaster moved reluctantly forward and supervised the fastening of the Defiant's bow lines.

Price came quietly to Lizbeth's side. "Now what do they plan to do?" he asked.

"I guess we go find Grigo," she said.

"And then?"

Lizbeth surveyed the waterlogged old yacht. "Then they take him back to Yugoslavia, or Serbia, or whatever they're calling it," she said.

"In this?"

"That was their plan," Lizbeth confirmed, "but I don't think they'll do it, not now, not after we've all been through."

"I wouldn't underestimate their foolishness," Price said. "I think you'd better go down and talk to the colonel."

The Serbian Solution

Lizbeth climbed down into the cabin, her nose wrinkling at the overwhelming odor of damp clothing, soggy carpets, spilled food, and diesel fumes. She spared a thought for Alex Perenyi, thinking that it would have taken a miracle drug to prevent him from being seasick in this chaos. Now that the adventure was drawing to a close she wished he was with her. They had started this journey together and they should finish it together.

"Lizzie," Bubani called to her, and she saw him struggling to sit upright on a water-soaked settee. His leg had been crudely splinted with sail battens tied with strips of cloth.

"We'll get you an ambulance, Uncle," she said immediately.

"No," the old man protested, "don't waste your time on me. You must go to your brother. Our crossing has taken too long. Josef will be ahead of us."

"But he doesn't know where to look," Lizbeth assured him.

"It's a small village," Bubani said, "and they all know each other, he will only have to ask enough of the right questions. Go ashore, Lizzie, rent a car and drive to Dragons Green. It's two miles inland from here, that's all, just two miles."

"Are you coming with me?" she asked.

Bubani shook his head. "I will slow you down. Take Paul, the prince will remember him."

He reached inside his soaked jacket and handed her a roll of paper money. "Pay with this," he said, "and hurry."

His attitude was so urgent that Lizbeth found herself back on deck and calling for Paul before she realized that she hadn't asked Bubani about his own future plans.

Bronwyn was sitting in the pilot house, looking out at the rain soaked little town.

She offered her unsolicited opinion. "It's even more lousy over here than it is in Swansea. I can't wait to get to where we're going."

"Where's my father?" Lizbeth asked.

"Oh, he's gone. He gave me a right old going-over about my language and then he buggered off."

"Gone?" Lizbeth repeated.

"Five minutes ago, while you were downstairs."

"Gone where?"

"How the hell should I know? He gave me all this grief, then he just climbed up onto the dock there and walked off."

"Damn," said Lizbeth.

She looked up at the black ribbon of road leading out of the harbor and over the hills to Dragons Green. They were all going there, she thought, Price, Joe and Flora, the Americans, they were all going to look, but she was the only one who knew what she was looking for. The thought gave her very little comfort.

CHAPTER FOURTEEN

Gibbons flung himself in through the back door of his house. He staggered back when the overwhelming smell of decay hit him. "Sorry Viktor," he said, "I don't have time to do anything about you."

He washed, shaved and trimmed his grey hair, then he put on his one and only suit. It was a little tight in the waist, he thought, but all in all a fine suit. He added a red tie. He cleaned his shoes and found his good raincoat. Before he went back out the door he checked himself in the hall mirror and was pleased with what he saw. The man who looked at him from the mirror was tall and slim and showed a slight resemblance to his distant cousins in the House of Windsor. His eyes were the only problem; they had a certain feverish quality which detracted from his general appearance.

And why shouldn't he look anxious he asked himself. They mustn't come and find him in this inadequate and smelly little house. Smelly and noisy little house, he corrected himself, because Jim was apparently awake and he could hear him crashing about in the attic. Gregory looked up at the ceiling for a moment. There's nothing I can do about him now, he thought.

He made a conscious effort to calm himself and then went out to the garage. He drove through the village at a sedate pace. People were awake. A police car came up behind him, sirens wailing, and he pulled aside to allow it to pass. An enormous black American car was parked outside the village store, and a small man stood on the doorstep, speaking to Mrs. Trewin. Neither of them looked up as Gregory drove by. As he rounded a corner on the outskirts of the village he nearly collided with a red Jaguar driving at high speed. He was surprised to see two such expensive cars in Dragons Green so early in the morning, but he soon forgot about them and concentrated instead on peering through the driving rain and locating the turn-off to Darundel.

He found the road he was looking for and floored the accelerator pushing the old car up to a reluctant 60 miles per hour. With the wind swirling around him and the curtains of rain opening before him, he felt as though he were flying, flying to his destiny!

He saw the next police car before they saw him. He slowed his car to a sedate thirty miles per hour and cruised down the main street of Darundel.

The little harbor town was waking to a gloomy day. The street lights would shine until way past noon, and the windows of the stores and tea shops would mist over, obscuring the view of the outside world. He saw that the fishing fleet had apparently decided to remain in port for the day. The half dozen rusty trawlers of the Darundel fleet rocked at anchor in the sheltered waters of the harbor. Beyond the harbor wall Gibbons could see the white spray of the breaking waves. The yacht that he had seen from the cliff tops lay tied up alongside the jetty, within plain view of the Harbor Master's office.

Gibbons pulled the Morris Minor into a parking space and reached into the glove compartment for his binoculars. He must be sure, quite sure.

The binoculars brought the yacht into sharp focus. She had taken a beating, that much was obvious. She sat very low in the water, and he saw water pouring from her bilges as though the pumps were working overtime. Her sails were down, and a couple of sailors struggled with a mass of red canvas on the foredeck, trying to stow it or mend it, he couldn't tell which.

Gibbons focused the binoculars on the stern of the boat and read her name, painted in ornate gold lettering. It was her,

HMS Defiant, his father's yacht.

He had last seen the Defiant in 1952 when he was eight years old. That was the summer when the Royal Navy had assembled every ship she possessed to sail past the young Queen Elizabeth on the occasion of her Coronation. The Queen had viewed the procession from a headland on the Isle of Wight and Gibbons and Viktor had been seated among the other royal European exiles. The Defiant had put on a good show with her flags flying and Colonel Bubani standing at attention to offer the royal salute, but the wheel had been in the hands of a British naval officer.

Gibbons remembered Viktor whispering in his ear, the tutor's voice came to him as clearly today as it did then, "She's yours," Viktor said. "She's not a possession of this British Queen. She is yours."

"She's mine," Gibbons repeated as he looked at the battered old schooner. "She's come for me," he said aloud.

"Go down there and claim her," Viktor urged. "You don't want them to go to your house, do you? You don't want them to see what you left behind, they won't understand."

"What about the boy?"

"Someone will find him."

"And you?"

"Oh, they'll find me," Viktor said. "They'll dispose of my remains. It won't matter, I'll still be with you, and once you're gone no one will know what happened to Gregory Gibbons. I've protected you. I've always protected you."

"The bones..."

"You know whose they are."

"No, I don't. They're nothing to do with me, they're something you did."

"You know what I did," Viktor said. "You've always known what I did. I had to, didn't I? You left me no choice."

"Shirley?"

"Yes, of course, who else would it be? How many other girls did you sleep with?"

"But..."

"You told her your secret. You knew what I'd do."

"I didn't think you'd kill her."

Viktor laughed inside Gregory's head. "Don't be so foolish. As soon as she disappeared you knew what had happened to her. When you told me what you'd done, you knew what the result would be. You've known for years what I did. Now stop thinking about it and go down to the dock, it's time to stop looking behind you."

Gibbons climbed out of his car and locked the doors carefully behind him. He would never see that little car again. From now on, he thought, he would drive nothing but brand new cars, perhaps a large black American car like the car he had seen outside Mrs. Trewin's village shop.

As he approached the waterfront the wind and rain stung his face, and he looked forward to the warmth and comfort of the Defiant's main cabin, its windows welcoming him through the rain with the comforting yellow glow of oil lamps.

He came to the end of the jetty and stood beside the sheltering wall of the Harbor Master's Office, watching the activity on the deck. The crew had finally managed to stow the sails and were clearing away the tangle of rigging left behind. A dark-haired girl came out on deck and looked around. He could see quite clearly her expression of impatience and boredom. There was something familiar about her face, he thought. He had seen that expression somewhere before.

A white-haired man joined the girl. Gibbons scrutinized him carefully, trying to place the face. Many years had passed since he'd seen any of his father's retainers and, of course, they had all aged, just as he had and they must now be quite ancient. Perhaps this white-haired man was the colonel he remembered - Colonel Bubani. He seemed to have the air of a person who was in control.

Gibbons decided that the time had come to reveal his presence. He stepped out from the shadow of the office wall holding himself upright and proud. If they had indeed come to make him king, then he must appear as a king.

The white-haired man looked up and saw him. Gibbons nodded his head slowly and the man nodded back. So, Gibbons thought, this must be the colonel.

The girl returned to the cabin and the colonel stepped down onto the jetty and walked towards Gibbons. Let the mountain come to Mahomet, Gibbons said to himself, and waited. As the old man came nearer, Gibbons was able to read the unwelcoming expression on his face. This, he thought, was not an old soldier eagerly greeting the return of his leader. This was an angry man, a vengeful man, a man whose face was flushed with fury and whose pale eyes burned with hatred.

Gibbons hastily ducked back into the shelter of the wall but the old man was too fast for him. A heavy hand descended, catching him by the collar, and a voice hissed in his ear. "Demon seed," the voice said.

Gibbons turned to look his attacker in the face. "Devil spawn," the man said, and at that moment the years rolled back and Gibbons found himself reunited with the man who had ruined his childhood, his stepfather, Jamie Price.

Viktor spoke loudly in Gibbons' head. "Kill him," Viktor said.

Lizbeth had no time to wonder where her father had gone or whether he was coming back. Uncle Paul seized her arm and hurried her across the street to the service station to negotiate for the car rental.

The mechanic, whose name, according to the label on his jacket, was Jack, came in from the service bay wiping his hands on a greasy rag. He was a ruddy-faced man whom nature had cursed not only with crooked teeth, but also a wandering eye which stared off to one side. His good eye focused on them suspiciously, taking in Paul's soaked tweed jacket and Lizbeth's pink sweat suit, but he accepted the driver's license and the roll of money that Paul offered.

"Paul Mihailovic," he said, mangling the pronunciation as he tapped the name into the computer, grease-stained fingers working grease-stained keys. Paul didn't correct him.

"You come in on that yacht?" the mechanic asked.

Paul nodded; Lizbeth said nothing.

"They're saying she's a navy ship," Jack said.

Paul said nothing. Lizbeth nodded.

Jack looked them up and down. "We don't get many navy ships in here," he said. They remained silent. "You don't look like navy," Jack added.

"We're not regular navy," Lizbeth said lamely, and turned away to discourage further questions. She concentrated on looking out of the rain-streaked window, hoping to catch a glimpse of her father. Where could he have gone, she wondered, and why? Two police cars cruised by, their lights flashing.

"More police cars," Jack commented. "They've been up and down all morning."

"What are they doing?" Lizbeth asked, glad of an opportunity to change the subject.

Jack's eyes, the good one and the wandering one, lit up. "There's a kiddie gone missing. Disappeared yesterday from Dragons Green. I don't doubt they'll be dragging the harbor as soon as the weather settles down."

"From Dragons Green?" Paul asked, breaking his silence.

"Just up the road a mile or two."

"Yes," said Paul, "I know."

"Why would they be looking for him or her here?" Lizbeth asked.

"Well now," said Jack, leaning forward across the counter and eager to share his little tid-bits of gossip, "seems like he was delivering newspapers up there in Dragons Green, and he told his last customer that he was coming down here to Darundel Bay. He told him he was going down on the beach to see what had washed up from that Japanese freighter."

The computer printer came to life, noisily printing Paul's rental contract. Jack began to talk faster. "The freighter went aground on the Darundel Rocks one evening last week. No good reason, really, I mean, not even bad weather and—"

"We saw it," Lizbeth said, seeing it again in her mind's eye, its bow reaching up to claw at the dark sky.

Jack greedily collected this new piece of information. "Oh, you saw it, did you, out there on the rocks?"

Lizbeth nodded.

"Broken up?"

Lizbeth was sorry to disappoint him, feeling that Jack would have liked a description of twisted metal and floating debris to pass on to his next customer.

"She seems to be in one piece," she said.

Jack lost interest in the Japanese freighter and returned to the subject of the missing boy. "Been gone all night, and his poor mother a nervous wreck."

"I'm sure they'll find him," Lizbeth said. "Maybe he's been trapped by the tide, or maybe he fell off his bicycle on the moor. I'm sure they'll find him."

"They didn't last time," said Jack gloomily. He pulled the papers from the printer and passed them to Paul for his signature. "He's not the first person to go missing up there."

Paul held the pen poised above the documents. "Not the first?" he said softly.

Jack shook his head. "It was a few years back; I was just a kid myself so you can see for yourself it was quite a few years ago. It was a girl that time but it makes no difference, I can put two and two together."

And make five, Lizbeth thought. The two incidents didn't have to be connected.

"Have there been any other boys?" Paul asked. He hadn't moved.

"Maybe," Jack said, "I mean, they don't make this sort of thing public, don't want to start a panic, but all I can say is that for tiny little place like Dragons Green, two murders we know about is two too many."

Paul scrawled his name across the paper. "You don't know

that they're murders." he said.

Jack shrugged his thin shoulders. "They're murders," he said. "I can tell. I got my own theories."

He handed Paul a set of car keys. "Are you sure that freighter isn't breaking up?" he asked.

"It's all in one piece," Lizbeth assured him.

"There'll be nothing coming ashore then," Jack said, "unless the boy washes up on the shore."

And wouldn't you just love that? Lizbeth thought.

"The car's right outside," Jack said, "the dark blue Rover."

Paul bundled Lizbeth into the passenger seat and climbed in behind the steering wheel, pushing the seat way back to compensate for his long legs. He was unusually silent and his face wore such a look of brooding concentration that Lizbeth was afraid to speak.

They reached the top of the cliff road and came out on the windswept moors. A police car passed them, going towards Darundel with its lights flashing. Paul sighed deeply, and for a few moments paid more attention to the receding police car than he did to the road ahead.

They arrived in Dragons Green by a different road than the one taken by Lizbeth and her mother thirty years earlier. Lizbeth recognized nothing until they reached the village green, and then she saw everything exactly as she had seen it in her opium dreams.

The village had hardly changed at all over the intervening years. There was the old stone church surrounded by its tumbled gravestones, the sign still screened by the spreading branches of the two holly bushes. The village store looked the same with its windows crowded with jars of candy and a Walls Ice Cream sign swinging above the door. The old pub squatted in the same position with its thatched roof defying the rain and its red painted dragon still rearing onto its hind legs and spouting fire.

Paul pulled into a parking space beside the rain-soaked and deserted cricket pitch that was the central feature of the green. He turned to face Lizbeth. His face was still set in an expression of great sadness. "Which way?" he asked.

Lizbeth looked around. "We went up the hill," she said, "beside the church. Up there, I guess."

Paul nodded, but the car didn't move.

"I'm certain of it," Lizbeth assured him.

Paul sighed, and looked straight ahead.

"Uncle Paul," Lizbeth asked, "is something the matter?"

The old man didn't look at her but stared straight ahead at the winding road leading up past the church. "What do you know about your brother?" he asked eventually.

"Not much," said Lizbeth.

"And what do you know about us?"

Lizbeth smiled. "You're the uncles," she said easily.

"Harmless old men, holding onto long-forgotten dreams?"

"No, no, that's not what I mean at all. I mean, look at what you've just done. How many other men your age could have brought the Defiant through that storm? Don't say your dream's forgotten; it isn't."

She patted his huge hand as it rested on his knee. "Your dream is about to come true. You're going to find Grigo, and who knows, maybe he'll still have supporters, and maybe he'll be the next leader. Anything could happen now that you've finally found him."

"And maybe young Joe is right," Paul said.

"Joe!" Lizbeth exclaimed. "I don't think so. Joe is never right."

Paul turned to look at her. "I have followed the colonel for all these years," he said, "and I have tried to keep my promise to the prince's father. We swore to him that we would give everything, even our lives, to put his son on the throne."

"You will," Lizbeth said reassuringly.

"We could have gone back," Paul continued, as though Lizbeth had never spoken. "We could have gone back five or six years ago, when the Communists left. We could have gone back and seen our families, seen our homes, seen our land one more time, but we didn't..."

"Because you were looking for Grigo," Lizbeth said.

"Because we were keeping our promise," Paul amended.

He ran his fingers through his thick grey hair in obvious agitation. "We knew about the rumors, but we ignored them. The colonel, he wouldn't even let us discuss them, so we didn't. Just lately young Joe has tried to get us to listen, but we ignored him because he was young, and like you say, not very intelligent. We blamed it on that woman..."

"Flora," Lizbeth prompted, wondering where Paul was headed with this strange conversation.

"She said terrible things," Paul said, "but it was all old history, because the prince had been missing for so long."
He looked Lizbeth in the eye. "To tell you the truth, Lizzie, I never expected to find him. I kept my promise because I'm a man of my word, but I expected to go to my grave without finding him, and without ever going home again."

"And now you can go home," Lizbeth said, but even to herself her cheerful tone sounded wrong as it fell onto the heavy air between them.

"Years ago," Paul said, "when your brother was fourteen, a young boy disappeared. He was the son of a bus driver from Newton."

Lizbeth waited.

"Newton, where your brother lived with his tutor," Paul added.

Lizbeth nodded her head.

The air between them grew very still.

"He was missing for three days, and the police thought that he may have run away up to London, or perhaps he had been caught by the tide and drowned."

Lizbeth heard the deliberate echo of the words the mechanic had spoken in Darundel.

"They found the boy eventually," Paul said, "or at least they found his body, washed up on the beach at Three Cliffs Bay."

"Did he drown?" Lizbeth asked.

Paul shook his head. "No," he said.

"What does this have to do with us?" Lizbeth asked. "I mean, just because he was in Newton..."

"He was a newspaper boy," Paul said, "and the last delivery he made that night was to a big old house in Newton where an orphaned foreign prince lived with his tutor."

"Oh, that doesn't mean a thing," Lizbeth protested.

"The police had a lot of questions to ask the tutor and the teenaged boy," Paul continued, "but they were nowhere to be found. They had vanished. They haven't been seen or heard of since, until now."

"No," said Lizbeth, "you're jumping to conclusions; there's no proof. It could have been anyone."

Paul nodded his head in agreement. "That's what we have all said, for all these years. We have said that Viktor, the tutor, panicked and took the boy away for no good reason. He was a strange man, and very protective of the prince, he could simply have resented the police coming around asking questions."

"Of course, of course," Lizbeth said, but her mind was reluctantly slotting the pieces of the puzzle together and forming an ugly picture.

"The people who questioned me," she asked, "I thought they were from the Foreign Office, but they weren't, were they?"

"Some of them were," said Paul.

"And some of them were police?"

"A lot of them were police."

"And they thought that Grigo—?"

Paul shook his head. "No," he said, "I think they suspected Viktor. They couldn't suspect the prince, he was just a boy."

Lizbeth seized the idea enthusiastically. "I hated Viktor, he scared me. Do you think he's still alive?"

"I hope so," said Paul, "because if Viktor isn't alive, then..." His voice faded away and he stared miserably ahead.

"This is ridiculous," Lizbeth said. "We don't know anything."

Paul eased the gear lever forward. "Now we can go on;

now that you know."

Know what? Lizbeth thought.

They drove on in silence, and any pleasure that Lizbeth might have felt in recognizing the country road with its high hedges and overhanging branches, was obliterated by the terrible suspicions rushing unbidden into her brain. She reprocessed her childhood memories. The kind men in dark suits who came to talk to her as she sat on her father's knee, they weren't diplomats looking for a lost leader; they were policemen looking for a criminal.

A clear image of her mother came into her mind, and, for the first time ever, she considered the possibility that her mother's death wasn't accidental. Viktor could have done that, she told herself. Viktor could have done that to protect himself. He could have killed her mother and the two uncles. "He meant to kill me as well," said a little voice deep inside her.

Where the hedgerows came to an end and the road began to run alongside the edge of the moor, the bungalow came into view. When she had seen it as a child it had been a new building of bright red brick with a sparse front lawn and a strip of land separated from the moors by a dry stone wall. In the intervening years the bricks had mellowed to a warm rust, roses had grown around the front gate, and ivy had climbed the walls. Behind the house lay a well-tended lawn, surrounded by flower beds, and the stone wall lay almost hidden in a thicket of flowering vines.

"This is it," Lizbeth said.

Paul pulled into the driveway and turned off the engine. Lizbeth surveyed the house nervously. If only they hadn't talked to the mechanic, she thought. If only Paul hadn't voiced his suspicions then she would have been free to run up to the front door and tell her brother the glad news. "We've come for you, Grigo. We're taking you home."

The bungalow looked deserted. Paul sighed deeply and climbed out of the car.

"How old would Viktor be, if he were still alive?" Lizbeth asked.

"As old as I am," said Paul.

He could still be here, Lizbeth thought. He could still be looking after Grigo.

There was no response to Paul's knock on the front door. Lizbeth rang the doorbell and heard its chime echoing inside the house.

Paul pressed his nose against the frosted glass of the window. "They're not home," he said.

"Maybe they don't live here anymore," Lizbeth said.

She stepped off the path and looked in through the windows. She recognized the room immediately, still the same, right down to the oriental rug on the floor.

"They still live here," she said, stepping back onto the doorstep. "Should we try the back door?"

They walked around to the back of the house, passing a detached one-car garage. Paul looked in at the garage window. "Empty," he said.

This was never part of Bubani's plan, Lizbeth thought wryly. When the cavalry came to rescue the prince in the ivory tower he was supposed to be at home waiting, not down the pub having a quick beer. The thought amused her, and her spirits lifted. Paul was wrong, surely he was wrong. Paul rattled the back door knob and then stepped back to listen. The silence was broken only by the pattering of the rain drops, the mournful calling of a curlew out on the open moor, and some muffled thumping sounds from within the bungalow.

"There's someone in there," Lizbeth said, "but they don't want to come out."

Out of their sight, in the front of the house, they heard a car approach and then stop. He was home.

Lizbeth was suddenly shy. Thirty years! What would he think of her after all these years? Would Viktor be with him?

Paul straightened his tie and his jacket.

"Forget your suspicions," Lizbeth urged. "This is it, Uncle, you've waited so long."

"The colonel should have been here," Paul whispered.

"The honor should have been his."

"Let's not greet him on the back door step," Lizbeth said, feeling that some formality was required of such an occasion.

They hurried around to the front of the house. A bright red Jaguar had pulled into the driveway behind their rental car, effectively blocking their exit.

Lizbeth was instantly suspicious, and her suspicions were confirmed when Joe Ralko climbed out of the driver's side of the car.

"No," she said.

"Is he in there?" Joe asked.

"I don't have to tell you anything," Lizbeth said.

Joe leaned down and spoke to the passengers in the car. "He's not there," he said.

The car doors opened and Flora appeared, followed by Milos and Peter.

"How did you know?"

"We were asking questions around the village," Joe said, "and getting nowhere, and then someone came into the village shop and said about this yacht that had turned up in Darundel with a crew of real old men. We knew it was you, and we knew that if we just sat at the crossroads and waited you'd come by and we could follow you. Pretty smart, huh?"

"He's not here," Lizbeth said.

"And we heard other things in the village," Flora said. "Rumors."

"You're wrong," Lizbeth said, "you're all wrong. How can you even think it?"

Flora turned to Joe. "I'm going inside."

"He's not there," Lizbeth said, "and the doors are locked."

Flora shot her an angry glance. "Do you think I've come so far to be stopped by a locked door?"

She leaned down and picked up a rock from the path, and before anyone had time to protest, she smashed the window pane in the front door. "Shall we go in," she asked, "or are you all going to be very British and go and have a nice cup of tea and come back later?"

Paul caught Lizbeth's arm and spoke softly in her ear. "I have a gun."

Who is he going to shoot, Lizbeth asked herself. We don't even know which side we're on any longer?

Flora reached in through the broken window and opened the front door. Joe stepped through into the hallway with the other crowding in behind him.

He stopped suddenly. "My God," he said, "what's that smell?"

The odor was overwhelming and like nothing Lizbeth had ever smelled before.

"Death," Flora said. "It's the smell of death."

Yes, Lizbeth thought, a smell like road kill on a hot day, but ten times worse.

"There's something dead in here," Flora said.

They huddled together in the hallway looking at the closed doors. Someone has to open a door, Lizbeth thought, someone has to look. In the sudden silence that surrounded them they heard the same muffled thumps they had heard outside the cottage. Paul's hand reached into his pocket and Lizbeth thought of the gun he was carrying.

"It's upstairs," Joe said.

Lizbeth shook her head impatiently. "It's a bungalow, there isn't an upstairs."

"An attic," Joe suggested.

Paul opened a door at random. "Kitchen," he said. He opened another. No one offered to help him. "Bathroom".

The smell, Lizbeth thought, the smell comes from behind one of those doors.

"Here's a bedroom," Paul said, "with a trapdoor in the ceiling."

They crowded into the bedroom. No, Lizbeth thought, this isn't where the smell comes from. The room looked like a young boy's bedroom with a narrow bed, rows of bookcases, and model airplanes displayed on the dresser.

"There should be a hook," Joe said, "to pull the ladder down."

Peter spoke for the first time. Still holding his handkerchief over his nose and mouth, he reached one long arm up towards the ceiling. "I can do it," he said.

He pulled the trapdoor down toward him and tugged at the bottom step of the folding stairs. The smell was no stronger with the trapdoor open. It's not up there, Lizbeth thought with relief. The smell didn't come from the attic but the noise did. They were greeted with a volley of thumps and bangs and an outbreak of muffled cries. Paul pulled the gun from his pocket and went up the stairs.

We're doing this together, Lizbeth thought. We're all so damned scared we've forgotten to hate each other.

Paul disappeared through the trapdoor. There was a moment of silence and then they all heard the voice of an angry young boy.

"Pervert," he shouted. "Stupid old pervert. Where's my Mum? You wait till I tell my Mum."

"Wait!" Paul shouted. "Wait a minute and I'll help you."

"I don't need no blooming help."

A pair of scuffed sneakers appeared at the top of the steps, followed by sturdy suntanned legs and then a very angry little boy.

"I'm gonna tell my Mum," he shouted back up the stairs. He turned and saw them all waiting for him at the foot of the stairs. For a brief moment sheer terror flashed across his grimy face.

"It's all right," Lizbeth said, "we're here to help you."

"You the police?"

"Not exactly."

"Where are the police? I'm gonna tell the police. He kept me all night, all night."

"I know," Lizbeth said.

She looked around the room. No one else said anything.

"I hate that smell," the boy said. "This house stinks."

"Yes," Lizbeth agreed, "it stinks. We'll get out of here as soon as we can. What's your name?"

"Jim."

"Can you tell us what happened, Jim?"

Jim glanced at the other people and then back at Lizbeth. Oh God, Lizbeth thought, I shouldn't have asked him that. He shouldn't be talking to me, he should be talking to someone who knows how to do this sort of thing.

"He locked me up," Jim said. "He's a retard you know, everyone in the village says he's a retard. He wanted me to play with him."

"Play!" Lizbeth gasped.

"Yeah, he wanted to play stupid card games. He said I had to keep him company. He said he didn't have anyone to play with. He wanted me to go away with him, and when I told him he was a stupid old pervert he put tape over my mouth."

"But he didn't do ... didn't do.... anything else?" Lizbeth asked. "He didn't do anything to you?"

Jim looked at her blankly. "He's just a stupid old retard," he said. "Are the police coming? Am I going to be on television? Where's my Mum?"

"We have to phone the police," Lizbeth said. "We have to tell someone we've found him. His mother must be worried to death."

Flora spoke for the first time. "Little boy, do you know where the men went?"

"It was only Mr. Gibbons," Jim said. "I didn't see the other old man. I haven't seen him all week."

Lizbeth couldn't bring herself to think what that meant, she could only think of Jim's mother pacing the floor and waiting for the phone to ring.

"We have to phone the police," she repeated. "There has to be a phone here somewhere."

She went out into the hall and flung open another door. As soon as the door was open the stench billowed out to meet her, and with it the sound of a thousand buzzing flies. There was something awful on the bed. She could hear herself screaming.

She prided herself on never crying, never behaving in a hysterical fashion, but now she screamed and screamed. She screamed until a pair of arms tightened around her and pulled her close.

She heard a blessedly familiar American voice said, "Don't do that, Miss Price, you'll split your stitches."

CHAPTER FIFTEEN

Gibbons had never before been in an actual fistfight and he was surprised at how hard it was to subdue the old man. *He has to be at least eighty years old,* Gibbons thought, *and yet he attacks with the strength and fury of a man half his age.* The two men fell to the ground in a struggling heap. Gibbons managed to raise his head for a moment to see if anyone was coming, but their struggles had brought them into the shadow of the Harbor Master's office where they would be invisible to any casual passerby.

"Devil," Price grunted, clawing for Gibbons' throat.

"Let him waste his breath on insults," Viktor advised.

Gibbons concentrated on fighting back the clutching fingers while the old man raged breathlessly.

What was Price doing here, he wondered? What on earth would possess the colonel to bring this miserable old fool along with him? Of course he was Lizzie's father, but that hardly gave him the right to be a part of Gibbons' triumphant return to his people, particularly in view of the fact that he had always treated Gibbons with disdain.

Gibbons freed himself from Price's claw-like hands and struggled to his feet. The old man launched himself at Gibbons' knees. Gibbons staggered and then managed to free one leg, allowing him to end the combat with an accidentally well-placed kick to the old man's balding head. Price collapsed.

Gibbons looked around again to make certain no one had

seen the struggle but they appeared to be alone on the jetty, lost in their own world of rain and cloud. He could see people moving about on the deck of the Defiant. A man and a woman left the boat and started to walk towards him.

"Not this time," Gibbons thought as he ducked back into the shadows. The couple hurried past him, heads down against the driving rain. Gibbons wanted to see their faces but as they passed by Price stirred and groaned and Gibbons turned away to silence him with another wild kick. When he looked back, the man and woman had crossed the street and disappeared from view.

Well, he thought, I can't stay here all day.

He would have to make his presence known to someone, but who would that be? Who could he trust? He moved out of the shadows again and looked at the waiting yacht. The dark haired girl came out on deck again, swathed in a yellow oil skin jacket. She appeared to be alone. She couldn't hurt him, he thought, not one girl, all alone.

Her head turned in his direction, and he waved a hand in greeting. She waved back and moved a hand to push her hair out of her eyes. She climbed onto the jetty and came towards him, alone.

He could see that she was smiling, her whole face alight with anticipation. This is better, he thought. In Belgrade there would be hundreds of girls like this, that's what Viktor had told him; there would be hundreds of girls casting flowers at his feet, and children singing songs of welcome, flags waving, bells ringing. This was what he had been born for.

"Are you him?" the girl called in a light, clear voice which carried easily towards him on the wind.

He nodded his head.

"I knew it! I knew it!" she shouted.

Gibbons remembered the inert body of Jamie Price slumped behind the office wall, amidst a tangle of ropes and crab pots. Got to get rid of him, he thought. He stepped sideways into the shadows. He slid his hands under the old man's arms and heaved him to the edge of the jetty. It was impossible to say whether the old man was dead or alive and Gibbons didn't care much either way. He rolled the body over and tumbled it into the cold grey ocean which was rising and falling in waves against the stone wall.

He was finished before the girl rounded the corner. She greeted him with a triumphant smile.

"She went looking for you, but I found you," the girl said. "Should I curtsey?"

"If you want to"" Gibbons replied, hoping that she would.

She did. It was only a small, token curtsey, but it was his first, and most probably her first, he thought.

"I'm your cousin," the girl said, "or sort-of cousin; Bronwyn Ralko."

Ralko! Ah, yes, the names were coming back. Josef Ralko, a boring man who walked one step behind the colonel and wrote constantly in a notebook. Was he a relation? Viktor had never said anything about him being a relation, but there were many things that Viktor had never explained. Gibbons noticed that the girl wore a diamond stud in her nose, which he thought most peculiar and very unattractive.

"Is the colonel here?" Gibbons asked.

"He's on board the boat," Bronwyn said. "He broke his leg on the way over here and that's why he didn't go to Dragons Green with ..." She hesitated and gave Gibbons a calculating look.

"I saw a man and a woman leave the ship," Gibbons said.

Bronwyn Ralko smiled, and although Gibbons knew very little about women, and almost nothing about teenaged girls, he thought there was something dishonest under that bright expression.

'Who were they? he asked

"Just one of the uncles, and his wife," Bronwyn said dismissively. "Come on, let's get on board. There's a bit of a mess down below, but we're getting it cleaned up. We had a hell of a crossing."

Gibbons looked back towards the shore and saw a little red car with a yellow surf board strapped to the roof cruise slowly past the end of the dock. He thought about Price and wondered if he'd done the right thing in dumping him into the water. Perhaps his body could be seen from the shore.

"We have to sail immediately," Gibbons said, following Bronwyn on board the Defiant. "We can't wait for the people who went ashore."

"Of course we can't," said Bronwyn, smiling to show her complete co-operation.

So this was what it meant to be a king, Gibbons thought.

Flora caught hold of Lizbeth's hand before she could lift the phone receiver. "Don't call the police."

Lizbeth recoiled from the contact. "I have to. They have to know about the little boy, and about ... him."

"Five minutes won't make any difference," Flora said. "The boy's safe, and whoever that is in there is as dead as he's ever going to be."

Alex came out of the bedroom where he had been alone with the body.

"Well?" Joe asked.

Alex shrugged his shoulders. "I can't tell. It's an old man, and he's been dead a while but I don't know what caused his death."

"Is it Grigo?" Lizbeth asked.

Alex shook his head. "I doubt it. It's an old man, a really old man. How's the kid doing?"

"Your friends from the CIA are keeping him busy," Lizbeth said. "He's outside looking at their guns."

"They're not my friends," Alex replied. "The kid should be looked at by a doctor. He seems to be tough as nails, but you never know. Has anyone called the police?"

Flora slapped her hand down over the phone receiver. "The police will keep us all here answering questions while Gruda gets clean away."

"We don't know it was him," Lizbeth protested.

"Don't be ridiculous," Joe said, "of course it was him."

"I talked with the little man from the Embassy," Flora said. "Apparently his name is Moe, a strange name."

"What's he doing here?" Lizbeth asked.

"I'll tell you later," Alex said. "What did Moe think?"

"I didn't ask his opinion," Flora replied. "I told him what we wanted and he agreed, on condition that he comes with us. He will leave his men here to take care of the details while we catch up with Gruda."

"We don't know where to look for him," Lizbeth said.

Flora shot her a withering look. "Don't pretend to be stupid," she said, "you know that he has gone to the harbor."

"He doesn't know about the boat," Lizbeth said, looking to Paul for support and finding none. Paul had been silent for a long time. He sat on a chair in the corner, his hands folded in his lap, staring straight ahead into nothingness.

"Uncle Paul," Lizbeth said, "what do you think?"

"I think someone should warn the colonel," Paul said.

"Everyone knows about the boat," Joe said. "The lady in the village shop was talking about it. The news is out. We can take that black car the Americans came in and be over there in ten minutes or less. "

"The doctor will wait with the body," Flora announced.

Alex shook his head. "That body doesn't need a doctor, and I'm tired of other people telling me where I have to go. I'm going with you."

"We can't leave the boy," Lizbeth protested.

"I think he's left us," Alex said.

Lizbeth followed his pointing finger and saw the boy running through the rain.

"He knows his own way home," Flora said. "And his mother will call the police. We have no time to waste. Let us go."

The embassy limo was enormous by British standards, but it wasn't designed to carry eight people in comfort. Lizbeth was crammed into a corner with Alex Perenyi beside her. She was quite surprised to find that instead of all the other things she should be thinking about, she was, in fact, thinking about the warmth of his leg as it pressed against her own, and the weight of his arm draped around her shoulder. She remembered how tightly he had held her, and how good it felt to be held.

She sneaked a sideways glance at his face, and found him looking at her. Their eyes locked and held, the pressure of his leg increased, and the arm around her shoulder pulled her closer. They said nothing.

"How did you get here?" she asked at last, when the intensity of his gaze had become truly uncomfortable.

"I arranged it," said Moe Ellington who was driving the limo.

"I know about you," Lizbeth said. "You said you were helping Alex, and then you, you..."

"Helped myself?" Moe asked. "Not really, Miss Price, although it must appear that way at the moment."

"Yes it does," Lizbeth agreed.

"I believe him," Alex said. "You'd better listen to what he has to say."

"I suppose it's more bad stuff about Grigo."

"Yes, I'm afraid so," Moe said.

Lizbeth sensed that the little man was trying to be kind but there was no way to sugarcoat the story he told. After he had been forced to leave Alex at the Motorway Rest Area, he had returned to find the Embassy buzzing with activity. Diplomats who were many rungs higher than Moe on the ladder of success had caused sealed files to be opened. They had conferred with their British counterparts, and they had found a suitably sympathetic titled gentleman to visit the Countess Iole and have a long talk with her. The Countess knew far more than she had told Alex and Moe about the prince's alleged crimes.

"You're talking about the boy who drowned, aren't you?" Lizbeth said.

"He didn't drown," Moe replied.

The Serbian Solution

Lizbeth nodded her head miserably. "But we don't know that was Grigo."

"No," said Moe, "we don't know, but even a suspicion is enough to start them all fighting again. You have to understand, Miss Price, that the prince has supporters in Serbia, powerful supporters. The war over there has been a horrible thing and it's not really over, just on hold. There are a surprisingly large number of people who think that the restoration of some kind of hereditary monarchy could be a unifying factor, it's been considered even at White House level."

"I didn't know that," Alex said.

"You wouldn't," Moe replied. "The whole thing was a bit of a moot point when the prince was nowhere to be found, but you have to remember that both Britain and the United States have had boots on the ground over there and they don't want to send them again. They'd really like a solution. When Dr. Perenyi came walking into the Embassy with his absurd-sounding story about being kidnapped by Yugoslav Serbs, and when I disappeared with him, it went all the way up the ladder to the people who were willing to take it seriously."

"It makes sense," Alex said.

"How nice of you to say so," Flora snapped. "How nice of your government to be so concerned about how our country is run. You don't want a king yourselves, but you think it would be just fine if we had one."

"Flora..." Joe said.

Flora refused to be interrupted. "The Americans had a revolution to rid themselves of a lunatic king and now they want to a lunatic on our throne."

"That's not what we want," Moe said. "The whole thing is really very embarrassing, and we have to find a way to stop him."

Flora nodded her head. "At least we agree on one thing."

Moe pulled over to the curb. "We're here," he said. "Let's see what's happening."

The weather had, if anything, grown worse. The wind had backed even further and was blowing straight out of the west, across the wide reaches of the Atlantic Ocean, bringing stronger winds and heavier rains. Even with the windshield wipers working at full speed, the visibility was practically zero.

"Do people really enjoy living in this country?" Alex asked, opening the car door and stepping out into the downpour.

"I didn't," Lizbeth said, climbing out behind him.

He reached out and took her hand. "Come on," he said, "lead the way."

Moe had parked illegally at the foot of the jetty. Farther on down the beach they could see the flashing lights of a police car, and silhouettes of people.

"They're still looking"" Lizbeth said softly. ""Shouldn't we tell them not to bother?"

"Not yet." Alex tightened his grip on her hand, and she led him out onto the jetty, with the rest of the party following closely behind. She peered ahead into the gloom, trying to catch sight of the Defiant.

Alex stopped suddenly, pulling her backwards. "We're at the end of the dock," he said.

Lizbeth looked around and realized that they were, indeed, at the very end of the jetty and ahead of them lay nothing but wind-whipped water.

"I don't understand," she said. "It was here. Do you think they might have moved it to another berth? The Harbor Master didn't want them to tie up here."

Moe came up behind them, hands thrust into his coat pockets, shoulders hunched against the wind. "Not here, huh?" he said.

"They must have moved her," Lizbeth repeated stubbornly, but she knew she was wrong. Oh, they'd moved her, no doubt about that, but not to another berth, they had moved her out to sea. HMS Defiant, with her ripped sails, her leaking hull, and her crew of foolish old men, was most certainly clawing her way back to open water.

"This is a job for the Coast Guard," Joe said, following the direction of Lizbeth's gaze as she stared out at the inhospitable ocean.

"Or the Royal Navy," Moe Ellington added. "We were in contact with them as soon as the Defiant left St. Caerog. She's a naval vessel and they don't like to find that their ships have put out to sea without so much as a by-your-leave."

"Was the Navy watching us all the time?" Lizbeth asked, thinking of the ordeal she had been through, and particularly of the jagged blackness of the Darundel Rocks.

"No," said Moe, "no one was watching you. They couldn't pick her up on radar, not enough metal on her I suppose, and they downright refused to fly their choppers in this weather." He patted her arm. "They'll take it more seriously now that they know who's on board."

He turned on his heel and headed back down the jetty. "Come on," he said, "let's get back to the limo. No point in standing around out here in the rain, and I bet the car phone's going crazy."

Flora hurried to keep pace with him. "Mr. Ellington, I have to talk to you. I can't afford to be found by the police. You understand, don't you?"

"No," said Moe, "I'm not sure I do understand, but for heaven sake come back to the car and let's talk about it somewhere where it's not raining."

Lizbeth hung back and watched disappear behind a curtain of rain, the tall silver-haired beauty talking earnestly to the little American, with Joe Ralko straggling along in the rear.

Alex turned to face her. "There's nothing to see out here."

Lizbeth was watching Paul who stood still as a statue at the end of the jetty. She moved to stand next to him. "Uncle Paul," she said, "come with us."

"They won't make it," he said softly. "You know they won't make it. The water was pouring in."

"Perhaps it's better that way," Lizbeth said.

Paul looked at her sharply.

She shrugged her shoulders. "I don't mean to sound callous, but don't you think this is easier? What do you think will happen to Grigo when the police catch up with him? And think of Uncle Stefan; this way he will never have to know the real story. This is better, cleaner."

"I should be with them," said Paul.

Yes, Lizbeth thought, you should be with them. What on earth are you going to do now?

"And there's Bronwyn," Paul said.

Lizbeth's hand flew to her mouth. "Bronwyn," she said. "Oh my God, how could I have forgotten her?"

She thought of the dark-haired girl, with her sullen expression, her in-your-face anger, and her ridiculous dreams of being a princess.

Poor kid, she thought, she must be terrified.

"Thank God Joe doesn't know what bad shape the Defiant is in," she said. "He'll be out of his mind."

"He won't worry about her;" Paul said, "he doesn't even like her."

"He may not like her," Lizbeth said, "she's pretty hard to like actually, but I'm sure he cares about her. She is his sister""

"Not really," said Paul. "She was adopted. I don't think he ever really thought of her as a sister."

"Adopted! Are you sure; I mean, they look so alike?"

"I'm sure."

Alex reappeared through the rain. "Come on," he said, "there's no point in standing here any longer."

Without a moment's hesitation he moved in beside Paul and took his arm. For the first time Lizbeth realized that the old man was wavering unsteadily and without Alex's arm he could easily have pitched forward into the water. Maybe that's was what he wanted to do, Lizbeth thought. Maybe he was realizing how much of his life had been wasted on the impossible dream.

Moe Ellington had not succeeded in reaching the shelter of the limousine; instead he was standing at the end of the dock talking to a couple of rain coated policemen.

"Parking problems?" Lizbeth said to Alex.

"So much for diplomatic immunity," Alex replied.

Moe turned away from the police and came towards them, smiling reassuringly.

"Trouble?" Alex asked.

Moe shook his head. "Nothing that concerns us," he said. "Some punk kid pushed an old derelict into the water."

He stopped to look around at the village, postcard pretty even in the rain. "You wouldn't think it, would you, not in a place like this?"

"Do they need any medical help?" Alex asked.

"Shouldn't think so," Moe replied.

Alex said that he would go and offer his services anyway, and he handed Paul into Moe's keeping, urging him to get the old soldier into the car.

"Give him some brandy. I know you have a bar in the back."

He turned his attention to the group of policemen and civilians gathered on the narrow and stony strip of beach alongside the jetty. Lizbeth followed him at a distance, unwilling to lose sight of him again. When he had first put his arms around her in the death room of the bungalow, she had felt herself relax, and now she realized that she was consumed with the very fact of his presence. Just watching the confident way he pushed through the crowd brought her pleasure, and a certain unjustified sense of ownership.

He's your doctor, that's all, she warned herself, so don't go making this something it isn't.

She pushed closer. She couldn't see the drowned derelict who was apparently lying on the beach out of view, but she could see the punk kid Moe had referred to. The boy's clothes were soaked, as were everyone's, and his shock of blond hair was plastered flat against his head. He was held in the firm grip of a helmeted policeman but he appeared to be struggling to break free and speak to Alex. She recognized him as he turned his face towards her.

"Chris!" she shouted. "Alex, it's Chris!"

She started to run.

Chris had lost his cool. The once laid-back surfing dude was panic-stricken. "It wasn't me," he kept repeating, "I didn't do it. Tell them who I am, Doc. Tell them it wasn't me."

Alex and Lizbeth both tried to speak to the stony-faced police constable, but they weren't helped by Chris' constant interruptions. "Twice in one day!" he yelled. "I've been arrested twice in one day for something I didn't do, and they say this isn't a police state!"

"Cool down," Alex said. "We'll explain everything."

"Like you explained what happened at St. Caerog?" Chris demanded. "I need a lawyer, that's what I need." He turned to the policeman. "I was trying to help him'"' he said. "Why won't anyone believe me? Is it 'cause of my hair? Would you believe me if I got a haircut?"

The wailing of an ambulance brought an end to Chris's complaints as he was jerked aside to make way for the paramedics and Lizbeth got her first glimpse of the derelict, lying face down on the beach.

The paramedics rolled him over and clamped an oxygen mask over his face, but not before Lizbeth recognized him. She hurled herself forward, ignoring the protests of the crowd. How much more could she take, she wondered? First her brother, and now her father.

"Is he dead?" she demanded. "someone tell me if he's dead."

CHAPTER SIXTEEN

The Emergency Room Physician came out to talk to them. She surveyed the row of worried faces with tired brown eyes set in a handsome hawk-like Indian face.

"How is he?" Lizbeth asked.

"Are you the daughter?"

"Yes I am. How is he?"

"He is having difficulty breathing. There is a slight concussion, some exposure..."

"Is he going to live?"

Alex took her hand. "They can't always answer that question," he said softly.

The doctor looked down her nose aa him. "This may not be a big American hospital but we do our best. I am sure the young lady's father will make a full recovery."

"Can we see him?" Lizbeth asked.

"Not yet."

The physician, turning on her heel and marched back into the examination room.

"Some bedside manner," said Alex. "What did I say wrong?"

Moe Ellington came up behind them, holding a disposable coffee cup. "She was the same with me. I was only trying to help but to hear her talk you'd think I'd insulted every woman doctor in the world, the National Health System, and the entire population of India. All I said to her was that the care of this patient involved a national security risk and I thought he should be given a private room, and I said that we had a prominent American surgeon with us, that's you, Doc, and she should feel free to consult with him."

"And she took that badly, did she?" Alex asked.

"Oh yeah; she took that real badly."

Moe drained his coffee cup. "I have to go," he said. "I've put in an emergency call to the Embassy and told them what's going on. They'll get some naval choppers out to look for the Defiant. Now I'm gonna go see if I can get that kid out of jail. What's his name?"

"Chris Evans," Alex said, "and he's having a really bad day, in fact nothing's gone right for him since he first met me."

"I know how he feels," Moe said. "I'll be back soon. Ciao for now."

Alone with Alex, Lizbeth was suddenly overcome with shyness. She had so much to say, such a need to apologize for everything that had happened to Alex, but she remained silent. The silence grew long and uncomfortable.

Alex cleared his throat as though he intended to speak first but then the doctor reappeared. "You can see him now," she said coldly.

Lizbeth was appalled at the sight of the bruises on her father's face and her first instinct was to rush to him and throw her arms around him. She suppressed the instinct, remembering that although she might now be an American, he was still British. He would have no idea how to respond to such a show of affection.

He was sitting up in bed in striped hospital pajamas. An IV tube snaked down to one of his sun browned hands, and an oxygen tube was clipped to his nostrils. His hair stood on end, and his face wore an expression of wariness.

"Dad," Lizbeth said, "how are you?" She stood close to the bed, her hands clasped together to resist the impulse to reach out and smooth his hair.

"How should I be?" he asked. "How should I be when I've been attacked by that demon?"

"So it was Grigo?"

"Of course it was."

"You're lucky you got out of it alive," Lizbeth said. "I think he meant to kill you."

"He thought I was one of them; one of his faithful followers. There he was walking along the dock, large as life, and looking the spitting image of his father and he gave me this sort of regal hand wave, like he expected me to bow down and fall all over him."

"And then he attacked you?" Lizbeth asked.

Her father glanced slyly away. "He's a devil;" he muttered, "he deserves to die."

Lizbeth sat down in the chair at the side of the bed, and felt Alex move to stand beside her. She guessed that he was itching to study the chart clipped to the foot of the bed, but she knew he wouldn't do it.

"Dad," Lizbeth said, "has anyone told you what we found at Dragons Green?"

"Presumably you found the serpent's nest, but the serpent wasn't home."

"The serpent had left a mess behind him," Alex said.

Briefly he explained what they had found in Gregory Gibbons' bungalow.

Far from being shocked, the old man seemed to be elated. "So," he said triumphantly, "I was right all along. I knew it. I knew he would come to nothing but bad!"

"You knew about the first case, didn't you?" Lizbeth asked. "You knew about the boy in Newton."

"Everyone knew about the boy in Newton," her father replied, "but they had to cover it up. They had to sweep it under the rug because he was their prince, their Messiah. Well, he wasn't my prince, and I didn't have to cover up for him."

He looked at Lizbeth for a long moment.

"So Viktor's dead is he?"

"Very dead," Lizbeth replied.

"He killed your mother," Price said, "and he meant to kill you."

"I know," said Lizbeth. "Uncle Paul told me."

"Paul Mihailovic?"

Lizbeth nodded her head.

"He showed signs of common sense," her father said. "I always thought he was a bit smarter than the others, but not that colonel. Oh no, there was no telling that colonel anything."

He waved his hand dismissively. "Well, you have what you came for, girl, you can go back to the States now."

"Not yet" Lizbeth protested.

"There's nothing to keep you here," her father said.

There's you, Lizbeth wanted to say. I want to stay and be with you. I want to make up for all the years of hate.

Her father's expression was so cold and distant that she couldn't make herself say the words.

"It's a pity the old man's dead," Price said. "He should have stayed alive long enough for the law to hang him."

"Dad!"

"I know, I know, we don't have hanging anymore. It'll be jail for the Prince of the Yugoslavs, let's see how he likes that."

Lizbeth shook her head. "They've taken him on the Defiant. They're all gone, all except Uncle Paul and he was with us."

"They sailed without Paul Mihailovic?" Price asked.

Lizbeth nodded her head.

"It'll break his heart," Price said, and Lizbeth thought she saw a small chink in his armor of resentment.

"Do you know where they'll go?" Alex asked.

"Straight to Hell," Price replied.

"We thought they might be heading for Montenegro," Lizbeth said, "going back the way they came."

"That old tub won't make it as far as the Bay of Biscay," Price replied. "She's leaking like a sieve, and there's not a man on board knows how to navigate."

"The Navy is sending out helicopters to look for them," Alex said.

"Your navy, or our navy?" Price asked.

"The British, I assume."

"Ah well," Price said, "it makes little difference, there'll be nothing for them to find, she'll break up and go down with all hands. The Devil will be rejoicing tonight."

"Dad …" Lizbeth started to say, but her father silenced her with a frown.

"I'm tired, and I'm going to sleep."

He gave her a long hard look tinged with an unfathomable sadness. "Go back to America, Lizzie. Don't dig any deeper, you won't find anything here to make you happy."

"I don't understand."

Price slid down in the bed and closed his eyes. "Go away. There's nothing for you here." he said softly.

Lizbeth didn't know where to go. For the first time since she had been removed from her hospital room in Pittsburgh, there was no one to tell her what to do. The freedom should have been exhilarating, but she was too tired to be exhilarated.

Moe awaited them in the corridor, a small, tense figure filled with so much pent-up excitement that he couldn't stand still. He paced restlessly as he talked to them.

"So how is he?"

"I think he'll be fine," Alex said.

If bitter and vengeful is fine, Lizbeth thought, then he'll be perfectly fine. She turned away to look out of the window and saw to her surprise that the gloom of the day had given way to a clear night. The rain had stopped. The wind was still blowing hard, but the cloud cover had lifted revealing a smattering of stars and a small sliver of moon.

It's bedtime, she thought, and I have no idea where to sleep. She realized that she was incredibly tired and looking back on the activities of the last forty-eight hours, this came as no surprise. She had to guess that Alex was equally tired, although he, of course, didn't have to deal with a constant, dull pain in his side.

"I've found us all somewhere to sleep," Moe said, as if reading her thoughts.

"Thank heaven," Lizbeth said.

Alex turned to look at her. His look could have been interpreted as a doctor's concern for his patient, but Lizbeth thought not and she felt blood rushing to her cheeks.

Moe, who seemed to miss nothing, paused for a moment and raised one sardonic eyebrow. He went on to explain that Darundel and its environs were very short of hotels that came up to the standards expected by American tourists. Fortunately, however, with the weather being so bad, the guest houses of Darundel had plenty of vacant rooms. Moe had bought up as many as he could for his group, which had become quite large. Joe, Flora and Paul were at the Bide-a-Wee Bed and Breakfast, Moe and the CIA agents were at the White Rose Inn, and Chris, Alex and Lizbeth had been allocated rooms at Long Barrow Farm.

Long Barrow Farm, seen through a curtain of rain, was a low stone building located at the dead end of a muddy lane. The welcoming porch light showed rambling roses climbing the walls and surrounding the windows, but the overwhelming smell was not of roses but of manure. When Moe brought the car to a halt outside the front gate they were greeted with high-pitched barks from a pair of black-and-white border collies, and an answering chorus of bleating and mooing from the outbuildings.

"Go right on in," Moe said. "They've left the door open for us."

The dogs let them pass without an argument and returned to the barn. Moe led the way up a narrow stairway to the upstairs landing and pointed out a series of doors.

"Chris Evans is in there, I should have him released pretty soon." he said. "That one is the bathroom, you have to share, sorry about that. And then these two are yours. Next to each other," he added heavily.

His remark fell into the silence between Alex and Lizbeth and for a moment Moe seemed lost for words. Eventually he smiled, and brought his hand out from behind his back, offering them a large plastic bag. "I know you don't have any luggage," he said, "but I took the liberty of buying you a couple of toothbrushes, and a change of clothes. I'm really tired of seeing you in the matching sweat suits. I took a guess at the sizes."

He handed the bag to Lizbeth. "Enjoy. I'll see you in the morning. They'll be starting the search at first light, but I don't suppose we'll hear anything for a while."

Lizbeth chose the closest door and stepped into the room, turning on the overhead light. She found herself in a low-ceilinged room with bare wooden floors, dormer windows, and a simple iron bedstead. The windows were open, admitting the damp night air and the odor of cows.

"I can do without that smell," she said, and crossed the room to close the window. She hesitated with her hand on the latch, looking out at the scudding clouds and the dark outline of the moors. She could hear the distant crashing of waves on a beach and feel the west wind whipping at her hair.

She thought about the Defiant struggling westward into the open Atlantic, with her ragged sails set and Bubani at the helm; or perhaps Grigori himself. She wondered what he looked like. She imagined him as a lean, confident figure driving the Defiant forward into the teeth of the wind, and she imagined poor Bronwyn, her tough exterior cracking as she faced another night of terror at sea.

She lifted her eyes upwards to send a prayer to the God that she hadn't spoken to in years, but she had no idea what to pray for. If it weren't for Bronwyn she would wish them all into a watery grave, knowing that the uncles could die happily without ever discovering that their hero had feet of clay.

"It's hard to know, isn't it?" said Alex, coming up behind her and speaking as if he could read her thoughts. She nodded her head and reached out to close the window. Her fingers fumbled unsteadily with the latch, and Alex reached out strong fingers to help her.

His hand brushed against hers and she blushed,

remembering where else his hands had been. He knows all about me, she thought. Not just what I look like without my clothes, he knows what my insides look like, my muscles, my intestines; he knows more than I do.

"You must be exhausted," Alex said. "You should get into bed."

"I don't think I can sleep."

She looked at Alex, drinking in his lean dark face, his tired brown eyes and stubbled chin, and thinking that she had never in her life seen such an attractive man. The air in the room was heavy with their desire. She could see it, feel it, breathe it, but someone had to make the move.

The Lizbeth Price who aggressively sold two million dollars' worth of real estate each year took over from the convalescent woman and decided to do what she always did, she made the first move.

"I don't want to be on my own," she said, and she reached out and slipped an arm around and behind his neck.

He hesitated, and she thought that she'd done the wrong thing. She remembered the aloof surgeon she had seen at Northern General Hospital, and the angry man who had chided her for her thoughtless ambition. She pulled his head down towards her own and the surgeon disappeared, revealing the real Alex Perenyi, who pulled her close and lowered his lips to her mouth.

They kissed for a long time and as they kissed their hands moved. Her hands wound themselves into his thick dark hair and his hands slid along her back, exploring the curves of her waist and her hips. They moved to the bed, shedding their clothes as they went. The pink sweatsuit and the navy blue sweatsuit fell to the floor.

Alex paused, staring at the brightly patterned bikini top. "It was him," he said, "I thought it was."

"What are you talking about?" Lizbeth asked.

He reached out for her, pulling her down onto the bed.

"I'll tell you later," he promised.

The Serbian Solution

Afterwards Lizbeth wanted to sleep, but she couldn't. Lovemaking had brought no relief from her tensions.

She had no right to complain, Alex was a caring and thoughtful lover. She guessed that he could also be passionate, but that he had held back in deference to her condition. He had fallen into an exhausted sleep and for a while she had been content to lie in his arms and think of the strange road that had brought them to this place, and to wonder where the road would lead them next.

Her thoughts turned inevitably to the horror of Viktor lying on his bed, his eyes open, and the flies crawling across his face. From there it was a simple step to think of HMS Defiant, steadily making her way out to sea. She knew she couldn't just lie in bed with her thoughts going round and round this way. She had to do something, although there was very little she could do in the middle of the night.

She slipped from the bed, picked up the bag of clothes and made her way stealthily to the bathroom. The farm house was an old one with thick walls and low ceilings. The bathroom door was made of massive oak planking. Lizbeth was pretty certain that she wouldn't be disturbing anyone in the sleeping household by taking a bath.

While she waited for the cast iron tub to fill she looked at the clothes chosen for her by Moe Ellington, holding them against herself to check their fit.

The little man had done remarkably well. He had bought her a white cotton brassiere and panties. She checked the label, Marks and Spencers, and the size was right. He had also chosen navy blue cotton pants, a white cotton blouse, and a pink sweatshirt. She considered the pink sweatshirt with some dismay. Pink was a difficult color for a red head, she thought, and she had been trapped in a pink sweatsuit for days. But perhaps Moe didn't know her hair was red. For the past couple of days her hair had been so dirty that he could be forgiven for thinking it was a dull brown.

Lizbeth slid into the warm water, poured shampoo onto her head, and started to wash her hair. She ducked under the water, and when she surfaced she could hear someone knocking at the bathroom door.

"Lizbeth," Alex called, "are you okay?"

"Fine," she answered

"Hi Liz," said another voice.

"Is that you, Chris?" Lizbeth asked. 'What do you both want?"

They were talking so loudly that she could only assume they weren't worried about waking the farmer and his wife. Maybe the farmer was already awake. Dawn came early in this part of the world, and the farmer's day started at dawn.

"We had a phone call," Alex said, "from the hospital."

Lizbeth leapt out of the bathtub, and wrapped herself as best she could in a small bath towel. She opened the door a couple of inches.

"Is something wrong?" she asked.

"Your father wants to talk to you," Alex said, "you and Joe Ralko. He says it's urgent."

"He wants us to come in the middle of the night?" Lizbeth asked.

"Chris says he'll take you," Alex said. "Can I have my new clothes, please, I think they're in that bag; I'm coming with you."

Lizbeth hurried out of the bathroom and into her own bedroom, leaving Alex to wash as quickly as he could. She slipped on her new clothes and stood looking out of the window. The first rays of dawn were lighting the sky, tinting the clouds red.

Red sky in the morning, she said to herself, sailors take warning.

Down below her window the farmer passed by driving his cows out to pasture. The border collies ran ahead of the herd, romping together in the long, lush grass. An old and timeless beauty hung over the landscape, from the gentle faces of the Guernsey cows, to the distant bleating of sheep, and even to the shapeless clothes of the farmer.

Chris brought the little red mini round to the front door,

and Lizbeth clambered into the back seat.

"What do you think he wants?" she asked.

Alex shook his head. "No idea."

They drove in silence to the Darundel Cottage Hospital. Chris dropped them off at the main entrance, and told them he'd be in after he parked the car. Lizbeth reached out for Alex's hand as they walked the long corridor to her father's room. They entered the room hand in hand to find Joe seated at the bedside.

Price was wide awake, sitting up in bed, and scowling.
"I don't need the doctor," he said. "I want to talk to Joe and Lizzie."

"I'd like him to stay," Lizbeth insisted, keeping hold of Alex's hand.

"So that's the lie of the land, is it?" Price said. "You've moved on to another one have you?"

"Dad!"

"Another American."

"What do you want, Dad?" Lizbeth asked.

"You and Ralko have unfinished business," Price said.

Joe looked at him blankly.

"Are you just going to abandon your child?" Price asked.

"Dad," Lizbeth said, "I don't know what you—"

Her father scowled at Alex. "I don't suppose she told you about the baby, did she? I don't suppose she told anyone about her shame.""

Alex tightened his grasp on Lizbeth's hand. "I know about the baby," he said.

"She told you?" Price asked.

"Of course she told me. It's part of her medical record. I used the scar from the C-Section as a reference point when I made my own incision." He looked innocently at the old man. "Why should she be ashamed of a baby?" he asked.

He's a gem, Lizbeth thought, an absolute gem.

"What baby?" Joe asked.

"Don't be any more stupid than you can help." Price snapped back. "What baby do you think I mean? I mean the baby you fathered on my daughter."

"Oh," said Joe, "I'd forgotten." He turned to Lizbeth and smiled. "I really had forgotten," he said, "I mean it was so long ago, and you had it adopted, didn't you?"

"Not it;" said Lizbeth, "she."

Joe turned back to look at the old man. "So what about the baby?" he asked. "What's so important that we have to come here in the middle of the night? I was asleep, you know, when they called. I thought you were dying or something."

Lizbeth looked at Joe and wondered how she could ever have been in love with him, but she had been desperately in love, and deeply wounded when he turned his back on her and the child he had fathered. So long ago, she thought, echoing Joe's own question. Why did her father want to talk about the baby now?

"I know where she is," Price said. "I made an arrangement with Joe's mother. It was our little secret."

"You gave her to the Ralkos?" Lizbeth asked.

"I did."

For Lizbeth the pieces of the puzzle fell into place immediately. Eighteen years ago Price had taken the baby girl from her arms and given her to the Ralko family. Mrs. Ralko had claimed her as her own child and told Joe he had an adopted sister.

"Bronwyn," she said softly, "Bronwyn is my child."

"Don't be ridiculous," Joe said, "she's my sister."

"Your adopted sister," Lizbeth said.

They looked at each other, momentarily bridging the gap made by many years and many miles. They were the parents of a daughter and now that daughter had a name and a face.

"I wasn't going to tell you," said Price. "I wasn't ever going to tell you, but... I mean, she wasn't the kind of granddaughter a man could be proud of. I thought it was the devil seed, passed down from Olwyn to Lizbeth, and then to her, but now I see it wasn't that at all."

Lizbeth saw a flicker of something in his eyes she didn't

know what; it could have been regret or hatred. Whatever it was, it was a deeply-felt passion.

"The bad seed comes from him," he said, "from Prince Grigori, not from Olwyn. The girl doesn't have the bad seed, she doesn't deserve to die."

"Doesn't deserve to die?" Lizbeth repeated. "What are you talking about? What gives you the right to pass judgment? She's just a kid."

"She won't die," Joe blustered. "They'll be rescued. The navy is out looking for them and the coast guard—"

"Are they?" Price said. "Are they really looking?"

Joe was shocked into silence.

"Would you look for them," Price asked, "if you were the British, or the Americans, or would you leave them to sink?"

Lizbeth saw Alex nodding his head and realized what her father was saying. How much easier it would be if Prince Grigori, his followers, and his yacht sank without a trace. There would be no need for the expense of an air-sea rescue mission, no need for a high profile arrest, no need to explain to the Royalists why the man who might be heir to their throne had been arrested.

Could he be right? she wondered. Could Moe Ellington be deceiving them all with his talk of helicopters, and lifeboats?

"That's why I wanted to see you," Price said, "I wanted to tell you that if you want your daughter back, you'll have to go and find her yourself."

CHAPTER SEVENTEEN

With a supreme effort Lizbeth controlled her panic. Think, she said to herself. Think and then act. Find the American and talk to him yourself.

They discovered Moe Ellington eating breakfast in a cafe on the waterfront. He sat alone, drinking coffee, and seemed pleased enough to see them as they crowded into the tiny cafe. He invited them to pull up a chair and sit down. He inquired if they had slept well, and commented on the improvement in the weather. He was, Lizbeth thought, the picture of innocence. She refused to sit.

"How's the search going?" she asked.

Moe appeared to consider the question. "I haven't heard anything. There's a lot of water out there, you know; it may take a while."

His face assumed a solemn expression. "We may have to face the fact that all we will find is some wreckage washed up on a beach."

"You'd like that, wouldn't you?" Lizbeth said.

Moe appeared not to understand what she meant. Lizbeth started to ask another question but Joe spoke first, coming straight to the point with his usual lack of finesse.

"Why don't you tell us the truth, shrimp?" he asked.

Moe paused to sip his coffee "I am telling you the truth, and don't call me shrimp."

"I'll call you whatever I like," Joe said. "Why don't you tell us what you're really doing?"

"And what is it you think I am really doing?"

"You're going to let that boat sink, aren't you?"

Alex interrupted before the confrontation degenerated into a brawl. "Moe," he said, "we really have to know what's going on. There are some new facts that have come to light and—"

"Don't humor the little creep," Joe said. "Get out of the way, I'll get the truth out of him."

Alex turned on Joe. "Shut up just shut up and be quiet for once. I've had nothing but trouble from you and I'm sick of it."

Lizbeth caught hold of his arm. "Let me talk to him."

She took a deep breath to calm herself and then sat at the table, pulling a chair close to Moe. "I have a daughter," she said, "She's on the Defiant."

"How can she be?" Moe asked, not unreasonably.

"Bronwyn Ralko is my daughter," Lizbeth said.

It sounded strange, even to her. Bronwyn Ralko is my daughter, she thought, how am I ever going to get used to that idea?

Moe looked at her. ""No shit?" he said softly.

"No shit," Alex confirmed.

"That's tough."

"You'll find her, won't you?" Lizbeth asked.

"We'll try, but we can't make any promises."

"How hard will you try?"

"Well," Moe muttered, "there are ... there are ... problems and..."

"You're not looking for them, are you?" Alex asked.

"No," said Moe, "we're not looking for them."

Lizbeth didn't wait for the explanations. She stormed out of the cafe, with Alex and Joe hard on her heels. Outside, she took in lungfuls of the rain-washed sea air and tried to wipe away her tears of frustration. I haven't cried yet, she told herself, and I'm not going to now.

"So, now what do we do?" Joe asked.

"How the hell do I know?"

"I think we go and see Flora," Alex said.

His answer was so surprising that Lizbeth forgot her tears for a moment and simply stared at him.

"Why Flora?" she asked.

"She has powerful friends," Alex said. "I don't know what her agenda is, but I'll be willing to bet that she doesn't want to see the Defiant disappear without a trace. I think she's just as interested as we are in knowing what happens to the crew, particularly the prince. I suggest that we go along to the place where she's staying and find out what she's up to"

"We're at the Bide a Wee Bed and Breakfast," Joe said, "it's just down the road. I'll show you the way."

Before they reached the door of the Bide a Wee, Chris had caught up with them. He tagged along asking question after question until he understood the implication of their news.

Lizbeth hung back as they reached the door of the Guest House. "I can't go in and talk to her," she said.

"Come on," Joe insisted, "don't waste time!"

"Are you forgetting that your lady friend has sworn to kill me?" Lizbeth asked him.

"She didn't mean it."

"I think she did."

They stared at each other over the great gap of the years, and then Joe shrugged his shoulders. "Okay, we'll go in without you."

Lizbeth grabbed his arm. "Don't tell her about me, about you and me, and Bronwyn""

"She won't care," Joe said.

"Believe me, I'm not worried about that," said Lizbeth. "I don't know how her mind works, and I don't understand this blood debt business, but if she knows Bronwyn is my daughter, and then she does nothing to save her, and Bronwyn dies, maybe that will satisfy the debt. Maybe in her code of honor that'll be enough and I don't want that to happen. I don't want Bronwyn to die because of me. Just tell her you care about Bronwyn because she's your sister and that ought to be a good enough reason; it would satisfy most people."

The men went inside and Lizbeth stood on the doorstep of the Bide a Wee looking at the sunshine sparkling on the waves in the harbor. She thought about the Defiant fighting the great Atlantic breakers as they roared across the Bay of Biscay and imagined the old men pumping and pumping with the water rising around their feet. She thought of Bubani clinging to the wheel and watching the wind tear away the tattered remains of the sails.

Alex came out alone. "She can't do anything," he said.

"Can't or won't?"

"Can't," said Alex. "She has contacts, a plane here, a boat there, but it would take a fleet of planes and an armada of boats."

"We can't just give up," Lizbeth muttered.

Alex put a comforting arm around her shoulder. "Maybe they'll make it," he said."Maybe you'll see them in Belgrade."

Lizbeth lifted her face to the wind, letting it dry the tears gathering at the corners of her eyes. A flight of seagulls swooped low over her head and landed a few feet from her. They formed a squabbling line along the sea wall, their beaks facing into the wind. Instinctively Lizbeth checked their position against the position of the morning sun and saw that the wind blew from the northwest. She thought of how the Defiant would have to struggle with the wind on her nose, and how they would have to run the engine flat out to make any headway out toward the open Atlantic.

"That's it," she said, "Alex, that's it! Where's Chris? Go get Chris. He has to drive me to the Harbor Master's Office. I have to see the local charts and a weather report."

"I'll come with you," Alex said.

Lizbeth pushed him away. "You go back in there and charm little Miss Flora into getting her hands on a fast boat," she said.

The Harbor Master was reluctant to show her his charts and the weather reports but he finally gave in to the desperation in her voice. . He spread the chart out on a desk in his office and pointed out the local landmarks with a nicotine stained finger.

Lizbeth was convinced that she was on the right track as she studied the chart.

"The Defiant can't run her engine for long." Lizbeth said. "She was almost on her last gasp of gas as we rounded the sea wall here, so by now she's going totally on wind power. Now, according to these reports we've had a northwest wind all night."

"Aye," said the Harbor Master, "and she's still blowing."

"Dead on her nose."

"Aye."

"So how will she handle that?" Lizbeth asked.

The Harbor Master's finger traced a course close in shore. "A good seaman would have her creeping along her. Best heading she can make will take her down the Cornish coast."

Lizbeth nodded her agreement. "That's what I think. The Defiant isn't out in the Atlantic, she's somewhere along the coast." She rose to her feet. "Come on, Chris," she ordered, "we're going back to the hospital. I have to talk to my father."

She scooped up the rolled charts and tucked them under her arm. "I'll bring them back," she promised, and then she was out the door.

She didn't hesitate to disturb her father's sleep. She thrust the charts under his nose as he sat up in the bed.

It took him only a couple of minutes to understand what she was saying. He looked up at her and actually smiled. "I think you're right. That's where they'll be heading."

"So where are they now? Where should we look for them?"

Price studied the chart of the rugged Cornish coast with its innumerable markings of rocks and headlands, swirling currents, and rushing tides.

"He'll stand out from shore as far as he can," he said, "but he'll be fighting for sea room. The wind will bring him right back in again. He'll be fighting a losing battle without his engine. He'll have to buy some fuel."

"Where?" Lizbeth asked.

"Wait, wait," her father said, "don't rush me. Hand me a pencil."

"They'll stay away from the big harbors," he muttered, "won't want to handle the traffic, not without an engine. They'll be looking for somewhere small and easy to reach."

Lizbeth passed him a pencil and watched as he drew intersecting lines on the chart and made scribbled calculations in the margins.

"If she's still afloat," he said at last, "I think she'll be rounding Minwinnon Head just after noon today, and if they clear the headland they'll be able to bring her into Tremouth Harbor, it's the only one for miles that he'll be able to get into under sail. They'll be able to take on fuel there and then they'll head out to sea, God help them all."

"Surely the engine will help," Lizbeth said.

Price shook his head. "If they keep running that old engine, she's rattle herself to pieces."

Lizbeth grabbed the charts again and kissed her father quickly on the forehead, ignoring his protests. "

"Thanks, Dad." She hesitated. "I love you," she added. She thought she saw him smile.

Chris waited for her at the hospital entrance. "Now where?" he asked.

"We have to go to Cornwall," she said.

"Cool! I'll need some petrol. Do you have any money?"

"Don't you have any?"

Chris shook his head. "I never have any money," he said.

Lizbeth took a couple of deep breaths. "Wait a minute," she said, "just wait a minute. I'm sorry, Chris, I'm being ridiculous. We can't go on our own, we'll have to take Alex and Joe, and we'll need a bigger car."

"The police took away the red Jag," Chris said "and they took that Milos guy with it."

"No problem," Lizbeth said. "We'll just have to take the car Uncle Paul rented, but we're not taking Uncle Paul. Whatever he says, we're not taking him."

251

Moe flagged them down outside the cafe. He pulled open the passenger door. "I have to talk to you, Miss Price," he said urgently.

"Not now."

"It's important. Trust me, please."

"Why should I?" Lizbeth asked.

"It's about Flora."

Lizbeth climbed out of the car. "Go get Alex?" she said to Chris. "I won't be long."

She allowed Moe to lead her back into the cafe. The three CIA men waited for them at a corner table.

"We're going to come clean with you," Moe said, "I think we owe you that much. I understand you talked to Flora Balka and she told you that she couldn't help you."

Lizbeth nodded her head.

"We've been investigating Miss Balka," Moe continued, "and I think that it's only fair to tell you what we've found out."

As soon as Moe started to explain, Lizbeth realized he was telling the truth. The facts were so obvious that she should have thought of them herself and her only excuse was that she'd been in the United States for a long time, and isolated from European news.

Flora Balka was not, as the Baroness had suspected, working to put some rival king on the throne. Flora was not interested in any form of democracy or any form of royalty. Flora was a Communist. She had been born into a Communist nation and educated in Communist schools. The Party had been mother and father to her and had promised her lifelong employment and security. Now the Party had collapsed and the nation had fallen apart, fractured into a mass of warring tribes and the disciplined peace that Flora and her generation had known was gone, replaced by bitter wars and uncertain cease-fires. Their land was patrolled by blue-helmeted capitalist troops and their future was in the hands of peace talks conducted by strangers.

"We call Flora and her friends Retro-Rebels," Moe said, "and we're seeing them all over Eastern Europe. Capitalism has been a big disappointment to them. They want things put back to the way they were."

"So what am I supposed to do about her?" Lizbeth asked.

"Keep an eye on her," Moe said. "I don't believe her when she says they're not looking for the Defiant. She wants to be a hundred percent sure that Prince Grigori is out of the way."

"Can you keep her here?" Lizbeth asked.

Moe shook his head. "I have no authority to hold her. I'm just warning you to be careful. In fact, I suggest you take her with you wherever it is you are planning to go. At least that way you'll know where she is and what she's up to."

Lizbeth left the cafe and walked the few yards to the Bide a Wee Guest House. She didn't know what scared her most, the thought of Flora plotting behind her back, or the thought of Flora sitting beside her in the car.

Fortunately she didn't have to ask Flora herself, Joe had already done it for her and Chris had them lined up and waiting in front of the Guest House; Joe, Flora, and Alex.

They were on the road within a couple of minutes, crammed into the rented Rover with Joe at the wheel. They headed out of Darundel and picked up the main road west.

Soon they left the rolling green hills and moors of Devon behind them and took to the high and rocky Cornish countryside. There were few trees here to show them the strength and direction of the wind, but they could see high white clouds moving fast across the pale blue sky, and the occasional glimpse of the ocean showed them white capped waves.

Lizbeth glanced frequently at her watch. Two hours to go, by her father's estimate, until the Defiant would be staggering past Minwinnon Head and into Tremouth Harbor.

Flora sat up front next to Joe, and Lizbeth could see only the back of her head. She wanted to tell Alex what she had found out from Moe, but there had been no opportunity. She couldn't talk about Flora, and she certainly couldn't talk about what had happened between them last night and so she could think of nothing at all to say.

Alex made a couple of comments on the scenery and the weather and then a heavy silence fell over them.

Despite her best efforts Lizbeth found her eyes closing and her mind wandering. Her head drooped against Alex's shoulder and she drifted off into sleep.

Arguing voices awoke her. She pulled herself from sleep to discover that Joe and Flora were involved in a loud disagreement.

She lifted her head from Alex's shoulder, greeted him with a half-smile and took stock of her surroundings. They were descending a steep and narrow cobbled roadway towards a tiny harbor. Granite cliffs towered above the harbor, and the same granite had been used to form the handful of cottages along the wharf. A tiny sea wall separated the harbor from the Atlantic breakers beyond. Seagulls perched on the wall, facing into the wind and occasionally the birds would take flight and be blown about like pieces of paper as they fought the high winds. At the end of the wall a trio of cormorants balanced precariously on a tiny harbor beacon.

"Just pull in down there," Flora ordered.

"It says NO ENTRY," Joe replied.

"Oh, for heaven sake," Flora said, "just pull in there and stop. There are the petrol pumps, you can see them from here."

"Is this Tremouth?" Lizbeth asked, still slightly fuddled from her sleep.

"This is it," Alex said "and it's not much of a place. There are a couple of boats in the harbor, but nothing that looks like the Defiant."

"Shark boats!" said Chris. "Cool!"

The shark boats reminded Lizbeth of the big game boats she had seen in the Bahamas. They were shiny and white, each equipped with a flying bridge raised high above the deck. A forest of fishing rods sprouted from the stern of each boat.

She had not been thinking about shark. Now she tried to put aside the picture forming in her mind of sharks surrounding the sinking remains of the Defiant.

"They don't get the really big ones," Chris said, as if reading her mind, "no Great Whites or anything like that."

Joe brought the Rover to a halt on the cobbled quay where a hand painted sign announced *Captain Frank, Fuel, Food, and Charters*.

Captain Frank appeared at the door of his shop, eager to do business and not in the least put out that Joe had parked underneath a NO PARKING sign. Lizbeth guessed that the last few days of lousy weather had resulted in very little business for Captain Frank.

"I'll go," said Flora.

"We'll all go," Alex said determinedly and opened the car door. "Come on, Lizbeth, the fresh air will wake you up."

"I'm awake," Lizbeth said, staggering out and allowing the cool wind to bludgeon her into wakefulness.

She watched Flora advance upon Captain Frank who was a young, sun bronzed Adonis and not at all immune to Flora's silver hair streaming behind her in the wind and the subtle shifting of her hips as she approached him.

"Keep up with her," Lizbeth said, "and make sure you hear everything they say."

"Do you know something?" Alex asked. "What did Moe tell you?"

"I'll tell you later, but don't trust her. Keep your eyes on her."

According to Captain Frank, there had been no sign of the Defiant. Lizbeth looked at her watch. Her father had said the Defiant should arrive by noon and it was not yet noon.

"I think we should wait," she said.

"I don't know what else to do," Joe agreed.

Lizbeth looked at her watch again.

"I have asked my contacts for a boat. Now I must ask them when it will arrive," Flora said. She took hold of Captain Frank's muscular arm. "Do you have a phone?"

"Wait a minute, wait a minute," Lizbeth interrupted. "Who said you could get a boat? Who said we needed your help?"

"You did," Flora replied. "You came to me and asked for help. I thought that even one boat was better than no boat."

"She's doing her best," Joe said.

Sure she is, Lizbeth thought.

"There's a phone in the shop," said Captain Frank leading Flora inside.

Alex patted Lizbeth on the shoulder and then followed them.

Chris wandered away out onto the sea wall, scaring the cormorants into flight and leaving Joe alone, leaning against the hood of the car and looking strangely forlorn. On an impulse Lizbeth went to stand beside him. She slipped her hand into the curve of his arm.

"I've been so bloody stupid," Joe said softly, not looking at Lizbeth but staring straight out to sea.

"We didn't know about the past," Lizbeth said. "No one told us what Grigo had done. It's not your fault, Joe."

"I don't care about him," Joe said. "Let the bastard drown. I mean, about Bronwyn. How could I have missed it? Mum told me she was adopted and I believed her. I just thought it was coincidence when everyone said she looked like me. I didn't like her, Lizzie. I thought she was a nuisance. What sort of a father does that make me?"

"We'll make up for it," Lizbeth promised. "We'll get her back and we'll make up for it."

Gibbons concluded that the girl was absolutely useless. His simple request for a cup of tea had gone unheeded for hours and now she was back in the pilot house whining to Colonel Bubani about the pumps.

"Where's my tea?" Gibbons demanded.

"Shut up about your bloody tea," Bronwyn said.

Gibbons rose to his feet with some difficulty as the deck was tilted at a ridiculous angle. "If you are expecting a place at court," he said, "you are going the wrong way about it."

"What bloody court?" asked Bronwyn, "Neptune's bloody court? Uncle Stefan, we have to do something, you have to come down and look."

The colonel shook his head. He was a scarecrow figure, with his soaked clothes and windblown hair. He perched uneasily in the helmsman's seat his splinted leg dangling uselessly and his face grey with fatigue.

"Go away, girl," Gibbons said.

"You'd best go, Bronwyn," said Bubani. "Just go and do whatever you can."

The girl gave Gibbons one more long, insolent look, and then retreated down the companionway to the cabin.

Gibbons moved closer to the colonel so that the old man would be sure to hear him. "She has to go," he said.

"She's doing her best," the colonel replied. "We're all doing our best, sir."

The "sir" seemed to be an afterthought, and Gibbons gave the colonel another demerit mark in the mental log he was keeping.

To say that the last few hours had been a disappointment would be putting it mildly. After the initial euphoria of his arrival on board the Defiant and the delightful way the old soldiers had jumped to attention, obeyed his commands, and whisked him away from Darundel, Gibbons had experienced nothing but disappointment.

His first surprise was the age of the crew. Of course he was flattered to find his father's old friends on board, but where were the young men? Where were the crack sailors needed to sail the boat? Where was his private cabin? Surely he was entitled to a private cabin. One of the old men had swung open an interior door and showed him a stateroom, but the room had been awash with water and the bed was piled high with supplies.

In fact, Gibbons concluded, the boat was in appalling condition, and his orders to the girl and the old men to tidy up and make things ship shape had been consistently ignored. They seemed totally distracted by their need to man the pumps and tend the sails, which he thought was probably the result of years of inadequate maintenance. He was deeply hurt that his father's yacht should have been placed in the hands of infidels who treated it with so little respect.

He had managed to doze a little during the night, and had awoken at dawn to find that the rain had ceased but that the crew had done very little to repair the boat. In fact, they had somehow managed to rip the forward sail, and were reduced to only one rather small area of canvas, and making very heavy weather of it. They were also still in sight of the coast, which was a major disappointment for Gibbons as he had expected to be well out to sea.

He looked at his watch. It was almost noon and all he'd been offered to eat was a handful of dry biscuits and a cup of water, all offered by the surly girl who expected to be a princess.

He unrolled the charts and looked at them, as he had been doing frequently all morning. Their route lay westward to Lands End at the very tip of the Cornish coast, and then onward to the Bay of Biscay. He traced the route along the coast of Portugal and back into the Mediterranean. How was he expected to undertake such a journey on a diet of dry biscuits and cold water? Surely the colonel could have done a better job of provisioning the boat?
He stared balefully at the old man, thinking how frail and tired he seemed to be, and hoping that the colonel would not be expecting an exalted position in the new administration. He would be needing new, young men. This band of senile old renegades would have to be put out to pasture and the sooner the better.

"Grigori," Viktor said.

Gibbons sighed. He had hoped that Viktor would leave him alone. He didn't need him now.

"The girl should be persuaded to fall overboard," Viktor said.

Gibbons ignored him.

Colonel Bubani raised the binoculars to his eyes and focused them on the rocky coastline, about a half-mile away. All morning they had been tacking in towards the land, and then out and away, and then back again, with their progress marked at a snail-like pace on the chart.

The colonel lowered the binoculars and rang the watch bell, bringing another of the doddering old fools onto the deck; this one, Gibbons believed, was named Mikhail. Mikhail bowed respectfully to the prince as he passed by, and Gibbons decided that Mikhail might be rewarded with some decorative, but meaningless, position at court. At least the man showed the correct amount of respect.

"Tell me if you see what I see," Bubani said to Mikhail. Mikhail raised the binoculars with trembling hands, focused them with extreme difficulty, and finally nodded his head.

"Tremouth," he said.

"That what I thought," said Bubani. "We'll have to put in there. We daren't risk putting in at Penzance, we'd never negotiate the harbor without an engine. Go on down and tell everyone we're almost there"

"Almost where?" Gibbons asked, rising to his feet again.

"Tremouth, sir. We'll put in there and get some fuel."

"Fuel for what?"

"For the engine, sir," said Mikhail.

"You mean we have an engine?" asked Gibbons, amazed at their stupidity. "Why have we been crawling along like this, when we have an engine?"

"We didn't have any fuel," said Bubani.

"My God," said Gibbons, "what kind of fools are you to come for me with no fuel?"

Bubani opened his mouth as if to explain, appeared to think better of it, and closed his mouth again.

"Once we've got the engine running," he said, "we can head out away from land and we can start using the automatic pumps, which will leave some of the men free to do other things."

"Like making breakfast, I sincerely hope," said Gibbons.

"Of course, sir," said the colonel, "if that is first on your list of priorities."

Gibbons thought he detected a hint of sarcasm in the

colonel's tone, and decided that he would keep a very careful eye on this cantankerous old man. Bubani turned the bow of the boat towards land, and for the first time in many hours the Defiant came upright on an even keel.

Gibbons settled back into his seat and watched the rocky coastline draw closer. "Give me the binoculars," he said.

The colonel unstrung the binoculars and handed them across. Gibbons raised them to his eyes and saw the little town with sudden clarity, right down to the short expanse of sea wall and the lone figure standing at the end of the wall. Perhaps, he thought, there'll be a restaurant, and I'll send that stupid girl to fetch me a cup of tea and a sandwich, or perhaps I'll go myself.

He saw several boats in the harbor, and some cottages surrounding the wharf.

"Quite civilized" he said aloud.

"Fool"" said Viktor's voice in his head, "you nearly made a terrible mistake, my boy."

Gibbons lowered the binoculars. "I want some hot food and a cup of tea," he pleaded silently.

"Civilized," Viktor said, "you called it civilized."

Gibbons waited for Viktor to explain. "Phones," said Viktor, "and radios. The police have phones and radios. They'll be looking for you, Grigori. You left some unfinished business behind, didn't you?"

"The boy," said Gibbons.

"And Jamie Price," Viktor added. "And, of course, if they've found the boy then they've found me. I don't suppose they'll understand. They won't like what they've found and they'll be looking for you. You can't go into that port. You can't set foot in England ever again. You have to go to Belgrade, Grigori. It won't matter in Belgrade."

"Turn the boat around," Gibbons ordered.

Colonel Bubani ignored him.

"Turn the boat around," Gibbons repeated, rising to his feet and coming to stand next to the colonel.

"Sir," said Bubani, "we have to go in there and get fuel.

We can't go on under sail. Look at the canvas, it's ripped."

"And whose fault is that?" asked Gibbons. "Turn this damned boat around."

"We won't make it, sir," Bubani argued. "The men are too tired to keep pumping, we have to get fuel."

Gibbons' patience deserted him, or was it Viktor's patience? One or the other of them lashed out with Gibbons' right hand and knocked the old man from his seat. They ignored the man's scream of pain as his broken leg hit the deck. Gibbons took hold of the wheel and steered the boat into a sharp turn. Waves crashed over the foredeck as the Defiant met the waves head on.

Bronwyn appeared at top of the steps. "What the hell are you doing?" she asked.

"I'm assuming command," said Gibbons.

"Good," said Viktor.

"You're a bloody fool!" Bronwyn shouted.

She grabbed hold of his arm. Gibbons hit her hard, and she collapsed at his feet. He looked back over his shoulder at the rapidly receding coast line.

"How am I doing, Viktor?" he asked aloud.

The only answer came from the howling of the wind and the groaning of the timbers. Defiant began a long descent into a wave trough. She was slow to come up again, and reluctant to shake the water from her foredeck. Gibbons heard a loud cracking sound from down below and moments later the old men swarmed up the companionway, their faces white with terror.

CHAPTER EIGHTEEN

Chris came back along the sea wall at a run, skipping nimbly over the wet rocks and shouting. The wind snatched away his words, and Lizbeth failed to understand what he was saying until he was back on the wharf.

"I saw them," he shouted. "I saw them out there!"

"Thank God," said Lizbeth, and found herself hugging Joe and crying.

"Oh thank God," she said again.

Chris pulled at her sleeve. "I don't know what they're doing," he said. "but I don't think they're coming in here."

"What are you talking about?" Lizbeth demanded, starting forward along the sea wall. Chris caught up with her in time to stop her from sliding into the water.

"They seemed to be coming this way, or at least I thought they were, and then it looked like they turned and headed back out to sea."

"Are you sure it's them?"

"Quite sure. I recognized the red sails and the two masts, there isn't another boat like that."

"Then we have to go after them," Lizbeth said, shaking off Chris's supporting arm. "I don't know what they're playing at, but we have to go after them. Flora said she was getting a boat, didn't she?"

Joe shrugged his shoulders. "I don't know," he managed to say before Lizbeth dragged him in through the front door of

The Serbian Solution

Captain Frank's little store to confront Flora.

Flora was perched on a corner of Captain Frank's desk, drinking coffee and smoking a cigarette. Lizbeth gasped out her news and demanded that Flora produce the boat she had promised.

Flora raised an eloquent eyebrow. "It's not here yet," she said, "I'm sorry, but that's the truth; my friends aren't here yet."

Captain Frank looked from one woman to the other. "Do you need a boat?" he asked.

"No," said Flora.

"Yes," said Lizbeth.

Captain Frank turned his attention to Lizbeth, offering her a dazzling smile. "The Lady Jane is available. She's tied up right outside, fully fueled, and ready to go."

Alex's hand appeared over Lizbeth's shoulder, offering Moe Ellington's American Express card. "We'll take it," he said.

His eyes roved over the meager supplies on Captain Frank's display shelves. "And we'll take a packet of these," he added, reaching for a bubble pack of seasickness pills. As they headed for the boat, Lizbeth saw him opening the pack and gulping down the pills.

The Lady Jane was the larger of the two shark fishing boats, a gleaming white-and-chromium beauty whose engines made a satisfying, deep-throated roar when Captain Frank cranked them up from his seat high up on the flying bridge.

They crowded aboard, dropping down from the dock to the deep well of the cockpit. Chris untied the mooring lines and then scrambled up the ladder to the flying bridge and took a seat next to Captain Frank. Within moments the Lady Jane was roaring out of the harbor, sending up a shower of spray from the bow and leaving a churning white wake behind her.

They rounded the harbor wall and met the force of the waves head on with the Lady Jane skimming across the wave crests and slamming into the troughs with a bone jarring thud.

"Good God," Alex said under his breath, and even Lizbeth, accustomed as she was to all kinds of sea conditions, found herself clinging to the railing. Looking in through the cabin door she saw Joe, standing up and looking out of a porthole.

Within a couple of minutes the harbor was lost from sight behind the rolling waves and Lizbeth could see nothing but water.

"How do we find them?" Alex gasped.

"I don't know," said Lizbeth. "Maybe they can see more from up on the bridge. I'm going up."

The climb was precarious and when she reached the top of the ladder she found that the rolling of the boat was magnified by the height of the bridge. She felt as though each wave would literally fling her from her perch. Captain Frank reached out a strong arm and pulled her into safety behind the windshield.

They were alone in the vast expanse of broken water with no sight of land behind them and no sight of the Defiant. Chris, however, seemed confident as to what he had seen and where, and he scanned the horizon expectantly from the crest of each wave. Lizbeth looked down into the cockpit and was rewarded with a weak smile from Alex who had sunk onto one of the cushioned bench seats. He was pale faced, but not green, so she assumed that the pills were having their effect.

"There," said Chris, pointing ahead.

The Lady Jane buried herself in a wave trough and then rose again, shaking water from her bow. As they crested the wave, Lizbeth saw a flash of red in the water.

"Got it," said Captain Frank, and the Lady Jane descended into another trough.

In this way they struggled forward with the engine running flat-out and Chris watching for the Defiant from every wave crest.

As they drew nearer, Lizbeth could see that the old boat was in serious trouble. The flash of red they had seen was the shredded remnant of a sail, flying like a tattered pennant from the head of the forward mast. The boat lay low in the water, rising and falling sluggishly with each wave. Water poured across the foredeck and the Defiant made little effort to shake it off.

As Lizbeth watched, a rogue wave roared out of the ocean

depths and defeated the Defiant's efforts to keep her bow into the wave. She turned sideways and the waves crashed across the deck, sweeping away the rear mast.

"She's going down," Lizbeth shrieked. She grabbed Captain Frank's arm, "Do something!" she pleaded.

"I'm not going in any closer," Captain Frank said, "or she'll take me with her. We'll stand by to pick up survivors." He turned to Chris. "Can you raise them on the radio?"

Chris spoke urgently into the microphone and then shook his head. "Nothing," he said.

Lizbeth could see activity on the deck of the Defiant. Someone with an axe was hacking at the rigging that had tangled the fallen mast so that it trailed the sail in the water alongside the boat and forced the Defiant over at a perilous angle. With a superhuman effort the lone sailor separated the mast from the rigging and the Defiant rolled sluggishly upright.

Captain Frank throttled back on the Lady Jane's engines, holding his place but going no closer. He called down to Alex and Joe, who were standing together in the cockpit, to get out the lifejackets.

"Here comes another boat," Chris said.

Liz followed the direction of his pointing finger and saw another powerful motor boat roaring towards them from the south. Chris keyed the microphone and spoke into it.

"They're not answering""

"That's strange." Captain Frank took the microphone from Chris's hand and spoke urgently.

"Are you sure your radio's working?" Chris asked.

"Radio's fine," Captain Frank replied. He looked long and hard at the motor boat. "What's that flag she's flying?" he asked.

"Who cares?" said Chris.

Lizbeth stared at the approaching boat, and at the red star on the blue and white pennant fluttering high up in the rigging. "I know what it is," she said, but neither Frank nor Chris were listening to her; they were too busy watching the Defiant as she rolled heavily with each passing wave.

Captain Frank had stopped all forward motion and held the bow of the Lady Jane into the waves. Lizbeth descended easily into the cockpit and found Joe and Alex unpacking lifejackets from the cockpit lockers. "Where's Flora?" she asked. "Did anyone see her come aboard?"

Alex stopped dead in his tracks. "Isn't she in the cabin?" he asked.

"I doubt it," said Lizbeth, but she looked in through the cabin door to make sure. There was no one in the cabin.

"Isn't she here?" Joe asked.

Lizbeth shook her head. "No," she said, "she's not here. She was never here. My guess is that she's on that boat out there, the one that's heading straight for us and flying a Yugoslavian Communist flag."

Suddenly Captain Frank gunned the Lady Jane's engines, sending the boat leaping forward and throwing Alex, Lizbeth and Joe into a heap on the floor of the cockpit. Before they could get back to their feet, Captain Frank had thrown the Lady Jane into a tight right hand turn, and Chris, who had been on his way down the ladder, landed hard on top of them.

"They're shooting at us," he panted. "Get the lifejackets on."

"Who's shooting?" Joe asked

"The people in the other boat," Chris said, crawling forward and grabbing lifejackets. "If they hit the fuel tank we'll go up like a firework."

Lizbeth staggered to her feet, clinging to the deck railing. Captain Frank threw the Lady Jane into another tight turn which brought them within a couple of yards of the crippled Defiant. Lizbeth could almost reach out and touch the weathered planking as they screamed past.

A bearded man watched her from the aft deck. For a brief moment their eyes met, and Lizbeth recognized him. After thirty four years she had finally found her brother.

Gibbons watched as the powerboat screamed past him and hoped that the crew had no plans to board the Defiant. They wouldn't, he told himself, because that would be piracy. He alone was master of this vessel and he alone would decide its fate, and the fate of the pitiful collection of old men trapped below in the waterlogged cabin.

He clung to the wheel and felt the water lapping at his ankles with each wave that broke across the deck. Since the last remnant of sail had ripped away and the Defiant had stopped her wild forward motion, he had experienced a sense of peace. The only impediments to his peace were the noise made by the crew as they pounded on the locked cabin door and the roar of the approaching powerboat. Another wave broke over the rail and poured into the pilot house, rolling over the inert figure of Bubani and soaking Gibbons to the knees. The wave drained away under the cabin doors and he heard renewed shouting from the men trapped below decks.

Moments earlier they had tried to disturb his peace by appearing at the cabin door and complaining that the fore hatch had given way and water was coming in. He had been ready for them. He pushed them back down the steps and threw the girl in after them. They were all below now, and nothing disturbed his peace except for the powerboat.

Gibbons watched the gleaming white boat make a sharp turn and come back towards him. As she screamed past for the second time he saw a red haired woman standing at the stern rail and staring at him. Suddenly the woman jumped from the speeding boat into the water. Gibbons watched in amazement as she was followed by the rest of the crew, leaping from the speeding boat into the heaving water. Seconds later the white boat exploded into a ball of flame.

For a moment there was silence, as though all the sound had been sucked out of the air, and then the air was filled with a hissing sound as burning wreckage began to fall into the sea around the Defiant. The remnants of the white boat remained afloat, burning furiously and sending up clouds of black smoke.

"That's strange," said Viktor.

Gibbons waited to find out what Viktor thought was so strange.

"I can hear an engine," Viktor said. "You should be very careful."

Viktor was quite correct. Gibbons could hear the deep hum of another boat engine. He climbed up onto the roof of the pilot house and looked at the surrounding ocean. The Defiant was no longer riding the crests of the waves and his view was severely limited. He thought he saw a flash of light in the water ahead of him, perhaps the sun reflecting from a windshield. He turned to look behind him and saw specks of bright orange in the water. Lifejackets, he thought. The crew of the powerboat had been wearing lifejackets when they jumped.

He felt safer up here on the cabin roof where he could look down god-like and see the waves breaking over the stern.

Bubani had crawled from the flooded pilot house to the stern deck. Gibbons watched the man's painful progress with complete indifference. He appeared to be heading for the stern rail.

"Perhaps he'll throw himself in,: Viktor said.

Gibbons thought that would be appropriate. After all the man was a complete incompetent and hurling himself into the sea would be the equivalent of falling on his sword. Bubani pulled himself to his feet and leaned forward over the rail.

"He could at least jump," Viktor said, "this is so undignified."

Gibbons began to feel uneasy. Bubani didn't look like a man about to commit suicide. He looked more as though he was trying to pull something into the boat. He saw a shock of blond hair, and then an orange lifejacket, and then a man rolled in over the rail and collapsed on the deck. Moments later another man appeared, a big man with huge muscular arms, and then a woman with long red hair, and then another man with a dark, furious face.

""Get off my ship," Gibbons yelled.

"Up yours," said the big man in a loud voice.

"Pirates!" Gibbons screamed.

The woman was on her feet. "Where's Bronwyn?" she shouted.

She started moving towards him. Gibbons stared at her face. She was angry, very angry.

"Where's Bronwyn?" she shouted again.

"It's your mother," said Viktor, "and she knows what you've done."

Gibbons moved forward, dropping from the roof of the pilot house onto the mass of splintered spars and tangled rigging that draped the foredeck. The waves were breaking here, crashing across the deck. The water was cold and unwelcoming.

The woman followed him, screaming his name. "Grigo," she said, "Grigo, listen to me. Where's Bronwyn?"

Gibbons was as far forward as he could go. Only the bowsprit remained, inches from the water. He turned to face his pursuer.

"Grigo," she said, "it's me, Lizzie."

"Lizzie?" Gibbons took a step towards her. Yes, he could see it now. Little Lizzie!

"Why has it taken you so long?" he asked.

The woman edged closer. The anger drained from her face. "What happened to you, Grigo?" she asked. "Why did you do it?"

"I didn't do anything," he said.

"Push her," Viktor said. "Push her in."

"No, it's Lizzie. I'm not going to hurt Lizzie. She'll understand."

"Come on," Lizzie said. "Come to me. We can fix it Grigo. Everything will be all right. Just come over here and tell me what you've done with Bronwyn."

"I don't know."

"The girl; the girl who was on board."

"She's in the cabin. She wants to be a princess."

Lizzie held out a hand. She smiled. "Come here, Grigo."

"Don't go," Viktor shouted.

Gibbons heard the roar of the engines behind him, and saw the shock on his sister's face. He thought she said something, but her words never reached him; something hit him hard in the chest. Pain filled his mind, his lungs screamed for air, and then he started to fall towards the welcoming waves.

Lizbeth watched as her brother threw his arms into the air and toppled into the water, then she turned and made her way aft. She could hear the roar of the power boat's engines as it made a sweeping turn and headed back towards them.

Alex was on his knees beside Bubani. He looked up questioningly.

"Gone. Maybe it's for the best. Where's Bronwyn?"

"Safe. He had them all locked in the cabin."

"Poor Grigo," said Lizbeth.

She looked around and saw the uncles huddled together in the false security of the pilot house. Chris and Captain Frank were passing out old fashioned cork lifejackets. Even above the roar of the rapidly approaching powerboat, Lizbeth could hear Bronwyn's voice.

"I'm not putting that bloody thing on!"

That's my girl, thought Lizbeth. She looked around for Joe but he was nowhere to be seen. She hadn't seen him since the Lady Jane exploded.

Captain Frank was filling the air with inventive curses, the gist of which was that Flora's boat was about to ram them.

"Out on deck," he yelled. "Everybody out on deck, now!"

The power boat, with the Yugoslavian flag fluttering boldly in the rigging, drove a carefully calculated course. It caught the Defiant a glancing blow on the port side, and another on the bow.

"Grab something," Captain Frank shouted, "anything that floats."

The Defiant buried her bow for the last time. The stern deck rose majestically into the air, and then the old yacht began her inexorable slide towards the ocean floor. For the second time that afternoon Lizbeth leaped into the sea, gasping as she hit the cold water.

"So she got me after all," Lizbeth said to herself as the water closed over her head.

There was no fight left in her, but she came to the surface anyway, hauled up by her lifejacket. For a moment she thought she was alone and then she was lifted on the crest of a wave and saw swimmers in the water around her.

She heard a blast on a whistle and saw Captain Frank clutching a hatch cover and blowing on a whistle tied to his lifejacket.

"Stay together," he shouted. "Over here."

She struck out towards him, swimming as strongly as she could, and saw other swimmers converging on the same point, even the old uncles, clumsy in their bulky cork life preservers.

"Find something that floats," Captain Frank was yelling, "those cork jackets won't keep you up for long."

A wave washed Lizbeth up next to one of the uncles and she caught hold of him, towing him towards the hatch cover. It was, she thought, Uncle Mikhail, but so changed by exhaustion and disappointment that she couldn't be sure.

She caught sight of another orange lifejacket and saw Alex towing the unresponsive form of the colonel. With a supreme effort Alex heaved the body across the hatch cover. "Hang on!" he shouted, but there was no reaction from the colonel.

"Hang on!" Alex said again, but Bubani's body rolled slowly off the floating platform. It was picked up by a breaking wave and carried away out of sight.

"Stay where you bloody well are," Captain Frank commanded as Alex started to give chase, and Alex returned to the hatch cover.

Lizbeth trod water and looked around, counting orange lifejackets from the Lady Jane. She saw Captain Frank, Alex, Chris, and the grey heads of the uncles in their cork life jackets, and she saw Bronwyn swimming amongst them, leading the old men to a floating hatch cover.

Lizbeth looked up. The sun was obscured by the pillar of smoke from the burning Lady Jane.

"Oh God," she thought, and the thought was quite definitely a prayer. ""I hope someone sees that."

A piece of wood broke the surface close by, and then another and another. Somewhere down below them the Defiant was breaking up and her loose timbers were drifting upwards.

Soon the survivors were surrounded by a mass of floating debris, and Captain Frank kept himself busy capturing spars and towing them over to the hatch cover where he was forming a raft of sorts.

The cold water was beginning to take its toll. The old men were losing their grip on the hatch cover. Chris and Captain Frank swam back and forth and heaved the old men out of the water onto the precarious raft, but Lizbeth knew this couldn't go on for long; she knew they would start to slip away, one by one. She did not even want to think about the sharks and the massive fishing rods carried by the Lady Jane, the enormous hooks, the heavy duty fishing line, and the sharpened hook of the gaff.

She kept an eye on Bronwyn, checking that the girl was safe. Should she speak to her, she wondered. If they were running out of time, should she go and make her peace with the girl, and tell her who she really was? She could think of no way to do it. Where would she even begin?

Alex swam up beside her, grabbed her arm and pushed her over towards a floating spar. "Have to talk to you," he gasped.

They clung side by side to the spar, their heads clear of the water. They were in sight of the other survivors, but very alone.

"In case we don't make it—" Alex said.

"We'll make it," Lizbeth assured him.

"In case we don't," he continued doggedly, "I want you to

know that, well, I'm not sorry about any of this."

He reached out and covered her hand with his own. There was no warmth in his skin and yet the touch was comforting.

Lizbeth thought she heard the roar of a powerful boat engine. "Oh my God," she shouted, "they're coming back. Haven't they done enough?"

"I just wanted you to know," Alex insisted "before it's all over".

They were lifted together on the crest of a wave, and Lizbeth saw the boat that was hurtling towards them in glorious Technicolor, its fluorescent orange hull flinging aside the waves, its decks crowded with volunteers in yellow rain slickers.

"It's the lifeboat," she heard Chris shout and from the next wave she heard Captain Frank shouting "About bloody time. I called you ten minutes ago".

The lifeboat crew searched for survivors until well after dark and then they turned and headed back towards Tremouth. Lizbeth only gave the Coxswain one name to write in his log, Colonel Stefan Bubani, Lost at Sea.

"What about Joe?" Alex whispered.

"I didn't see him," she said. "I don't know what happened to him."

"He's Bronwyn's father."

"I'll never tell her."

"And your brother?"

She smiled. "The prince is still missing." she said. "It's better that way."

CHAPTER NINETEEN

Lizbeth packed her new clothes into her new suitcase, and carefully placed her new passport into her purse alongside her boarding pass. On the other side of the king-sized hotel bed she saw that Alex was admiring his new documents. They grinned at each other.

"Home," she said.

"Back to work," Alex said.

She shook her head. "Not yet," she said, "first we get a few days off. You and I, somewhere quiet".

He laughed. "Not a cruise," he said, "I am never going to sea again."

"Not even a beach?" she asked, "Somewhere tropical?"

He leaned across the bed and kissed her, comfortable at last with their relationship. "Maybe a beach," he conceded.

Whatever was going to happen next was interrupted by a sharp knock at the door.

"Moe," said Lizbeth.

"One last time," Alex said. "You'll like the Countess, she's a class act."

The Countess was indeed a class act, Lizbeth thought, as the old lady gripped her hand and looked into her eyes.

"Your mother was a beauty," said the Countess, "but the doctor didn't seem to be sure about you."

"I'm sure now," Alex interrupted.

"Good," said the Countess. She looked sideways at Lizbeth. "Of course you have no royal blood, so we can assume that your life will be long and happy, and uninterrupted by revolutions, and kidnappings, and clandestine plots."

"I intend to see to that," Alex said.

The Countess smiled, but continued to look at Lizbeth. "There is the question of the blood feud," she said, "and I don't think the doctor can take care of that."

"I'll do my best," Alex said.

"And you will fail."

Lizbeth's heart sank. The blood feud was something that was rarely out of her mind. She had no assurance that Flora Balka had gone down with the rest of the crew, and no idea if any other member of the Balka family would pick up the responsibility.

Worrying about the blood feud was number two on her list of concerns, the first being the question of how Bronwyn would react to the idea of Lizbeth being her mother. For the time being Lizbeth was still a kind stranger who had offered to pay Bronwyn's way through university. Everything else would come later, she thought, when they knew each other better.

"There is someone who wishes to speak to you," the Countess said.

She inclined her head slightly to the ancient manservant, and the man shuffled over and opened an inner door. A tall man in a dark suit entered the room. Grey haired, handsome, and expensively suited, he approached the Countess with serene dignity.

"Normally," the Countess said, "we would make a formal introduction, but on this occasion I will simply say that you are meeting a representative of the true King of Yugoslavia, and the descendants of Queen Victoria."

Lizbeth looked at the nameless man with curiosity. How many kings were there, she thought?

The King's representative spoke perfect English. He smiled at Lizbeth showing gleaming white teeth.

"I admit it must be confusing for you," he said, "because

you were brought up to believe some very misguided individuals. I must tell you, Miss Price, that there was never any possibility of your brother having any role in the government. We are currently in exile and it is possible we will remain in exile, although we are hoping for the restoration of some of our property, but your brother had no legitimate claim and neither did his father."

"I understood his father was—"

The courtier finished her sentence. "He was very popular for a few months during World War II, but his claim was totally false. The lineage is well established and accepted by the many exiled courts of Europe. When it is time to restore a King, we will be prepared. I'm sorry for the loss of your brother, and of your friend Colonel Bubani, but perhaps it is better that you put this behind you."

"I'd be happy to put it behind me," said Lizbeth, "but what about the blood feud? I'm not safe, and neither is my..."

"Daughter," the man concluded. "Yes, we know about her, she is indeed a very distant relative of the Crown Prince, and in time, after you have made her acquainted with her true identity, perhaps she may come and meet the Court. We are mostly in Italy these days."

"I haven't told her..."

"You will in time," the courtier said. "As for the matter of the Balka family; we have taken care of that issue."

"Blood feuds, indeed," said the Countess.

"Indeed," said the courtier. "We are a modern people, and that is what we have told the Balka family. They fully understand and you will hear no more from them."

Lizbeth felt a surge of relief. The thought of Flora had been weighing on her day and night since the Coast Guard search had failed to come up with any trace of her.

"I will leave you now," the courtier said. "It is not appropriate for me to say more. I wish you well Miss Price, and I urge you to watch the newspapers. One day you will hear that we have been able to go home. Perhaps we won't live as kings, but we will live in our own land again."

He inclined his head gracefully to the group and then stooped to bow over the hand of the Countess. To Lizbeth's amazement the old lady rose slowly to her feet, and as the courtier left the room she performed a trembling curtsey.

"Was that...?" Lizbeth asked.

"No need for you to know," said Moe.

THE END

Author's note: This story is a work of fiction and the characters portrayed within are purely fictional. However, the story is inspired by elements of truth including proposals made in 1991 to restore European monarchies as a means of obtaining peace. The children of several European monarchs were carried out of Europe as the Nazis advanced and were given shelter by the British Royal family. They are now scattered throughout Europe still in possession of their titles but not of their thrones.

Eileen Enwright Hodgetts

Also available from the same author.

The Girl on the Carpathia – The Titanic Novels
Historical fiction - in the aftermath of the sinking the U.S. Senate launches an investigation and a search for a scapegoat. Based on historical records of the 1912 Hearings.

The Girl in the Lifeboat – The Titanic Novels
After the sinking of the Titanic, the surviving crew returns to Britain to face an investigation into their actions

The Toby Whitby Mystery Series – cozy mysteries set in England in 1952. Lawyer Toby Whitby's poor eyesight kept him out of active service during the war but now he is making up for lost time. For some people the shadow of war lingers as crimes committed during the war are only just coming to light, and the victims look to Toby for solutions. Air Raid, Imposter, and Nameless are the first three books in the series. Air Raid was named in the Best Books of 2019 by Kirkus Reviews.

Excalibur Rising a four book edge-of-your-seat fantasy-suspense series laced with wit and history. If you like unusual characters, dramatic plot twists, and the myth of King Arthur, then you'll love *Excalibur Rising*.

You may also enjoy
The Girl in the Barrel – suspense and romance at the brink of Niagara Falls
Afric When flooding traps two American women in an African village, they find themselves at the mercy of a war lord and in the center of the CIA's war on terror.

Find additional information and updates at
www.eileenenwrighthodgetts.com

Made in the USA
Middletown, DE
03 March 2023

26124226R00156